'We can start by declaring a truce.'

With some hesitation, Claire placed her hand in his. But instead of shaking it Jack slowly raised it to his lips, then turned it to plant a kiss on her palm. Heat flowed through her at the warm pressure of his lips. She yanked her hand away, stunned at her reaction.

His lips curved in a lazy smile, and she suddenly saw the young man he'd been. 'I would have preferred to seal our truce with a proper kiss, but somehow I doubt if you would co-operate.'

'Friends do not kiss each other!'

'It depends on the sort of friend.'

'I have no intention of ever being that sort of friend with you, my lord.'

He gave her a smile that looked rather wicked. 'No?'

Ann Elizabeth Cree is married and lives in Boise, Idaho, with her family. She has worked as a nutritionist and an accountant. Her favourite form of daydreaming has always been weaving romantic stories in her head. With the encouragement of a friend, she started putting those stories to paper. In addition to writing and caring for two lively boys, two cats and two dogs, she enjoys gardening, playing the piano, and, of course, reading.

Recent titles by the same author:

LORD ROTHAM'S WAGER

Ann Elizabeth Cree

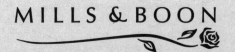

MILLS & BOON

First published in Great Britain 2000
Harlequin Mills & Boon Limited,
Eton House, 18-24 Paradise Road, Richmond, Surrey TW9 1SR

© Annemarie Hasnain 2000

ISBN 0 263 82297 4

Set in Times Roman 10½ on 12 pt.
04-0004-76247

Printed and bound in Spain
by Litografia Rosés S.A., Barcelona

Prologue

John Alexander Grenville, the sixth Earl of Rotham, threw down his hand. 'Your game.' He leaned back in his chair and, with a short laugh, shoved his vowels towards his second cousin, the Honourable Frederick Brenton.

Frederick stared at the vowels as if he thought they would bite. 'Damn it, Jack. You're more drunk than I thought! You never lose!'

'That or he is in love,' Harry Devlin drawled. He raised a negligent brow in Jack's direction. 'I've never seen you play so poorly.'

'It's hardly love.' A scowl marred Jack's dark brow. He motioned to the passing waiter and ordered another bottle of the establishment's excellent claret.

The three men sat in a private room in Weston's—one of London's most notorious and exclusive gaming hells. They had been playing since early evening and now, at past three in the morning, seemed unlikely to quit. Several empty bottles sat on the table. All three men had removed their coats. Frederick looked rumpled, Harry had lost none of his splendid elegance, and Jack looked untouched by the amount of alcohol he'd consumed. Only the rather wild look in his usually cool grey eyes betrayed the fact that he was perhaps less than sober.

'Well, I won't question my luck,' Harry said. He was a tall, broad-shouldered man with blond hair and a pair of lazy blue eyes. 'However, I do question the wisdom of consuming a fourth bottle of claret. No plans for tomorrow, I take it?'

'No.' Except a visit from his stepmother and maternal grandmother. Separately, of course, since they had little love for one another. The combination was enough to make him consider the possibility of drinking himself under the table, except they'd probably take advantage of his helpless state.

Suddenly Jack lost his indifferent pose and sat straighter. An alert expression popped into his eyes. 'Damn! The will! I'd nearly forgotten. It was read today.'

'What will?' Frederick asked.

'My great-uncle's,' Jack said. He watched the waiter set the bottle down, then reached for it and poured himself another glass.

'I assume you are drinking yourself to oblivion in celebration, then?' Harry enquired.

Jack raised his glass. 'Yes, most certainly in celebration to the terms of Great-Uncle Hugh's will.'

'Not too favourable? But you're rich enough. Don't know why you need more,' Frederick said.

'So you didn't get Blydon Castle?' Harry asked.

Jack laughed shortly. 'Oh, yes. It is mine. But there are certain conditions attached.' He was surprised to find his voice as articulate as it was.

Harry leaned forward. 'Such as?'

'Such as I marry within six weeks and my bride and I must reside for the next six months in the castle.'

Frederick's mouth dropped open. 'Good God!'

'Yes.' Jack grinned sardonically.

Harry stared at him. 'How very interesting. Great-Uncle Hugh found a way to make you toe the line after all. Do you want the place that much?'

Jack looked away. 'I do.' He had fallen in love with Blydon the first time he'd seen it as a boy. Grey and windswept, near the sea in Kent, it looked like the embodiment of all his romantic boyhood imaginings of knights and dragons and fair ladies. No matter that the halls were often draughty or it lacked many modern conveniences; he'd felt at home. Much more than at the staid and respectable seat of his own family.

'Leg-shackled! Good God!' Frederick said again. He looked revolted. 'Not you!'

'So, who is the fortunate woman to be? Sylvia?' Harry asked.

'You can't! She's the widow of a Cit!' Frederick exclaimed.

Jack cast him a dark look. 'That matters little to me. Although I doubt she'd want to ruin our friendship with marriage.' His last mistress, as warm and intelligent as she was, had no desire to give up her independence. And she still mourned her husband, who had been the love of her life.

'I've no doubt once it's known you're seeking a more permanent connection you'll have no lack of applicants,' Harry said.

'I am certain any woman will be delighted to spend six months in a draughty castle.' As much as he looked forward to spending six months with a bride.

'The end result of a title and a fortune should more than make up for any inconveniences.'

Jack grinned sardonically. 'Such a charming way of putting it.'

'Dare say the Duchess will be all over you now, trying to pick a bride.' Frederick shuddered and took a sip from Jack's glass.

Jack plucked the glass from Frederick's hand. 'Undoubtedly.'

'You don't have much time.' Harry was clearly enjoying himself. It filled Jack with the desire to leap at his friend's throat and wipe the smirk off his face. 'So how will you choose? Beauty? Wit? Fortune? Figure?'

'How the devil should I know? Perhaps each candidate should submit a written dossier of her qualifications. I'd have as much luck choosing a wife by one of my grandmother's damnable fan lotteries!'

That was one of the Duchess of Arundel's favourite ballroom rituals. Ladies were invited to toss their fans on a table and each man would pick a fan. The owner would then become his partner for the dance. Last time, he'd had more than one lady before the dance give him hints about which fan he should choose.

A cool smile curled his lip. Why not? The results would make little difference. His father's marriages—the first, a marriage of convenience to a woman he had little in common with, and the second a love match to a beautiful but selfish girl less than half his age—had taught Jack well.

He realised Harry and Freddie were both staring at him. He leaned back again, stretching his legs. 'I have decided I will choose my bride by fan lottery. My grandmother is holding one at her ball next week. The woman whose fan I choose will be my bride.'

Freddie gaped. 'You can't do that! No woman will marry someone who picked her from a lottery.'

'She doesn't need to know that.'

Harry's eyes held speculation. 'How will you make certain she is not married and fifty? I assume you will want an heir.'

Jack frowned. An heir? He hadn't thought that far. 'I will tell my grandmother only unmarried ladies between eighteen and thirty may participate.'

Harry laughed. 'That still leaves many possibilities for error open. What if she is thin and freckled with an annoying laugh? Or a widow with an unsavoury reputation? Will you do it?' Without waiting for an answer he said, 'Five thousand pounds if you marry the woman you choose. And that filly you've wanted.'

'And if I don't?'

'You owe me five thousand pounds and your black stallion.'

Satan? For a moment, Jack hesitated. He'd had the horse since it was a young colt. But his gambler's instincts took over. He'd never had a problem obtaining any woman that interested him. And there had been no shortage of respectable ladies and matchmaking mamas who had hinted that a proposal of marriage from him would not be unwelcome. 'Done.'

But as he was leaving Weston's, with the pale red of early morning light streaking the sky, he realised he was quite wrong. For there was one lady who had refused to marry him. His mouth twisted as a stab of unexpected bitterness hit him. She had refused, even at the cost of her reputation.

Chapter One

Claire Ellison peered into the saloon off the Duchess of Arundel's ballroom. To her great relief the small room was empty. Most of the guests were probably enjoying the lavish supper the Duchess had provided in the adjoining apartments.

Claire slipped inside and quickly made her way over to the striped chaise longue on which she'd been seated. She looked around. There was no sign of her old faded fan.

She bit her lip, not wanting to give up hope. Perhaps it had slipped under the chaise longue when she'd been talking to Harry. She was always dropping things—gloves and fans and hairpins.

Careful not to crush the fine muslin of her ball dress, she lowered herself to her knees. But a quick look showed no fan lay under the sofa. She rocked back on her heels, with the idiotic feeling she was about to cry. She had excused herself from the supper in the hopes that she could find it before the ball resumed, certain it would be here.

The fan had been her mother's, given to Claire on her eleventh birthday. Claire rarely carried it, but tonight

was the first ball she'd attended since coming to London
with her sister-in-law and niece. At the last moment, she
had grabbed the fan, for some reason needing the comfort it represented.

She rose to her feet, and tried to smooth down the
front of her gown, which now had a series of fine wrinkles. Had someone taken it? But who would want such
an old, faded fan with a chip in one corner of the ivory
handle? She could ask one of the Duchess's footmen.
Or…perhaps Harry had picked it up.

He had still been standing here when she'd dashed up
from the chaise longue and fled the room. The only reason she had done so was because Harry had suddenly
informed her, in his bland way, that Lord Rotham had
just arrived. The small saloon with its one doorway had
suddenly closed in on her. Her only thought had been to
escape to the safety of the crowded ballroom, where she
could lose herself in the crowd of guests.

Not that Lord Rotham would remember her anyway.
She was probably nothing more than an inconvenient
memory. Nonetheless, she began to wish she had never
agreed to come to this ball. The Duchess of Arundel was
Lord Rotham's grandmother and of course he would put
in an appearance. Claire would have declined the invitation, but the Duchess was Jane's godmother and had
always been quite kind to Claire, so Claire had felt obligated to attend.

A sigh escaped her. She should probably look for
Harry and see if he had her fan. Then she could spend
the rest of the evening hidden away in a corner, hoping
to avoid Lord Rotham.

'I beg your pardon. I had no idea the room was occupied.' The cool male voice came from behind her.

She froze, her heart nearly thudding to a halt. Oh, no!

It couldn't possibly be him! No fate would be unkind enough to bring them together like this.

'Well? Are you tongue-tied?'

That well-bred voice was unmistakable, even after six years.

'No.' Slowly, she turned and forced herself to look at the Earl of Rotham.

He had changed. She saw that at once. He had matured, of course; the planes of his face were now lean and hard. His shoulders, under his corbeau coat, seemed much broader. But it was his eyes that had altered the most. They were cool and impenetrable with no trace of the laughter she remembered.

His dispassionate gaze swept over her face. For a brief moment, there was no sign he remembered her. Then shocked recognition leapt into his eyes.

'Claire! What the devil are you doing here?'

'I…I was invited.'

His eyes were locked on her face. 'I would have thought this house would be the last place in London you would set foot in, barring my own house, of course.'

'I had no idea you would be here.' She hardly knew what she was saying.

His expression cooled. 'Why wouldn't I be? This is my grandmother's ball.'

'Of course.' She attempted to gather her scattered wits together. 'If you will excuse me, my…my lord.' Her tongue tripped over the title she had rarely used.

Instead of moving to let her pass, he took a step closer. She found herself backed against the chaise longue.

'So, why are you here?' he asked.

'I told you, I was invited.'

'That was not my question. Why are you in London at all?'

His tone of voice seemed to imply she had no business anywhere near him. She lifted her chin. 'I am staying with my sister-in-law while Edward is away in Brussels. I trust you have no objections to that?'

'None at all. It matters little to me what you do.'

'Then perhaps you will let me pass.' She tried to keep her voice steady, not wanting him to know how much his words hurt. She attempted to move around him.

His hand shot out and closed around her wrist. 'No.'

'What?' She stared down at his lean, strong fingers on her arm, a shiver darting through her. She looked up at him, and caught a whiff of brandy on his breath.

'No.' He stared at her, a peculiar, almost reckless, look in his eyes. 'Will you participate in the fan lottery?'

'The fan lottery?' What was he talking about? Then she remembered there was to be one tonight. Her niece, Dorothea, had talked about little else for the past three days. 'No. I…I don't care for such things.'

'Don't you? Perhaps it is for the best after all.'

'Please let me go.' She was beginning to tremble, but she had no idea if it was from fear, or something else entirely.

'Not until you promise me the next dance.'

'The next dance?' He must be drunk. She attempted to pull her wrist out of his grasp, but his fingers only tightened. 'Why…why would you possibly want to dance with me?'

'Curiosity, perhaps.' His voice was bored.

'I'm afraid I do not share the same curiosity. I have no desire to dance with you.' She could hear voices and laughter from the ballroom. The supper had finished.

Sudden panic shot through her. 'Will you let go of me? You're bruising my wrist!'

He dropped her hand as if it burned him. Over his shoulder, Claire saw two women enter the saloon. They stopped abruptly and stared. With a sinking feeling, Claire recognised one as Lady Coleridge, an acquaintance of her sister-in-law's. Lady Coleridge's brow arched. 'I fear we've interrupted a tête-à-tête.'

Claire flushed. 'I was merely leaving. If you will excuse me, my lord.' This time he allowed her to step aside. She darted past him, not daring to look at his face.

Reaction set in once she reached the ballroom. She found she was trembling, her heart beating as fast as if she'd escaped from an enemy. Which perhaps she had. She found a vacant spot behind a pillar, and leaned against the wall, trying to compose herself as the musicians struck up the lively notes of a country dance.

Oh, why must she encounter him alone? She had imagined if she did chance to meet him she would be in company. She had planned to coolly acknowledge him as if she scarcely remembered him, not stand there in tongue-tied shock. And, after six years, she had never thought the sight of him would fill her with such confusion.

The last notes of the dance died away and the dancers began to disperse. She must find Jane, who by now was probably worried about her.

For not the first time, Claire wished she were several inches taller for she could scarcely see the other side of the room. She slowly made her way through the crowd, finally spotting Jane standing with Dorothea near the edge of the room.

Her sister-in-law turned as Claire reached her side. She was petite and blonde and lovely in a gown of pale pink silk. 'Claire! You were gone so long I feared something had happened.' Then she peered more closely at Claire, concern showing in her soft blue eyes. 'What is it? Oh, Claire! Something did happen!'

Claire tried to smile. She didn't want to worry Jane by her encounter with Rotham. 'Nothing of significance, except I did not find my fan. I thought perhaps Harry had it.'

A little frown creased Jane's brow. 'He said nothing about it when we saw him before this dance. Although he may have it.' Jane touched Claire's hand. 'Please, don't worry. We can ask one of the servants about it. I am quite certain we'll find it.'

'I hope so.'

Dorothea smiled at her from Jane's other side. She was as fair as her mother with a pair of sparkling blue eyes and a lively manner that boded well for her first season. 'The fan lottery is next, Aunt Claire! I think it should be great fun!'

'I hope so.' Rotham's odd question about whether she would throw her fan in the lottery darted through Claire's mind. But the entire conversation had been so disconcerting, she could scarcely remember what they had said.

Just then the tall double doors to the ballroom opened. Two bewigged footmen staggered in carrying a carved cherry table. The crowd parted so they could carry the table to the centre of the room.

The Duchess of Arundel stepped forward. Plump and pink-cheeked, she hardly looked her sixty years. She waited until the room was silent before speaking. 'It is time for the gentlemen to draw fans for their next lady. However, we will proceed differently tonight. First, all unmarried ladies between the ages of eighteen and thirty will toss their fans on the table.'

There was a collective gasp. 'Why, that is quite unfair!' a plump matron in purple satin exclaimed.

'Wait!' The Duchess held up her hand. 'To make it more equitable, only unmarried men will draw the fans.'

'Does that mean we're obligated for more than a dance?' a male voice called out. His remark was greeted with laughter.

'No, unless it is mutually satisfactory to both parties.' She smiled. 'My grandson has asked to choose the first fan.'

There was a chorus of masculine groans. 'He'll have an unfair advantage!' one man protested.

Claire's heart lurched as she saw him leaning against a pillar near the back of the room, arms folded across his chest. He looked as if the whole affair was a source of boredom. He straightened up and sauntered towards the centre of the room. The guests nearest him moved so he could pass.

He stopped next to the table and looked down. Fans scattered across its smooth surface, jewels in ivory and satin and lace. Claire watched as he circled the table. He picked up one fan and set it down. His face showed nothing but indifference, but the set of his shoulders indicated some sort of tension. It was most peculiar, almost as if it really mattered which one he chose. The room had gone dead silent as if collectively holding its breath.

Finally he extracted a fan from the table and opened it. He held it up. 'Would the owner please claim her fan?'

No one said a thing. A tall woman wearing a large turban had stepped in front of Claire, blocking her view.

Dorothea craned her head around. Suddenly, she caught Claire's arm.

'Claire, I think he has your fan!' Dorothea said.

'My…my fan? He can't have it!'

'But it is. I am quite certain of it. You must look.'

Stunned, Claire pushed past the lady with the turban. Her heart stopped. It was indeed her fan, or, she prayed, one just like it. Even from halfway across the ballroom its faded roses and yellowed ivory were all too familiar. But it couldn't be possible!

Jane was behind her. 'Oh, Claire, I fear she is right. It is your fan.'

Claire was frozen to the spot. The guests near them were beginning to rustle and look at her. Rotham waited, his face impassive.

Dorothea touched her arm. 'You must go, Aunt Claire. You cannot keep him standing there.'

'I can't possibly,' Claire whispered.

'Claire, you must,' Jane said. She looked almost as pale as Claire felt. 'It would be an unforgivable insult if you do not.'

Claire forced her shaking legs to move across the floor, feeling as if she was in a dream. Her heart was pounding so hard, she felt light-headed. She only prayed she wouldn't completely disgrace herself by swooning in front of half of society.

Rotham stood as if carved in stone, his eyes locked on her face. He looked down at her as she reached his side. She had no idea what he thought; his eyes were hard and unreadable. 'So, you will be dancing with me after all,' he said coldly.

'It appears so, my lord.' She tried to keep her voice equally cool.

The footman cleared his throat. Rotham looked startled, as if he'd forgotten they were in the middle of a ballroom. He turned to the guests. 'Gentlemen, please choose a fan.'

He took her arm and drew her away from the table as the men pounced on the remaining fans. He dropped her arm, then looked down at her, a mocking expression in his grey eyes. 'How unfortunate that you changed your mind and decided to toss your fan in the lottery.'

'I did not toss my fan in the lottery.'

He glanced down at the fan he still held. 'This is not your fan? Then why did you come forward?'

'Of course it is my fan. I only meant that I did not throw it in the lottery.'

He raised his brow in disbelief. 'No? I suppose it made its own way in.'

She flushed, but raised her chin. 'If you must know, I dropped it. I suppose someone found it and…'

'Obligingly tossed it in,' he finished. He managed to make it sound as if he didn't believe a word she said.

The anger she heard behind his words bewildered her. He should have been grateful to escape a forced marriage six years ago to a young girl he cared nothing for. She knotted her hands together.

'Please, my lord, we cannot quarrel here.'

'Shall we continue this conversation elsewhere, then?'

'No,' she whispered. She glanced around, feeling helpless. The footmen were removing the table. She saw Dorothea standing with a slight young man in a pale blue coat. The musicians began the opening notes of a minuet.

Rotham took her arm. 'As much as it pains you, you are obligated to me for this dance.'

She stopped, insulted by his drawling tone. 'I have no

desire to dance with you, my lord. Will you please return my fan?'

He smiled coolly. 'No. Not until we have finished this dance. You have no choice. Unless you want to create a scene.'

He led her into position. He bowed, graceful as ever, then stepped forward to take her hand. A smile touched his lips, but his eyes were ice-cold. 'You should at least look pleased to be dancing with me, Mrs Ellison. Even if you did not throw your fan in the lottery.'

'Please don't,' she whispered. Her bravado was starting to crumble under his continued assault. Why was he doing this to her? In all the imaginary conversations she'd concocted about this moment, she had never thought he would be angry. Indifferent, perhaps even contemptuous, but not so coldly angry.

'I am merely attempting conversation. Is there a topic you wish to discuss?'

'No.' She almost felt physically ill, as she had when her husband had belittled her. Somehow, her feet moved through the steps of the dance.

His mouth curved in that dangerous, cruel smile. 'Very well, perhaps I should choose a topic since you cannot seem to think of one. I was sorry to hear of your husband's untimely death. How…?'

She jerked her hand out of his grasp, the blood draining from her face. 'How dare you? Is it not enough you must insult me and now you mock me? I wish I had never laid eyes on you again!'

His face stiffened, a spot of colour appearing in his cheeks. She whirled around and, heedless of the stares and gasps from the guests, somehow made it through the dancers towards the doors leading from the ballroom. She had just reached the hallway when someone touched her arm. Her heart stopped and for a wild moment she thought it was Rotham.

But it was not. She looked up into Harry Devlin's imperturbable and welcome face. 'I take it your first meeting with Rotham was not exactly cordial?'

'Oh, Harry! It…it was horrible!' To her shame, her voice trembled.

He raised a cool brow, but his voice was kind. 'That bad? My dear, shall I call him out for you?'

'No!' She took a deep breath. 'No. Please, will you see Jane and Thea home? I…I just want to leave.'

Jack finally managed to make his way through the crowd after extricating himself from his stepmother's scathing condemnation of Claire. The dance had continued but without its former spirit. Most of the guests were too occupied in craning their heads around to stare at Jack.

He paid them little attention as he left the ballroom. The hallway was empty except for a few couples conversing. He dashed down the winding staircase to the main hallway. He reached the last few steps just as Harry stepped in from the cool night.

Jack stopped and stared down at his friend. 'Where is she?'

Harry raised a brow. 'You are referring to Claire? I just saw her off in her carriage. I doubt if she'd care to stand up with you again at any rate.' He opened an elaborate snuffbox and took a pinch. 'Or marry you.'

'If I didn't know better, I might be inclined to believe you had a hand in this affair.' Jack looked more sharply at Harry. 'Or perhaps you did. She claimed she has no idea how her fan came to be in the lottery.'

Harry shrugged. 'Perhaps, but I couldn't control which fan you picked. Unless you are crediting me with supernatural powers.' A slight smile touched his lips. 'Amazing how history repeats itself. We are almost in the same position as six years ago. But with much higher stakes on all accounts.'

Jack glanced down at the fan he still held. He looked back up at Harry. 'It is indeed ironic.'

'I shall be interested to see what happens this time. Shall you forfeit again, I wonder?'

Jack's mouth curved in a grim smile. 'No. I fully intend to win this wager.'

Chapter Two

'Well, really!' Lady Billingsley paused in the doorway of the drawing room and looked back at Claire. Her double chin quivered. 'I had hoped after last night you would have the decency to do the right thing and leave London immediately.' Her gaze shifted to her niece. 'And I cannot believe, Jane, that you actually mean to defend her! Dorothea's season is quite ruined!' She marched out, her large hips swaying with indignation.

'Oh, the dreadful woman!' Jane exclaimed. She brought her hands to her burning cheeks. She sank back down on the sofa. Her face was pale and Claire saw that her hands shook.

Claire left her chair and went to Jane. 'Oh, dear! I…I am so sorry to have brought this upon you.' Claire knelt beside her. She had been stricken with remorse ever since last night. Lady Billingsley's words, as harsh as they might seem, were only too true. Claire had brought disgrace upon her family. Edward would be furious with her. But then, she hardly ever pleased her brother no matter what she tried to do.

Jane looked unhappy. ''Tis hardly your doing. Lord Rotham should not have behaved in such a despicable manner. I can't imagine what possessed him. Oh, Claire, I fear he has never forgiven you for refusing him.'

'No.' Claire bit her lip. She couldn't imagine why. He had not been in love with her; in fact, she was not even certain he had liked her. She had thought they were friends, but his perfidy had destroyed even that illusion. And that had hurt even more than the shame she had found herself in.

She covered Jane's hand with her own. 'Perhaps I should quit London. I fear Lady Billingsley is right. I have brought disgrace upon you and Dorothea. I fear I am destined to ruin myself, but I cannot forgive myself if I ruin you in the process.'

'Oh, Claire, you have not.'

'But we have already had one invitation withdrawn. And there are certain to be others.'

'I would never even think of attending Lady Hawke's ball if she refuses to receive you.'

'But Dorothea…'

'Dorothea quite agrees with me,' Jane said. She turned and gave Claire a little hug. 'Do not trouble yourself. I have quite made up my mind this will not affect us at all. And I forbid you to leave London. Now, why don't you go upstairs and inform Dorothea that Aunt has left and it is safe to come down? And then you must rest. We will not be receiving any more visitors today.'

Claire gave Thea Jane's message, then wandered back to her bedchamber. She stood looking out over the formal garden at the back of the house. She couldn't leave matters as they stood. Lord Rotham would undoubtedly cut her, but what if he cut Jane or Dorothea? Dorothea's season would be ruined. What if Lady Billingsley was right and no one offered for Dorothea? It would be dreadful.

And Edward. Her brother would be furious if news of this reached his ears. Thank goodness he was in Brussels on a diplomatic mission. Perhaps, if Rotham could be convinced to acknowledge Jane and Dorothea, and if Claire left London, the whole affair could be hushed before Edward caught wind of it.

She turned from the window and sank down on her bed. Oh, why must he have pulled her fan among all the others? Had he recognised it and purposely done so? She could think of no reason why he would, unless he wanted to taunt her. Even now, the thought of his cold, mocking words made her shrivel inside.

If only she had kept her wits about her and smiled coolly at Rotham as if she scarcely cared what he said to her. But, no, as usual her emotions had burst to the fore and she had reacted without thinking. And now Dorothea's season was at stake.

And, to make matters worse, he still had her fan.

There was only one thing to do: she must beg his forgiveness, no matter how painful it might be.

Jack waited impatiently while his valet helped him into his morning coat. Hobbes then stepped in front of Jack and ran a critical eye down his handiwork. 'Very nice, my lord. The coat fits splendidly, although the cravat has the slightest of creases. Perhaps I might…'

'No.' Jack scowled. 'I'm in no mood to worry about my cravat.' The slight but persistent headache in the back of his head was an uncomfortable reminder of last night's excesses. His reputation for remaining sober was due to the very fact he always woke up with a blasted headache that could last an entire day after drinking too much.

'Perhaps it would be wiser to postpone your lordship's

business for a more suitable time,' Hobbes suggested delicately. The expression on his long, imperturbable face was not unsympathetic.

'This business cannot wait.'

'Very well. If that is all…'

'Yes. Thank you.'

Hobbes silently departed, undoubtedly relieved to return to his favourite task of cleaning and polishing Jack's boots.

Jack went to his dressing-table and picked up the gloves Hobbes had laid out for him. His gaze fell on the delicate folded fan next to a diamond cravat pin. He ran a hand through his hair with a groan. It wasn't only the brandy that was troubling him this morning.

What devil had possessed him to torment her like that? Until the moment he'd seen her in the saloon and recognised her, he'd thought she meant nothing to him. Then all the anger and bitterness he'd thought long gone had sprung to the surface. He'd looked into her face, even prettier than he'd remembered with her clear eyes and generous mouth, and felt something twist within him. He'd wanted to punish her for the hurt she'd caused him six years ago.

Oh, he'd had his revenge all right. And ended up creating an unforgivable scene in the middle of his grandmother's ball. The gossip circulating by now would probably be fascinating.

He wondered what damnable luck had drawn him to her fan. Or had it only been bad luck? He picked up the fan, running his finger down the ivory, finding the small chip in one corner. It had stood out among the other glittering fans by its faded looks, as if its owner had loved and used it well. He'd had some vague thought that perhaps the lady would be different from most of the shallow, frivolous women of the *ton*.

He'd never expected Claire. The odd relief he'd felt when she had come forward had been quickly replaced by anger. She'd made it very clear she detested him.

His lip curled and he put the fan down with an impatient movement. Undoubtedly, the brandy he'd consumed before the lottery had addled his mind. He was rarely given to such sentimental idiocies.

He picked up his gloves, wondering what the devil he was to do now. Unless he wanted to lose his horse, he was now obligated to convince her to marry him. Last night, the anger combined with the alcohol he'd consumed before the fan lottery had given him the false bravado to declare she'd marry him this time. But, in the sobering light of day, the possibility appeared remote.

He scowled and rubbed the back of his neck. Headache or not, he had little choice about his next move. He was going to call on Claire and hope he'd be allowed to set foot in the house.

His first order of business with Claire was offering her an apology.

The day was sunny with only a few lazy clouds floating in a cerulean-blue sky. Jack walked to St James's Square, hoping the exercise would help clear his head. He arrived at Lord Dunford's mansion. A fashionably dressed lady was just leaving the house accompanied by another female. When the lady turned her face, he was stunned to see it was Claire. She paid little heed to him until he stepped directly into her path.

'Claire.'

She gasped. 'Wh-what are you doing here, Ja...my lord?' she asked. A flush spread over her cheeks.

'I was hoping to call on you.'

'Call on me?' She backed away as if he'd suggested a seduction.

'Yes. You are leaving?' An idiotic question. Unfortunately, Claire had always had this effect on him. His gaze travelled over her. Her face was still a perfect oval, the few strands escaping from her bonnet the same warm golden-brown he remembered. She had always reminded him of a quiet autumn day.

'Yes, that is, I...I was.' She looked even more flustered as if he'd caught her in some misdeed.

'For a walk?' There was no carriage in sight. Green Park was adjacent to St James's Square so it was reasonable to think that was her destination.

'I suppose.' She bit her lip as if she was at a loss as to what to do next.

He raised a brow. 'You suppose? You don't know?'

She took a deep breath. 'Actually, I had been planning to call on you.'

'Call on me?' It was his turn to start. He frowned at her. 'What the devil for?'

She looked around as if she feared someone would see them together. 'Perhaps we should discuss this elsewhere.'

'We can walk in Green Park.'

She glanced up at his face, her soft hazel eyes uncertain beneath the wide brim of her bonnet. 'Very well, my lord.'

They started off, with the maid, who appeared little more than a girl, trailing behind them. He waited until they reached Green Park before stopping under the shade of a tree.

He looked down at her, a slight frown on his brow. 'I trust you were not serious about calling on me. Unless you want your reputation torn to shreds.'

'I doubt if I have much reputation left to ruin after last night.'

'You most certainly wouldn't have if something like that ever got around.' He fixed her with an ominous look. 'Ladies do not call on men, my dear.'

'I would have had my maid with me.'

He glanced over at the girl, who had wandered off and was staring with a dreamy expression at a herd of cows. He snorted. 'She barely looks capable of washing her own face, much less acting as a suitable chaperon.'

'Well, really!' She gave him an indignant look. 'I assure you she is perfectly capable. And I hardly think it is any of your concern what I do, my lord.'

My lord. He raised his brow, irritated at the formal address. She had rarely used it before, and only to tease him when he became too top-lofty. He folded his arms across his chest. 'It is. Most certainly if I am involved.'

'You are not…' She glared at him and then gathered herself together. 'This conversation is ridiculous. I have something I want to say to you.'

'What is it? If you want an apology, I will own I was in the wrong to behave in such an objectionable manner,' he said stiffly.

'Oh.' She appeared completely taken aback.

'Well? Do you accept my apology?'

Her eyes flashed with sudden anger. She looked as if she wanted to rip him up, but instead she frowned. 'Very well, but only for Thea's sake.'

'Thea?'

'Dorothea. My niece.' She took a deep breath, clasping her hands in front of her. 'I fear because of last night

I…I have disgraced myself and ruined her season. Mrs Billingsley—she is Jane's aunt—has already informed me that no one will receive me, and Thea will never make a decent match because her aunt has insulted a peer of the realm. And Lady Hawkes has withdrawn an invitation to her ball. Jane is horribly distressed, but declares she does not care, and Thea is vowing to cut anyone who dares to cut me. And when Edward finds out he will probably banish me for ever. So, I wanted to apologise and ask if…'

She looked vulnerable, suddenly reminding him of the girl she had been. Jack felt his temper flare. The damnable mess was hardly her fault, no more than it had been her doing last time.

'They're both fools,' he snapped. 'Don't worry. I'll make sure Dorothea's season isn't ruined. Nor shall you be banished. God only knows, I don't want to have that hanging over my head.'

'You don't mean to cut them?' She almost seemed to sag with relief.

'No, why the devil would I?'

'I don't know. Lady Billingsley said…'

'Lady Billingsley knows nothing. Five minutes in her company should tell you that.' He clasped his hands behind his back as he thought. 'Are you going to Lady Melton's rout tonight?'

'No. I don't think…'

'You will. When you arrive, I will escort you to the drawing-room where we will have an amicable conversation. We'd best be seen together as much as possible.'

'Oh, dear.' Dismay showed on her face. 'Is that really necessary? I rather thought if you would just speak to Jane and Dorothea…'

He raised a brow. 'Yes, it is most necessary. What

better way to still the gossip than to appear together? No one will dare cut you if you're with me. And my grand-mother will be there. I've no doubt she holds me entirely responsible for last night's debacle.' His grandmother had shot him more than one look of blatant disapproval after he'd returned to the ballroom.

'That is very kind of you, my lord.' Her words were stiff. And she looked completely apprehensive as if she feared what would happen in his company. The same feeling of bitter hurt that had hit him last night shot through him.

His mouth twisted. 'Not at all. I am never kind. And I always have my price.'

The flash of fear he saw in her eyes should have been gratifying. Instead, he felt even more bitter. He kept his face carefully indifferent. He held out his arm. 'I will escort you home.'

Her own face had shut down. 'No, I think I would rather walk alone.'

He dropped his arm. 'Very well. Until tonight.' He turned on his heel and left, not caring to know whether she watched him or not.

Lady Melton greeted her guests at the top of the wind-ing staircase on the first floor. Her eyes lit up with sup-pressed excitement when she saw Jane, Dorothea, Claire, and Harry, who had escorted them, come up the stairs. She was a short, petite brunette, with a vivacious man-ner. She grasped Jane's hand. 'Dear Jane! This is quite splendid. How lovely you look as always. I wonder that Edward has left you alone! And Thea. You will turn the heads of all the young men. It is quite unfair to the other young ladies.' She dropped Jane's hand and then took Claire's. 'My poor dear! It was so brave of you to come.

After last night… But the Duchess of Arundel has explained it all. How dreadful to feel so unwell that you must dash out of the ballroom!'

'I beg your pardon?' Claire said, feeling as if she'd missed part of the conversation.

'Yes, it was dreadful,' Jane said quickly. 'Poor Claire, the heat and noise of a ballroom always makes her feel so faint. And she is still recovering from a bout of influenza.'

Claire heard Harry emit a choked cough from behind them.

'You still look rather pale. No doubt you felt you must come so no one would think you meant to hide away!' Lady Melton lowered her voice. 'Lord Rotham is already here. Everyone is anxiously waiting to see what he will do when he sees you. I do hope he will behave!'

Jane managed to extricate Claire from Lady Melton's grip. 'I am certain everyone will be quite civil.'

'We must hope,' Harry said. He said something to Lady Melton which made her titter and then joined them inside the crowded drawing room. He looked down at Claire with a lazy smile. 'So, the Duchess of Arundel has decided you were struck with a sudden bout of illness. I wonder why?'

Claire gave him a swift smile. 'I…I really have no idea.'

'I must admit it is an interesting explanation for your sudden departure.'

'It is very clever. I wish we had thought of it,' Thea said.

'I wonder if Jack knows of it?' Harry's eye held a speculative gleam.

Claire flushed. She was trying to think of a way to

divert Harry from the topic, when the Duchess appeared at her side.

'Mrs Ellison, how nice to see you.' Her smile was warm. 'Are you better, my dear? You still appear a trifle pale, but then it is understandable.'

'I...I feel much better.'

'Splendid.' She smiled at Jane. 'I hope you won't object if I steal Mrs Ellison away? My grandson has been impatiently waiting to see her.'

The other three stared at Claire in surprise. They knew nothing about her visit to Rotham. 'Why, yes,' Jane finally said.

'There is nothing to worry about,' the Duchess said reassuringly. She took Claire's arm and led her across the room.

He stood near the tall windows of the saloon with a man Claire did not recognise. He turned as they approached, his face expressionless.

The Duchess propelled Claire forward. She smiled at the man with Rotham. 'Dear Frederick, how do you do? Have you met Mrs Ellison? My dear, allow me to present the Honourable Frederick Brenton. He is a cousin of John's.'

Mr Brenton had a pleasant round face under light brown hair cut in a fashionable Brutus crop. He stared at Claire, then seemed to remember he was supposed to say something. He bowed over Claire's hand and quickly released it. 'Delighted to make your acquaintance, Mrs Ellison.'

'Thank you.'

'And of course, you know my grandson,' the Duchess said.

Rotham stepped forward in a lazy movement and took Claire's hand. He lifted it to his lips, the kiss lingering a touch longer than was proper. A shiver ran through her. She resisted the urge to snatch her hand away.

A slight smile curved his lips. 'Mrs Ellison, I do hope you are better.'

'Y-yes. My lord.' Why must she stammer like a schoolgirl around him? It was just he looked so unapproachable again.

'Well? Are you?'

'Oh, yes. I'm afraid the heat in ballrooms affects me dreadfully,' she blurted out.

His mouth quirked, and for the first time amusement flashed in his face. 'Does it? Then next time we must be certain we dance near a window.'

Claire flushed, aware that Mr Brenton was eyeing them with a great deal of curiosity. The Duchess linked her arm through his. 'Come, Frederick, I must introduce you to Miss Morton. A charming young lady although she is rather like a rabbit—or is it a kitten?' She led him away.

Claire looked down at her fan, her mind blank. She had to think of something to say. Already, she could see two ladies had given up all pretence of conversation and were watching them. She took a deep breath and looked up at Rotham.

'There seems to be a number of people here,' she said, unnerved by his silent regard.

'Yes,' he replied, his voice polite. He didn't look very agreeable.

'I think it would be best if we entered into some sort of conversation,' she said desperately. 'I fear people will think we're about to quarrel again if we stand here without saying a word.'

'You are undoubtedly right. Do you have a topic you wish to discuss?'

'You are not being particularly helpful, my lord.' Really, she would almost rather have him walk away than stand here in this awkward silence.

'I beg your pardon.' He frowned. 'So, do you see Devlin often?'

'Harry?' She was taken aback by the question. 'Well, yes. He is a neighbour and has always been a very good friend.' She smiled a little. 'He has promised to look after us since Edward is in Brussels. And, of course, since he inherited Charing Hall we see him quite often.'

'I see.' His voice was clipped as if her answer hadn't pleased him at all. He folded his arms. 'So, you are living with your brother?'

'Yes.'

'How long have you been there?'

'Since Marcus died. For the past two years. Edward very kindly offered me a home.'

'Kind?' His mouth tightened. 'That was the least he could do. Were you happy with Ellison?'

What business was it of his? Especially when he sounded as if he was interrogating her for some misdeed. 'I really don't care to discuss my marriage with you, my lord. Perhaps we could discuss something more impersonal.'

'Such as what?'

'I have no idea. In fact, there is no point in continuing this idiotic conversation if you're going to stand there and…and glare at me!' Claire turned, colour rising in her cheeks.

'Wait. You can't go.' His fingers closed around her wrist.

'Let go of me!' She attempted to shake off his hand, barely aware of the gasp of one of the ladies next to them.

He dropped her hand as if it burned him. His brows snapped together in a ferocious scowl. 'Claire,' he said warningly.

'Kindly cease to address me by my given name! And will you have the goodness to return my fan?' She glared at him and started to stalk off.

She found herself face to face with his stepmother, Lady Rotham. 'I beg your pardon,' Claire said.

Lady Rotham's chilly blue gaze swept over Claire, a mixture of dislike and triumph in her eyes as she stepped aside. 'Of course. How very delightful to see you again, Mrs Ellison. But I see it is not only balls where you feel faint.'

'I find it quite depends on the company!' Claire snapped, and then wanted to bite her tongue when she saw two spots of furious colour appear on the other's face. 'Please excuse me, my lady.'

Claire made her way through the crowded room, wanting only to escape. She saw no sign of Jane or Thea—they had probably circulated to the next room. Harry was nowhere in sight. She reached the hallway, despair replacing her anger. She sank against a wall, next to a heavily carved table, and briefly closed her eyes. Nothing could ever redeem her from society's censure now. Lady Rotham had never liked her and now she had managed to insult one of society's leading hostesses as well as an earl. She'd best leave London and hope Lady Billingsley would be able to repair the damage she'd done.

She sniffed, refusing to give in to the sudden desire to burst into tears. Why must she always act so irrationally when she was with him? Losing her temper, running off on him in the middle of balls and routs, allowing him to kiss her in a moonlit garden.

'Claire. Damn, don't look like that.'

Her head jerked up, her heart nearly slammed to a halt. Rotham stood in front of her, a frown on his brow. She attempted to regain her composure and glared at him. 'I am not looking like anything in particular, my lord.'

'Then what is this?' With a gentle finger, at odds with the roughness in his voice, he brushed a tear that had managed to escape onto her cheek.

She flinched. 'Don't. Please, can't you just go away?'

'I want to talk to you. I know a room where we can be private.'

'I really do not think conversation between us is possible. You do nothing but…but glare at me.'

A wry smile touched his lips. 'If I promise not to glare at you, will you come with me?' He held out his hand.

She stared at his long, strong fingers, with the heavy signet-ring he wore on one finger. 'I don't want to talk to you.'

'But you must. We cannot continue like this.'

'We won't. I am leaving London as soon as possible.'

He dropped his hand. 'No. You can't leave.'

She raised her chin. 'I most certainly can, my lord.'

He made an impatient sound. 'I don't remember you as so stubborn. Will you come with me now, or must I force you?'

He looked perfectly capable of doing so. His face had that dark look again as if nothing she said pleased him. And the last thing she wanted was another scene. How could she have forgotten how odious he could be when he wanted something? Although she had no idea what he really wanted from her. She sagged against the wall, suddenly feeling exhausted. 'Please, can it not wait?'

His eyes searched her face. 'Very well. I will call on

you tomorrow.' He hesitated. 'Claire, there is no need for us to be enemies.'

She looked into his dark, intense eyes, hardly knowing what to think. Once she had thought they were friends, perhaps even more, but it had turned out to be nothing but a lie. She had been nothing more to him than a means to win a wager.

She could not fall into that trap again. He was no more interested in her now than he had been in the plump, plain girl she had been at seventeen.

He waited for her to speak. She moistened her lips, wishing she could tell him that they would never be anything but enemies.

'So, am I in time to prevent another battle?'

Harry's voice jerked them apart. His brow was raised quizzically as he looked from one to the other. 'I take it the pistols are cocked but the signal has not yet been given.'

Rotham moved away. The cool expression had returned to his face. 'On the contrary, the weapons have been dropped—at least for the moment.' His gaze returned to Claire. 'I hope to convince Claire there is no need for weapons at all,' he said softly.

'Do you? Of course, it is never wise to completely disarm until you are convinced your enemy is no longer a danger.'

Rotham met Harry's gaze, a distinct challenge in his own. 'There will be no danger.'

'I trust not.' Harry looked over at Claire, who had been listening to the exchange in increasing confusion. 'Come, Claire, it is time to bid our hostess farewell. Jane wishes to leave.'

'Oh, yes, of course.'

Rotham stopped in front of them, blocking their way. 'Tomorrow, Claire.'

She flushed and nodded. And hoped she could find the resolution to resist whatever it was he wanted.

Chapter Three

The next morning, Jack entered his drawing-room where his stepmother sat on the yellow and cream striped sofa. In her early thirties, she was an elegant brunette with a cool, composed beauty. She put down her delicate china cup when she saw him. 'I almost thought you'd ridden out of town. Do you always ride so long?'

'Sometimes.' He pulled off his riding gloves with a brisk motion. 'What brings you here so early, Celeste?'

A cool smile lit her perfect features. 'I have no doubt you know quite well.'

'Do I?'

'I pray you will sit down. I cannot converse with you pacing the room. It makes me quite nervous.'

Jack threw himself down in a wing chair across from her, stretching his booted legs in front of him. She looked at them, her nose wrinkling in distaste, before turning her attention back to him. 'I will come right to the point. You would be quite foolish to have anything more to do with Claire Ellison. It should be quite obvious after last night she intends to publicly humiliate you.'

'I doubt Mrs Ellison wished to humiliate me.' He'd briefly entertained the thought, but then the image of the tear trickling down Claire's cheek rose before him.

'Then how else can you explain her behaviour? I hope you won't tell me some tale of her taking ill again. No one believes that for a minute. Perhaps Maria could make that story credible once, but not a second time.'

'I did attempt to detain her by force. If anything, I would expect you to censure me.'

She gave a small laugh. 'I very much fear you still have some odd infatuation with the creature. I can't imagine why. She is no beauty and has nothing to recommend her. And she nearly trapped you into marriage six years ago. I dare say it is revenge.'

'I have no idea what you're talking about.'

'She wants revenge. For your refusing to marry her six years ago, of course.'

'You are mistaken. She refused to marry me.'

'Really! How chivalrous of you to say so.' She gave him an arch, disbelieving look which made him want to snarl. 'You've acted foolishly in this matter. Everyone is starting to speculate about what happened between you. I had to assure Emma Fenshaw last night that of course you did not seduce her. I told her the girl had a silly schoolgirl *tendre* for you and believed you wanted to marry her and then became spiteful when you did not.'

He gave her a level look. 'I trust you will spread no more rumours about Claire Ellison.'

Her eyes opened wide. 'Rumours? I was merely telling the truth.'

'You will spread no more rumours.' His voice was deadly quiet. 'If you recall, I am the trustee of your not insignificant allowance.' His father's infatuation with his new wife had not extended to allowing her control over her funds after his death.

She raised a brow. Her laugh was husky. 'Are you threatening me?'

'Yes.'

She stared at him, her expression calculating as if she couldn't quite decide whether he was serious or not.

He rose, not wanting to give her the opportunity to argue. 'I cannot spare you any more time. I have another appointment.'

She also stood and pulled on her kid gloves. 'You can't afford to waste time with Mrs Ellison. You must marry, you know. You will need to decide soon.'

She made an exasperated face when he said nothing. 'Alicia has arrived. It is time I found her a suitable husband.'

'She is only a schoolgirl.'

'She is seventeen. She has quite grown up and is very lovely. I hope you will befriend her as she has few acquaintances in London.'

'She will undoubtedly find many more under your wing.' Jack did not want to pursue the topic of his stepmother's ward, for he'd recently begun to suspect Celeste had some idea Alicia would make him a suitable wife. At least Celeste preferred to live in her own newly decorated town house in Bedford Square so he was not forced to have either one of them under his roof.

Celeste finally left. He watched her go, then flung himself down into a wing chair. He frowned. His threat would most likely stop Celeste from spreading new rumours, but he had no doubt she would do her best to worsen the gossip already circulating. For some reason, she had detested Claire from the very first. He had been invited to a house party given by Harry's parents that summer. Celeste had come down a week later and had taken an instant dislike to Claire.

Not that his behaviour was any better than Celeste's. He'd gone to the damnable rout last night with every intention of making polite conversation, but the sight of Claire smiling at Harry had made him want to mill his friend down. And then when she'd spoken of Harry's kindness all his good intentions had snapped.

She'd always had that effect on him. Six years ago he had only intended to kiss her and instead had come close to seducing her. She had refused to let him behave honourably and had instead thrown herself away on Marcus Ellison. Ellison had been a house guest of her brother's that summer. A cold, upright man of nearly forty, Jack had sensed from the first he wanted Claire. The man had no doubt taken advantage of her disgrace to offer his own proposal of marriage. Every time Jack envisaged her in Ellison's bony arms he'd been filled with a mixture of fury and despair.

Who knew what rash thing she'd do now? His lips curved in a grim smile. He wasn't waiting to find out. This time she was going to marry him if he had to abduct her. She might hate him, but at least she'd be safe from herself.

Thea dropped the curtain back and looked over at Claire and Jane who sat side by side on the sofa. 'He is here! He's ridden up on the most splendid black horse. I wish I had a horse like that! You must admit, Claire, he is quite dashing.'

'I don't think I've ever seen his horse.'

'Not the horse, Aunt Claire! Lord Rotham!' Thea giggled. 'You are teasing, I hope! But, don't you think he is handsome?'

'I've really never given the matter much thought. I suppose some might think so.' Claire ignored Thea's look of disbelief. There might have been a time when Claire had found him a trifle attractive, but certainly not now.

The sound of brisk footsteps on the stairway and then masculine voices made her freeze. She looked away from the door, not wanting him to think she was waiting for him. She snatched up a book sitting on the side-table and flipped it open.

He entered the room with a firm tread, then paused in the doorway. His eyes flickered over the room, coming to rest on Claire. She flushed and looked away, wishing she could present a cool, remote appearance.

Jane rose, a pleased smile on her face. 'Lord Rotham, how kind of you to call.' She held out her hand.

He looked a little startled at her warm reception. He took her hand and bowed over it, then released it. 'Thank you. It is kind of you to receive me.'

'Of course. I believe you have met my daughter.'

'Yes.' His face relaxed. His mouth quirked as he looked at Thea. 'Although I would not recognise you. I last remember you climbing trees and ripping around the countryside on a pony.'

Thea blushed. 'I no longer do such things.'

'I expect not. You have quite grown up.'

Thea looked even more flustered at the compliment in his voice. Claire felt an unwelcome surge of jealousy. She instantly quelled it. How could she ever be jealous of Thea, whom she had loved since a tiny baby? It was only that he had smiled at Thea in the teasing way he once had smiled at Claire.

'I dare say you wish to speak to Claire,' Jane said. She looked over at her daughter. 'Come, Dorothea. I wanted to show you the length of silk I found yesterday. I think it would make a splendid ballgown.'

Claire shot Jane a pleading look, which she ignored. For some reason, Jane had not been the least bit dismayed when Claire had reluctantly told her he was to call.

Dorothea followed her mother out of the room after flashing Claire a smile.

'I don't bite, Claire. And you may look at me.'

Her gaze flew to his face. To her surprise, a slight smile touched his lips.

'May I sit?' he asked.

'Sit? Oh, yes. Please do.'

For a horrible moment she thought he planned to sit next to her, but he settled his long frame in the gilt chair across from her. He seemed much too close despite the proper distance between them.

'What are you reading?' he asked.

'Reading?'

'You have a book open on your lap. I assume you're reading it.'

'It is…' Her mind was a complete blank. She looked down at the leather cover and finally remembered. 'It is *Clarissa*. By Richardson.'

'An interesting tale,' he said dryly.

'Well, I find it interesting even if you think it's dull.'

'I didn't say I found it dull.'

'No, but your particular tone of voice implied you found it dull.' She had no idea why she was sparring with him except it seemed a safe way to keep him at a distance as it had years ago.

'Not dull. Merely overly melodramatic.'

'I suppose you still only read dry history and Greek philosophy!'

His sudden grin erased the hardness in his face. 'And you still while away your time with improbable tales of distressed heroines caught in the clutches of wicked villains.'

'You will be glad to know Marcus quite shared your views. He forbade me to read anything except a few select scriptures.'

The humour faded from his face. 'I might tease you about reading novels, but I would never forbid you to do so,' he said harshly.

Claire looked away. The intensity of his words and the sudden change in his face made her feel afraid. She must keep the conversation on impersonal subjects. 'What did you want to say to me? I suppose you are not here to discuss my taste in books.'

He rose and came to stand over her. She resisted the impulse to jump up and move so she was safe behind the sofa. He looked down at her. 'I don't want you to leave London.'

'It can hardly matter to you whether I do or not.'

'But it does.'

'I can't imagine why. I've done nothing but cause trouble. I'm afraid even the Duchess's kindness cannot undo the fact I ran away again.' She took a deep breath. 'I suppose you wish for an apology. Very well, I…I am sorry.'

'I don't want an apology. You were right—I was not behaving well last night.'

'Oh.' For the second time in two days he'd surprised her.

He scowled down at her. 'There is no reason for you to run away from London. It will accomplish nothing.'

'I'm not running away. I am taking a prudent course of action.'

'For whom? Your niece? How will it help her if you leave London? It will only confirm the rumours that there was some reason for us to quarrel. And your sister-in-law. Do you think she will be happy knowing you've left London in this way? Or your brother. I assume he wanted you here for a reason.'

'To watch after Jane,' she said without thinking, and then flushed with guilt. How dare he try to shame her into staying? 'Lady Billingsley has offered to act as a chaperon.'

He raised a sardonic brow. 'Ah, the delightful Lady Billingsley again. She's more likely to drive Lady Dunford to distraction than be of any help.'

Claire bit her lip. 'I suppose she means well.'

'I doubt it. And there is my reputation to consider.'

'Your reputation?' Claire stared at him.

'Yes.' He folded his arms across his chest and gave her a hard look. 'My stepmother has already informed me that many think you wish to publicly humiliate me. The reasons you would wish to do so are of some speculation. Such as I seduced you and then refused to marry you,' he said deliberately.

She flushed. 'How…how perfectly idiotic.'

'Yes, isn't it? And rather ironic. So, I've no desire to have you leave London. That would only prove the rumours true.'

'Oh, dear…' Agitated, Claire rose. It was so dreadful, almost as if their past had risen up to haunt them, thrusting them into another impossible situation. And, as last time, he was taking the blame for a situation that was not entirely of his doing.

There was Jane and Thea to consider. Such gossip would only hurt them.

'What do you wish me to do?' she asked.

His face relaxed. 'We can start by declaring a truce. I think it might be possible for us to be in the same room together without a quarrel.'

'We don't seem to deal very well together.'

'We did once.'

'We've changed.'

'Not that much. Come, Claire, what do you say to a truce? A cessation of hostilities between us?'

She looked into his face. Today his eyes were a warm grey. They had been one of the things she had first liked about him—his eyes. A changeable grey, surrounded by long dark lashes. She had never seen such fascinating eyes on a man.

'Claire?'

She dropped her gaze. 'If you wish.' She undoubtedly sounded ungracious, but she felt reluctant to give him this small victory.

'Shall we shake on it?' He held out his hand.

With some hesitation, she placed her hand in his. But instead of shaking it he slowly raised it to his lips, then turned it to plant a kiss on her palm. Heat flowed through her at the warm pressure of his lips. She yanked her hand away, stunned at her reaction.

She frowned at him. 'That was hardly a handshake.'

His lips curved in a lazy smile, and she suddenly saw traces of the young man he'd been. She had thought him a terrible flirt. 'No, but much more binding, don't you agree? Of course, I would have preferred to seal our truce with a proper kiss, but somehow I doubt if you would co-operate.'

Claire flushed to the roots of her hair. 'No, never!' She backed away. 'Why are you even saying such things? Friends do not kiss each other.'

'It depends on the sort of friend.'

'I have no intention of ever being that sort of friend with you, my lord.'

He gave her a smile that looked rather wicked. 'No?'

'Most certainly not! If you continue to talk in this vein, then I will withdraw any pretence of friendship with you, my lord.' Claire frowned at him. Whatever was wrong with him now?

'Very well, I will try to restrain myself. Although I used to enjoy teasing you. You would turn a charming pink and then glare at me as you are doing now.'

'I would prefer not to talk about the past,' Claire informed him with cold dignity.

'Why not, Claire?' His lips still smiled, but his eyes were watchful.

'I don't owe you any reason. And please refrain from addressing me by my Christian name.'

'You granted me permission once to do so.'

She looked at him, feeling helpless and angry. Why was he bringing this up? She couldn't read him at all. 'I was young and very foolish. I don't wish to speak of the past. It is best forgotten.'

'Is it?' he asked softly.

'Yes!' She realised she was trembling. 'Yes.' She tried to recover herself. 'Is there anything else you wish to speak about? I...I do have other things I must do.'

'I think it would be best if we were seen together soon. Come riding with me.'

'Riding?' She started.

'Yes—on a horse? I remember you loved to ride.'

He was bringing up the past again. She looked away from him. 'I have no horse in London. And I have ridden very little for years.' Marcus had forbidden her to ride. And after his death she had lost interest, instead preferring long, solitary walks.

'Then come driving with me.'

Why was he so persistent? The thought of sitting next to him in a carriage was unnerving. 'I don't think it would be such a good idea.'

His brows snapped together. 'I think it would be. What better way for society to see us together?'

'I...' She bit her lip. Who knew what speculations would arise from that? But he looked so determined, she found herself unable to think of a polite way of refusing.

'And think of your niece and Lady Dunford,' he added softly.

'You're not playing fair.'

'No. I warned you, I never do.' He stepped closer, and she backed up against the sofa. 'Come, Claire, will it be so bad?'

He was too close. She was aware of his scent, a mixture of sandalwood and maleness, of how broad his shoulders were under the fine cloth of his coat. And his strong cheekbones and well-formed mouth.

'I...I don't know.'

'It won't be.' His eyes seemed to change as they moved over her face. Then his hand touched her cheek almost as if he couldn't help himself. 'You are even more lovely than I remembered.'

Her blood pounded in her ears and she felt dizzy at his touch. Her heart pounded in panic. 'Please don't!'

He stared at her, then his expression changed. 'Claire, what is it?'

'You're...you're too close.'

'Did you think I would hurt you?'

She shook her head. 'I...I don't like anyone too close to me.' Confused and ashamed, she looked away. For a moment, she'd felt the same stunned panic Marcus had aroused in her when he'd touched her face in that same way.

'Claire…' he began. She looked up at him, afraid to see the contempt in his eyes. Instead, she saw a peculiar anger.

The door opened behind them. Startled, she looked around. Harry entered. Then he stopped, one brow cocked. 'Still armed, are you?'

'No.' Rotham's voice was curt. 'I want Claire to drive with me today.'

'Indeed.' Harry's eyes went to Claire's face. He looked faintly amused. 'I fear you are out of luck, then. She has already promised to drive with me.'

Claire could scarcely look at Rotham, certain he would question the truth of Harry's statement.

He didn't. He gave her a hard look, then his lip curled. 'Very well. Perhaps another time? I trust you will not always be occupied?'

'I—I…no,' Claire stammered. He paused, then briefly raised her hand to his lips. And then he was gone.

She should have felt relieved. Instead, she felt horribly uncomfortable. She looked up at Harry to find a slight smile on his face. 'You looked so desperate, I thought I must come to your rescue. I trust you really did not wish to drive with Jack?'

'No, of course not.' But she wondered if that was really the truth.

Chapter Four

Claire picked up her gloves from her dressing-table and wondered why she felt so apprehensive about driving with Harry. There was no reason to be; she'd known him before she could walk. His family's estate marched next to her family's. He had always been like another brother, closer to her than Edward had ever been.

But her apprehension was not really due to Harry at all, but to Jack. Lord Rotham, she corrected herself. She bit her lip. She suspected he knew very well she had never agreed to drive with Harry before this morning. And he'd been extremely displeased. Which shouldn't matter a whit to her. He'd caused her more than a little displeasure ever since she met him. It was only that she had always quailed under displeasure, her brother had made life uncomfortable when she crossed him, and, with Marcus, the consequences had been devastating.

And then there was her reaction to his touch. Her cheeks burned whenever she thought of it. But Jack was not like Marcus; there were no cruel words, no brutal kisses. He had stopped as soon as he'd seen the fear in her face and said he would not hurt her. And she had believed him.

Her apprehension returned when they entered Hyde Park in Harry's phaeton. She had never been to the park during the fashionable hour and was astounded at the crush of people, horses and carriages. Most of society appeared to be here. To her chagrin, she found her heart thudding uncomfortably as she looked around. She mentally chastised herself. This was ridiculous. She had no reason to think he would even be here.

Harry cocked a brow at her expression. He looked quite elegant in a light blue coat over a buff-striped waistcoat, his cravat tied in a complicated knot. 'Must you look so apprehensive? I've not overturned a vehicle yet. At least not in Hyde Park.'

'I was thinking of something else.'

'While you are with me? My dear, I am insulted.' He nodded to a lady in a phaeton. 'Particularly since I suspect it was of another man.'

'Another man?'

'Rotham.' His lips curved in a slight smile at her startled look. 'Who or what else would bring such a frown to your lovely countenance?'

'Why would you ever think that? I really give him very little thought at all.' Claire was embarrassed her thoughts were so transparent.

'Don't you?' His horses started as a dog darted out in front of them. Claire clutched the side of the carriage. Harry deftly brought the horses under control. 'They are a bit fresh today.' He looked back down at Claire. 'I never did know why you turned him down. Was his… er…embrace so distasteful?'

'No!' Heat suffused her cheeks. 'I…I didn't want to trap him into marriage.'

'Trap him? You mean you were the one who lured him out to the garden?'

'No, of course not!'

'Then he lured you out to the garden. So, I would say he wanted to trap you.'

'He…he didn't lure me. He asked me if I would like to see the stars.' Oh, she sounded so terribly naïve. But, at seventeen, she had been. Jack had wanted to show her the constellations, and the July night had been clear and cool after the stuffy ballroom. He had led her to the formal garden and had spread his coat on the grass. They had sat on his coat, the scents of the garden, the peace of the evening enveloping them. She had felt so unlike her normal cautious self in the dark garden. He had reclined back on his elbows and pointed out the constellations, his voice warm and low.

The memory hurt. She forced her thoughts back to the present. 'I really don't wish to discuss him.'

He gave her a curious look. 'Don't you?'

He concentrated on manoeuvring around a trio of carriages blocking their path while their occupants conversed. And then she saw him.

He sat astride one of the most beautiful animals Claire had laid eyes on—a magnificent horse the colour of midnight. He was with another rider—a woman in a red riding habit mounted on a pretty chestnut. As she watched, the lady smiled up at Jack. Even from the short distance, Claire could see she was lovely. Then Jack looked down at her, his mouth lifting in a familiar smile.

Claire tore her eyes away with that same odd feeling she'd experienced when he'd smiled at Thea earlier.

'Mrs Robards,' Harry said. He also watched the couple.

'I beg your pardon?'

'The woman he is with is Sylvia Robards.'

There was little use in denying she was watching them. Harry knew her too well. 'She is very pretty.'

'Yes. They are very good friends.'

'Are they? How nice,' Claire said vaguely.

Harry looked amused. 'They are only friends, my dear.'

She gave him a swift frown. 'I really do not care.'

But inside she felt strangely hurt. Of course Jack would have female friends, and undoubtedly a beautiful mistress somewhere. Even six years ago, there had been rumours of his liaisons. Which was why she should have known he would never have an interest in someone as ordinary as herself.

She couldn't help glancing back towards them. Then her heart leapt to her throat as she saw he had left Mrs Robards and was trotting towards Harry's carriage.

'Oh, dear,' Claire whispered. If only she could jump out and run or fold herself away in a tight ball. If only masks were still fashionable.

'I fear it's too late to hide,' Harry murmured. 'Don't worry, he's unlikely to abduct you—at least here.'

Abduction was the least of her worries. Jack looked more as if he was inclined to strangle her as he came upon them. His face wore the cool, arrogant mask that she was beginning to realise hid anger. Was he really so angry she was riding with Harry? But that hardly made any sense unless he was jealous, which was impossible.

He reined his horse around neatly so he was riding alongside Claire. She looked straight ahead, trying to pretend he was not there.

'I trust you have no objections if I accompany you?' he said. His voice was smooth and silky. He wore no hat and in his black riding coat, his dark hair ruffled by the faint breeze, he looked dangerous and out of place in the civilised surroundings of the park.

'I don't, although I suspect Claire might,' Harry said.

'Claire can speak for herself.'

She forced herself to look at him. 'Would it do any good if I did object?'

His eyes held hers in a challenge. 'No.'

'About to go another round? Should I place a bet on the outcome?' Harry enquired. He brought his horses to a halt.

'There's no need. Claire and I have declared a truce. Haven't we, Claire?' he asked softly.

The intimate tone of his voice set her back up. He probably had been speaking to Mrs Robards in the same way. 'Of sorts,' she said coldly.

'So, she will converse amicably with me as we ride through the park.'

She looked at him. 'Will I, my lord?'

'You will, Mrs Ellison.' A slight smile played about his lips, but his eyes dared her to argue. 'Have you been to Hyde Park before, Claire?'

She gave him a false smile. She would show him how amicable she could be. 'No, it is my very first time. How lovely it is! And so many trees and people.'

'You forgot the horses and carriages,' Jack said. His eyes had begun to glitter in an ominous way.

'Oh, yes! There are so many!' She looked at his horse. 'What a pretty creature. Does he have a name?'

'Satan.'

The horse flicked his ears back at the sound of Jack's voice.

'That is not a very nice name.' It really wasn't. The horse had a refined, intelligent face.

'No?' Jack's brows snapped together.

Harry made a choking sound. Claire turned to look at him. The smirk on his face only increased her annoyance. Why wasn't he helping her? Instead, he was obviously enjoying the whole show. 'I would like to return home,' she told Harry.

'So soon?' he asked blandly.

'It cannot be too soon as far as I am concerned.'

'Trying to run again, Claire?' Jack asked softly. 'I wouldn't suggest it. I'll come after you.'

He was serious; of that she had no doubt. She clenched her hands together. She would not give him the satisfaction of another quarrel.

She was almost relieved to see Lady Rotham dressed in a stylish riding habit trot towards them on a dainty grey mare. She was accompanied by Frederick Brenton and another lady. As they came to a halt next to Harry's phaeton, Claire saw the second rider could hardly be more than seventeen. She had the cool beauty of a marble statue. Her complexion was smooth and pale, and her eyes a light clear blue.

Lady Rotham's gaze slid past Claire as if she weren't there. She smiled at Harry. 'Mr Devlin, how pleasant to see you. I believe you have met my ward, Miss Snowden?'

'I have had the delightful pleasure,' Harry said. He turned one of his most charming smiles on Miss Snowden. She gave him a cold look, then turned her gaze on Jack.

Lady Rotham steadied her mare who had bared her teeth at Jack's horse. She gave Jack an arch smile. 'I have been looking for you, Rotham. You promised to ride with us today. I was forced to impose upon dear Frederick instead.'

'No imposition at all. My pleasure,' Frederick said.

'Perhaps if I had been informed of the fact it would not have slipped my mind, ma'am.' Jack's voice was cool.

'Oh? I was quite certain you told Alicia, but perhaps I was mistaken.'

The grey mare danced into Harry's team. The horses jerked forward, causing Claire to lose her balance. Her chip-brimmed hat tumbled off her head, falling towards Harry's horses. She half stood, trying to reach it, afraid it would be trampled. The horses suddenly leapt forward. The next thing she knew, she was knocked breathless as she hit the ground.

She closed her eyes, pain and humiliation searing through her.

'Claire, damn it, look at me!' Jack's impatient voice penetrated her haze. He seemed to be leaning over her. How dare he scold her at a time like this? She kept her eyes squeezed shut, willing him to go away.

'Claire?' A gentle hand brushed over her face. 'Can you open your eyes?'

He was worried? She slowly forced her eyes open, and found his dark face hovering over hers. In her dazed condition, she suddenly recalled the last time they'd been in this position, only he had bent his head closer, until his lips covered hers.

She groaned and closed her eyes, trying to force the memory away.

'Claire, open your eyes!'

'No, go…go away.' Undoubtedly she had injured her head. Why would she even be thinking about such a thing unless her mind was addled?

'Claire? Wake up!' This time it was Harry.

From the sound of voices, there seemed to be a crowd gathered around. She reluctantly decided she'd best open her eyes before someone declared her dead. For the second time, she forced her eyes open, this time to find Harry and Jack both kneeling over her.

She tried to sit up, her head spinning. Instantly, Jack's arm was around her. 'I'm…I'm fine,' she whispered, her head sinking back into his arm.

'Hardly. I'm taking you home.'

'Oh, no. I…I came with Harry.'

Jack gave her a quelling look. 'You're insane if you think I'm letting you back in that carriage.' Before she could protest, he swung her up in his arms.

Claire wished she could swoon. She'd always detested scenes and now she was the centre of one taking place in the middle of Hyde Park. She could struggle to free herself but that would create even more of a scene. And, from the stubborn set of Jack's jaw, she had no doubt he'd force her to comply with his wishes.

'This is ridiculous. You cannot carry me home.'

'I'm not planning to carry you home.' Without preamble, he lifted her up on his horse. She clutched at the pommel, stunned to find herself atop the horse. Dizzy, she swayed a little. In a quick motion, he mounted behind her, his arm going around her waist to pull her back against him.

Despite her spinning head, Claire managed to speak. 'Let me down, now! What will everyone think?'

'Whatever they want, I imagine,' he said dryly.

'Rotham, don't you think you are carrying this a bit too far?' Lady Rotham said, her voice coolly amused. 'I doubt Mrs Ellison's life is in danger. And she is quite right—the gossips will construe the most damaging interpretation.'

'Let them.' He sounded completely indifferent.

'Harry?' Claire looked down at him, praying he would do something.

He merely shrugged, a faint smile at his lips. 'Sorry, Claire; I value my life too much to protest.'

'Wise of you.' Jack nudged his horse into a slow walk.

Claire closed her eyes, not wanting to see the stares and curious looks. If only it were possible to simply disappear. Whatever was wrong with him? Was he still so angry with her he planned to humiliate her at every opportunity without regard to the damage it did?

Unfortunately, her closed eyes made her only too aware of him. His heartbeat was strong and steady beneath her ear. The fine fabric of his coat caressed her cheek. His arm held her close to him, the horse's movements causing it to brush the underside of her breast. He smelled of horse and cologne and maleness, and, to her chagrin, she felt as if her body was on fire.

Which was ridiculous. She shifted, trying to move away from his arm which was threatening to send her out of her skin. His response was to tighten his hold.

Her eyes shot open. She squeaked. 'Th-there is no need to hold me so tightly. I…I can't breathe.'

'I didn't want you to try and escape.'

'I am hardly about to do that.' The sound of his voice so close made her dizzy.

'As much as you'd like to.'

'I can't imagine anyone who'd like to be dragged through the streets of London atop a horse like some sort of…of parcel.'

'I usually send my parcels with a servant.'

'That is not the point.'

'What is the point?'

'You are impossible!'

'Allow me to return the compliment.' At least she had

the satisfaction of hearing he sounded just as exasperated as she felt.

Claire clamped her lips tight, not wanting to say any more to him. By now they had made their way through the streets and had turned into St James's Square. She only prayed none of the neighbours were looking out of their windows.

In front of her brother's home, he halted the horse, After he'd dismounted, he turned and held out his arms. The sight of him waiting for her, his dark face expressionless, made her feel dizzy again. Perhaps it was only that the horse was so tall, or she had hit her head too hard.

'Are you planning to sit on Satan the rest of the day?' The impatience in his voice jolted her out of her reverie.

She scowled down at him. 'No. I was merely recovering my balance. Besides, he is a very tall horse.'

He looked startled and then his mouth quirked. 'I can't remember you being afraid of heights before.'

'I did suffer a jolt to my head, if you recall,' she informed him with icy dignity.

'Yes, but apparently not to your tongue.'

A stab of hurt shot through her. She slid off the horse. Jack caught her, his arms closing around her as she stumbled. She shoved away from him, wanting only to escape before he saw how his words had affected her.

But it was too late. 'Claire? What the devil is wrong?'

'N-nothing.'

She turned and started up the steps. The butler opened the door and Jane appeared behind him, her face full of concern.

'Claire? What has happened? Are you unwell?' she asked, coming to catch Claire's hands.

'I am fine.'

'Lord Rotham?' Jane looked over Claire's shoulder.

'She fell from Devlin's carriage. I decided to bring her home.'

'Oh, no! You were hurt!'

Claire tried to smile. ''Twas nothing. Please, Jane, I…I think I will just go in.' Avoiding Jack's eyes, she gathered up her skirts and hobbled in.

Jack stood against the wall in Lady Denbigh's Chinese drawing-room and fought back a yawn of boredom. He prayed the soprano would soon halt her piercing run, or he'd be tempted to put an end to it himself.

He shifted, folding his arms across his chest. The only reason he'd shown up at such a dull affair was in the hopes of seeing Claire. But when Lady Dunford and Thea had arrived with Harry just before the concert started Claire had not been with them. He shouldn't be surprised. After he'd carted her off like some sort of savage claiming a bride, he wouldn't be surprised if she never spoke to him again.

The sound of applause startled him out of his thoughts. He waited until the crowd dispersed before making his way towards Jane. He encountered the disapproving gaze of Lady Bellam, who barely gave him a nod. She was a stickler for the proprieties. Undoubtedly his latest exploit with Claire had marked him. From the turned heads and the whispers, he had no doubt all of society had heard by now.

To his surprise, Jane smiled at him. 'Lord Rotham, how nice to see you again.'

He bowed over her hand, then released it. 'Is it? I must own that surprises me. I would have expected you to consider cutting me.'

'If I did not think that you had Claire's best interests

at heart, I might do so, but under the circumstances I quite understand.'

'Do you?' Jack was startled. He was not exactly certain what circumstances she referred to. He wasn't about to ask. 'I doubt if your husband would be quite so generous.'

'I would hope he would be.' She gave him a reassuring smile. 'I suppose you are worried about Claire. She has a few bruises, but that is all. She was rather tired, so I insisted she stay at home.'

'I see.' So, Jane had insisted she not come. Would she have been here otherwise? Perhaps it was just as well. The thought of her soft curves crushed against him had almost been his undoing during that interminable ride to St James's Square.

He realised Jane was speaking. 'I am holding a small rout in a few days. I would like to send you an invitation. I would be very pleased if you would come.'

He was even more surprised. 'You are very kind, but I don't think it would be wise. I doubt your husband would approve.'

'I am certain my husband would agree it is time to put the past behind us.' She smiled at him.

'I fear you are overly optimistic. I would not want to cause you trouble.'

'You would not.' Under her soft appearance, he sensed an amazingly stubborn streak.

'Then there is your sister-in-law. I hardly think she would consider me a welcome guest.'

A little crease marred her brow. 'You must not think that. The past few years have been difficult for Claire. She has been very hurt—I do not think trust comes very easily to her now. She needs kindness and patience.'

Anger mixed with guilt assailed him. 'I fear, ma'am,

I am to blame. I wonder more than ever that you speak to me.'

'Oh, no. I never meant to cast the blame on you.' Her blue eyes were sincere. 'We were all at fault. I should have tried harder to prevent Edward from forcing Claire into such a hasty and unwise marriage.'

'An impossible task.' He caught himself and frowned. 'I beg your pardon, Lady Dunford. I have no business casting aspersions on your husband's character.'

'Edward sometimes only sees what he wants,' she said gently. 'But he is a good man.'

'I cannot imagine you would have married him otherwise.'

'No.' She smiled a little. 'So you will come to the rout, then?'

The guests were making their way back to the saloon. He hesitated for a moment. 'Yes.'

He bowed and moved away from her. He wondered if she'd be so pleased if she knew he intended to marry Claire. He knew if Edward Dunford found out he would go to hell and back to stop him.

Chapter Five

Four days after her fall, Claire sat on her bed and tried to force a measure of enthusiasm for Lady Hawke's ball. The withdrawn invitation had been restored with a vague apology about some sort of confusion. Jane had tried to persuade her to stay home for another night of rest, but Claire had insisted she was well enough to attend.

She had no idea why she wanted to go. Her wrist still hurt and her right side felt sore where she'd landed on it. Her latest breach of propriety probably had every tongue in London wagging. Perhaps it was to show Lady Hawke and the rest of society she had no intention of hiding away. Perhaps her wits were addled from her fall. Or perhaps she wanted to see Jack.

Her cheeks flamed at the traitorous thought. She was as ridiculous as she had been at seventeen when she'd had a schoolgirlish *tendre* for Mr Poyton and had hoped to see him everywhere. She really had no desire to see Jack at all.

She forced herself to rise, hoping she hadn't wrinkled the back of her new silk gown too badly. She picked up her gloves and fan from her dressing-table. She scowled at the last item. He still had her mother's fan. For some reason, every time she saw him, all thoughts of it fled her mind. Perhaps she should send him a note, demanding its immediate return. Then she wouldn't have to speak to him at all. Of course, if she did happen to see him, she would greet him in a cool civil manner. That should still the gossip and prove to society he was nothing more than a mere acquaintance.

He was the first person Claire noticed when she entered Lady Hawke's ballroom. He stood near the wall, masculine and elegant in a midnight-blue coat and tight-fitting pantaloons. As she watched, a tall woman in pale green came to his side, laying a hand on his sleeve. He looked down at her, a slight smile curving his lips.

Claire fanned her hot cheeks, angry at herself for noticing him straight away, angrier still for wondering who the woman was. She turned and followed Jane and Thea through the crowd, forcing herself to smile at the acquaintances she'd made since coming to London. She tried to ignore some of the more curious stares cast her way.

Harry solicited Thea for the first set of dances. Jane and Claire had barely reached an empty corner when Lady Billingsley appeared. She wasted no time on the niceties of polite conversation. 'I must speak with you, Jane.'

'Can it not wait, Aunt?'

'No.' Lady Billingsley's cold gaze fell on Claire. 'I am surprised you were brazen enough to come. After the spectacle you made of yourself the other day.'

Claire froze. Jane moved closer to her side.

'I won't allow you to speak to my sister-in-law like that,' Jane said quietly.

'Her behaviour will ruin Dorothea and shame the rest

of us.' Lady Billingsley's chin quivered in self-righteous indignation. 'Even now there have been bets laid as to whether she will quarrel with Rotham tonight!'

'Have there?' Jack's coolly amused voice came from behind Claire. 'Which way did you bet, Lady Billingsley?'

Her face turned a peculiar red and her mouth fell open. Then she snapped it shut. 'I never place bets.'

The smile on his face made Claire shiver. 'Very wise of you.'

Lady Billingsley stared at him, anger in her eyes. Then she seemed to fold up and, in huffy dignity, departed.

'Oh, dear,' Jane said. She looked at Jack. 'I am so sorry. She should not have been repeating such malicious gossip.'

'It is hardly your fault.'

'Perhaps not, but…' Jane still looked mortified. She tried to smile. 'I suppose you wish to ask Claire to stand up with you?'

'With your permission.'

'Of course you have it.'

Claire flushed, taken aback by Jane's warmth of manner towards Jack. It was almost as if Jane was promoting him as a possible suitor. But that was impossible—Jane knew Edward detested Jack and surely she could not think Claire would ever want him! Not that Jack was the least interested in Claire.

'Claire, will you honour me with a dance?'

She stared at him, her mind blank. 'A dance?'

'Yes, a dance.' His mouth quirked. 'The peculiar set of movements performed in time to music. I believe we attempted the exercise at my grandmother's ball.'

'I do know what a dance is, my lord. I…I was merely surprised you asked me.'

'Why? The conversation seems to have been leading up to this point.'

His voice was impatient. As usual. He undoubtedly felt forced into asking her by Jane. And was still trying to save her reputation. ''Tis very kind of you to ask, but I really do not care to dance.'

To her surprise a tinge of colour crept into his cheeks. Almost as if she'd slapped him. 'Don't you? Then I won't trouble you again.'

'I…I only meant I don't care to dance now. Country dances are so lively. I still feel a little bruised from my fall. Perhaps a minuet; they are more sedate.' She was babbling, trying to erase her rude words, erase the stab of hurt she'd glimpsed on his face.

His expression was blank. 'Very well. The next minuet, then.' He bowed. 'If you will pardon me, I have another obligation.'

Jane waited until his tall figure was out of earshot before she spoke. 'Claire! How could you speak to him in such a manner? After he was so gracious about Aunt's rude words! I never thought you could be so unfeeling!'

'It was only I thought he felt obligated… I am sorry.'

'I should hope so.' Jane looked at her with an odd expression. 'Oh, Claire, I think he must still be in love with you!'

'He…he is not. He never was!'

'I am certain of it. Why else would he defend you? And the way he looked at you when he carried you home the other day!'

'Jane, please don't say such things,' Claire begged.

Jane's expression was sympathetic. 'You mustn't be afraid, Claire.'

'I am not afraid.' But she felt a shiver, nonetheless. She would never, ever want Jack or any man to be in love with her. To look at her as an object of desire.

Harry returned with Thea. Her next partner soon claimed Thea, and Jane's attention was diverted by Lady Bothwell, an acquaintance of hers. Harry stood next to Claire as the country dances began.

'I see Rotham is partnering Miss Snowden,' Harry remarked.

Claire quickly spotted Jack in one of the sets with Miss Snowden. She wore a gauze gown in a pale blue, which complemented her cool beauty. Her blonde hair was pulled back in an elegant knot. They made a striking couple, his darkness and her lightness, moving gracefully in time to the music.

'She is Lady Rotham's ward?' Claire asked carefully.

'Yes, the daughter of Lady Rotham's bosom friend, according to the gossip. Although I find it difficult to picture Lady Rotham with such a friend,' he said dryly. 'At any rate, Miss Snowden's mother was well-connected, but married beneath her. When Mrs Snowden died, Lady Rotham rescued the girl from the vulgar clutches of her paternal relatives. No one quite knows what happened to her father.'

'That was very kind of Lady Rotham,' Claire said, trying to be fair to the older woman. Perhaps she did have some generous impulses. Certainly, Lady Rotham seemed determined to provide her ward with all the advantages she most likely had never known. And, watching Miss Snowden gracefully move through the steps of the dance, no one would ever suspect she had been born in less than noble circumstances.

'Perhaps.' Harry looked down at Claire. 'I have heard

Lady Rotham hopes Miss Snowden will become the next Lady Rotham.'

'Oh.' Claire felt stunned for a moment, then recovered. 'She would certainly make a…a lovely countess,' she said with as much indifference as possible.

'Albeit a rather icy one. It may be she would melt in the right man's arms. However, I'd not wager a fortune on it.'

'Harry!' Claire stared at him, shocked by his callous speculations on Miss Snowden's sensual nature. 'She is only a girl.'

'She is on the marriage market.' His brow inched up a fraction at her expression. 'My innocent, you surely must know that is on the mind of most of the gentlemen present who might consider Miss Snowden as a future wife. And probably those who don't.'

'I suppose. I really don't know.' Her face must be crimson by now. Harry had a proclivity for blunt speaking, but usually not about such matters. Worse, into her mind popped a vivid image of Miss Snowden in Jack's arms, her cool composure melting under his fiery kiss.

'Don't worry, my dear,' Harry said, reading her mind. 'I doubt if Jack is interested in such an ice princess. He prefers a bit more passion in his women.'

Claire turned to stare at him, her mouth open. He met her look with a bland one of his own.

She snapped her mouth shut. If she had not already been in disgrace for quarrelling with Jack, she'd have been very tempted to start one with Harry.

Jack pushed open the door to Lord Hawke's study and stepped inside. The room was empty. A low light burned on the massive mahogany desk. He had no idea why

Claire would send him a message asking him to meet her here, particularly as their dance together was next.

A grim smile twisted his mouth. It was unlikely she wanted a tête-à-tête with him. She had made that clear enough. More likely she wanted to refuse him the dance in private.

He flung himself down in Lord Hawke's chair and scowled at the ink-well sitting in front of him. Unfortunately for him, the attraction he'd felt for her when she was seventeen had erupted into desire for the woman she'd become. He wanted to possess her. He wanted all of her—her softly curved body, her lovely face. He wanted her to smile for him and talk to him as she once had.

He still had no idea why she'd refused his offer six years ago. Had his passionate kiss scared her so much she was afraid of marriage to him? Had her brother filled her ears with tales of his liaisons? He couldn't deny he'd had a scandalous affair with a married woman, but it had lasted only a few months.

He rose. Brooding about it would not help.

He started at the sound of a key turning in the lock. With a curse, he strode to the door and tried the knob. It was locked. He rattled it harder. The faint strains of a minuet reached his ears. The dance had started.

'Damn!' Who in the hell would lock him in the study, and for what purpose? More to the point, where the devil was Claire? Had something happened to her? Or had the message been nothing but a ruse to get him here?

He tried the door again, but it refused to budge. The last thing he intended to do was wait here until someone discovered him. He glanced around the room and saw the window near the desk. He went to it, pushed up the sash and climbed through.

* * *

Claire watched the dancers with a mixture of anxiety and annoyance. Had he decided to deliberately forget their dance as punishment for turning him down? Or had something happened to him? But whatever could happen at a ball?

She looked around the crowded ballroom again. There was no sign of him. Perhaps he'd gone off to play cards. Or he had just forgotten. Frowning, she turned away and decided to find Jane. Certainly she had no intention of dancing with him if he should show up later.

She was halfway across the room when he appeared at her side.

'Claire.' He touched her arm.

She started then looked up, ready to tell him exactly what she thought of his effrontery. The words died on her lips when she saw the angry red scratch across his lean cheekbone.

'What happened? How did you come to be scratched?' she asked, suddenly anxious.

'An encounter with a rosebush.'

'A rosebush? Here?'

'Not precisely in the ballroom.' A cool smile played on his lips. 'While I waited for you in the study, I somehow came to be locked in. I was forced to make my exit through the window. Unfortunately, there was a rosebush below.'

'But why were you waiting for me in the study?'

'The message you sent. You wished to meet me there.'

Claire felt the colour drain from her face. 'But I sent no such message.'

'Didn't you?'

'But why would I? I would never even think of asking to meet a man privately, certainly not at a ball,' Claire said, torn between indignation that he would think that and worry at who would send such a message in her name.

A slight smile curled his lip. 'A pity. I'll admit I was surprised. Perhaps you wished to cut me up for forcing you to dance. I hardly thought it was for a romantic tryst.'

'I should hope not!' She flushed anyway, looking at his firm mouth, and wondered why the last encounter she had had with him, before everything had fallen apart, should enter her mind.

'I fear we missed our minuet. Promenade with me instead.' His fingers lightly pressed her arm. 'Come.'

She looked down to where his hand rested on her white kid gloves. The sleeve of his coat did not quite conceal the fine scratches covering his hand. She looked back up at him. 'Shouldn't you have a servant fetch some ointment? I fear your scratches may become infected.'

This time his eyes held genuine amusement. 'I doubt it. I've been injured much worse without ill effects.'

'But your cheek. I am certain it must hurt.'

'A little.' His eyes had softened. 'So you are concerned about me?'

'I would be concerned about anyone in the same circumstances,' she said lightly. She looked away, not wanting him to see how the look in his eyes made her feel slightly breathless.

'I see.' He raised a mocking brow. 'I suggest we take a turn about the room. The rest of the company is undoubtedly waiting to see if we're about to quarrel again.' His voice was cool.

She bit her lip, hurt by his abrupt change in manner. So, they were back to being seen together merely to appease the rest of society. It had nothing to do with his actually wanting her company.

He held out his arm. She placed her fingers stiffly on the fine cloth of his coat. They began a slow promenade around the edge of the room.

She felt his eyes on her face. 'Smile,' he said. 'You look as if you've been sentenced to Newgate.'

'Very well, my lord.' She plastered a smile to her face. His muscle tightened under her fingers, and she could almost feel the rising anger emanating from him.

She looked into his face. 'Now what is amiss, my lord?'

'Now you look as if someone's held a pistol to your back to make you smile.'

'Haven't you?' It was all she could do to keep her temper.

'Hardly. If you recall I am attempting to redeem your reputation.'

'Well, if you insist on glaring at me in that odious way, I would rather be completely ruined.'

Although he too was smiling, he had an ominous look in his eyes. For the first time in her life, Claire felt like hitting someone. She removed her hand from his coat. 'You have done your distasteful duty, my lord. I think my reputation will survive without further assistance.'

He looked down at her with a frown. 'Distasteful duty? What the devil are you talking about now?'

'It is quite obvious you are only in my company because of some misguided sense of duty. Or perhaps you merely wish to punish me for what happened six years ago. I really don't care which it is, but I have no desire to spend any more time in your company.'

'You're wrong.' He was forced to step aside to let a

matron in puce silk and a purple turban pass. She gave him a cool nod.

He took Claire's arm. 'We can't talk here. Come with me.'

'I really have nothing more to say to you.'

'Good. Then you can listen to what I have to say.'

His fingers gripped her arm as he led her across the floor. She saw they were heading towards the doors leading to the terrace off the ballroom.

'My lord, perhaps I did not make myself clear. I don't want to be in your company.'

'Be quiet, Claire.' He gave her an exasperated look.

'Will you at least release my arm?'

'And risk having you escape?'

She cast him a furious look. 'I will most likely have bruises after this.'

His grip only slackened a little after he'd hauled her through the doors. The terrace and garden below were well lit with lanterns. Several couples strolled along the balustrade. She expected him to pause and was startled when he started to lead her down the steps to the small garden. She balked at the second step. 'I am not going to the garden with you.'

He raised a brow. 'Why not? Are you worried I'm planning to ravish you?'

The impatience in his voice was enough to dampen any thoughts she might have entertained along those lines. 'That is the last thing I would ever think. At any rate I cannot imagine why anyone would attempt to ravish someone in a garden behind a private home during a ball.' Then she turned crimson, for that was exactly what had happened between them. No, not exactly, for he hadn't attempted to ravish her, but it had been a thoroughly shocking kiss. Except, she had liked it.

He looked at her oddly, and she knew he also remembered. 'Don't worry, Claire, I've no intention of repeating the past.'

'I didn't think you did.' She found her hands were trembling. 'What is it you wish to discuss with me?'

'Not here.' He looked behind her and she realised she was blocking the steps. She followed him down to the garden and stepped to the side to allow a couple to pass. He pulled her around a large shrub and found a niche next to the terrace wall.

'What is it?'

'What happened six years ago.' He shifted so his shoulders rested against the wall.

'I don't want to discuss it. I've forgotten about it.'

'That's a damned lie. You would not have brought it up a few minutes ago if you'd forgotten.' His voice was rough. 'You think I'm trying to punish you for refusing my offer?'

She looked away from him. She could make out a couple strolling hand in hand through the garden, the light of the moon casting a soft glow on the lady's pale dress. She finally spoke. 'Yes, I sometimes think that. You have been so angry with me, ever since I saw you at your grandmother's ball.' She turned to look at him. 'I have no idea why. I did what I thought was best. I know you did not want to be trapped in marriage to me.'

He started. 'You refused me because you did not want to trap me?'

She knotted her hands. 'Yes, particularly after…'

'After what?' He looked at her hard. 'Claire?'

'After I found out about the bet.'

'The bet?' He became very still. 'What bet?'

'The bet you made with Harry. I knew I could never marry a man who would make such a loathsome wager.'

He stepped towards her. 'Who told you?'

So it was true. What had she been hoping? That after all this time she would discover he had never made such a wager? That Lady Rotham had lied when she'd told Claire he had only kissed her to win a bet? 'It hardly matters now, does it?'

'Claire, listen to me; it wasn't like that. Not then.' He stepped towards her. Even in the moonlight, she could see his face was pale, the mantle of haughty indifference gone from him. His eyes pleaded with her to hear him.

'I really don't care to listen to any more.' Her voice trembled. 'I…I had thought you were my friend!'

He made a move as if to reach for her. Then his hand dropped to his side.

She stumbled up the terrace steps and into the ballroom. The guests were milling around, waiting for the next set of dances. She made her way around the edge of the room, hardly noticing what she was doing. She should have been gratified she had managed to hurt him as much as he had hurt her. But instead she felt only a shocked numbness.

Jack stared after Claire's retreating figure.

I had thought you were my friend. The words twisted his gut as if he'd been knifed. She had refused his offer because she thought he'd betrayed her. Not because she detested him for some unknown reason. Although, God knew, he would hardly blame her if she did hate him.

She had no way of knowing that by the time he'd kissed her the bet was the last thing on his mind. That by then he'd found himself inexplicably drawn to her warm brown eyes flecked with gold, and her smiling mouth, her pretty, rounded figure. She was the first woman he'd met who seemed less interested in his title and wealth than in his views and pursuits, and who seemed oblivious to his reputed charm.

Which was how the damnable bet had come about in the first place. He'd come down from London for the house party and had met Claire at a local assembly. She had been no more than polite when she'd met Jack, which had, for some inexplicable reason, annoyed him. Later that evening he'd seen her dancing with Mr Poyton, a guest of the vicar's, and from the smile on her face anyone but a fool could see she had a *tendre* for the man—a thin, scholarly fellow who was unaware of her regard. After the assembly, over too much brandy, Harry had dared Jack to divert Claire's *tendre* from Poyton to himself. Jack had taken up the challenge.

And now there was another bet involved. His chances of winning her trust would go to the devil if she discovered this bet. If he had an ounce of decency, he'd call the bet off. But then he'd lose his horse. That would be almost like losing part of himself.

A couple coming up from the shrubbery startled him out of his thoughts. He must find Claire. He could not let things stand as they were, even if he had to lock her up and force her to listen to him.

Jack rapidly mounted the terrace steps and entered the ballroom. A cotillion was in full progress. He scanned the crowd for a glimpse of her light green gown and tawny hair amidst the mass of whites and creams and pastels. He finally saw Jane standing with his godmother. Claire was not with them.

His gaze swept over the dancers. He froze. She was in one of the sets, and Harry was her partner. As he watched, Harry leaned forward and spoke to her. Her lips parted in an answering smile.

The powerful desire to knock Harry flat then yank her

off the floor surged through Jack. Instead, he swore viciously, alarming an elderly lady standing next to him who stared at him, eyes wide with disapproval.

'I beg your pardon.' He gave her a stiff bow and stalked off. And when his stepmother accosted him to ask if he could accompany Alicia home as she had the headache he complied without protest.

She was running and running through the mist. The footsteps were behind her. She had no idea where she was going, only that she must get to the child first. The path opened before her, and suddenly she was on the parapet of a castle.

The footsteps came closer. She hid, but it was too late. The figure came towards her and then she screamed....

'Claire! Claire!' Someone touched her shoulder.

Her eyes shot open. For a moment the room, bright with morning light and pale green panelled walls, confused her. Then Jane spoke again and her mind cleared. She was not in Marcus's silent, cold home, but in her brother's house in St James's Square.

'It is all right, dear. You were only dreaming.' Jane sat down next to her on the bed.

Claire forced herself to sit up. The terrible feeling of loss she always experienced after the dream enveloped her. 'Did I cry out again?'

'Yes, but it is nothing to worry about.' Jane gently brushed the hair from Claire's face. 'I am only grateful I heard you. I was just leaving my bedchamber.' She took Claire's hand. 'You haven't had the dream for a long time now.'

Claire shook her head. 'No.' She shivered. It had been months, perhaps nearly a year since she'd dreamed of the carriage accident. Sometimes, she was running, sometimes riding in a carriage. And always through a cold, swirling mist.

Jane's face was kind. 'Will you take some chocolate and toast? And then after that I have quite decided you should remain in bed today. You should not have gone to the ball last night; I knew you hadn't recovered from your dreadful fall. There is no need for you to show up at every affair merely to prove you no longer have a quarrel with Lord Rotham.'

The mention of his name made Claire feel even more out of spirits. 'I am hardly doing it for that reason. I promised Edward I would help you look after Thea. I cannot do that if I'm hiding away.'

'Nonsense.' She looked carefully at Claire. 'Did something happen between you and Lord Rotham last night? I saw you leave the ballroom with him, but then you came in alone. And he left very abruptly while you danced with Harry.'

''Twas nothing. We merely do not deal well together,' Claire said.

'Did he say something to you?'

'No. Jane, please, I do not want to talk about him.'

'Of course. But if you should wish to…'

'I know.' She attempted a smile.

Jane still looked worried. 'Claire, I must tell you I have invited him to our rout tomorrow. He accepted.'

Rout? Claire had nearly forgotten about it. And Jane had invited Jack? She realised her sister-in-law looked anxious, as if she feared Claire might burst into tears over the news. 'You must invite anyone you wish. I promise I will behave and not run away from him.'

'Oh, Claire! That is not what I meant!'

'I know. Please, don't worry; I really don't mind.'

Claire settled back against the pillows after Jane left.

The thought of hiding away in bed was tempting except it wouldn't solve a thing. The sadness from her dream would linger and then fade away as it always had.

But would the regret and disappointment from last night disappear as well?

After dressing in a jonquil morning gown, Claire left her room and wandered into the library, feeling rather useless. The house was quiet, the servants going about their work in an orderly fashion.

Claire had once dreamed of her own home, but living with Marcus had buried that. His housekeeper had been grim and jealous of her territory, with no intention of yielding any authority to a girl of seventeen. And Marcus himself had considered Claire frivolous and disorganised and had made it clear her efforts displeased him.

Why was she even thinking of these things? She stood on the library steps and absently pulled down a book of Shakespeare's sonnets. For two years, she'd tried to lay the memories to rest, but ever since she'd met Jack again the memories had returned. Not only had he betrayed her and ruined her life once, but he seemed determined to do so again.

This was idiotic! She was not going to feel sorry for herself. Nor should she feel the least bit sorry for Jack. Except the image of the stunned, almost stricken expression on his face last night continued to haunt her. Had he really regretted the wager? But why hadn't he come after her instead of leaving the ball entirely?

'This is nonsense!' she said aloud.

'You haven't even heard what I have to say.'

She gasped and lost her footing, the book tumbling to the floor. The next thing she knew, she had slammed against a hard masculine chest. Strong arms caught her as Jack staggered a few steps back with the impact of her weight.

'I must admit, I never expected you to fling yourself into my arms.' He managed to regain his balance, but his arms still clasped her to him.

'I didn't. I stumbled.' She knew she should be struggling to escape, instead of enjoying the feel of the cloth of his coat under her cheek, and the sound of his strong heartbeat in her ear.

'You were fortunate, then, I was here to catch you,' he murmured. His voice was husky. His arms seemed to tighten around her.

An unfamiliar warmth had begun to spread from her chest down through her lower body. She pushed against him. He slowly dropped his arms away.

She stepped back, not quite looking at him. 'If you hadn't startled me in the first place, then I would hardly have needed your assistance.' Her voice, she noted with relief, at least sounded normal.

'And then I would have missed the pleasure of coming to your rescue.' His voice still held a tinge of that odd huskiness that made her knees weak.

She backed up another pace and finally looked at him. He looked dangerously virile, the deep blue of his coat turning his eyes a dark smoky grey, its perfect cut emphasising his broad shoulders and narrow hips. She knotted her hands together. 'What are you doing here?'

'Calling on you.' He looked back at her with the same intense regard.

'Oh.' She should be informing him she had no desire to speak to him and then exiting the room in cold dignity. But the tumble into his arms had thrown her off.

He clasped his hands behind his back. 'I want to talk to you about last night.'

'Do you? We always seem to be discussing the prior evening,' she said.

A faint smile touched his mouth. 'I've noticed. Along with the observation that any discussion we have together in a public place usually results in your fleeing away from me.'

Claire flushed. 'Yes.' She twisted her hands tighter. 'What have you come for?'

He looked straight at her. 'The wager I made six years ago.'

She turned away, her hand going to the lace neckerchief at her breast. 'Is there anything to say? It all seems very clear; you made a bet to…to seduce me and I suppose you nearly succeeded.'

'Who the devil told you that?'

The harshness in his voice made her spin around. 'I beg your pardon?'

He scowled at her. 'I made no bet to seduce you.'

'Didn't you?'

'No.' A tinge of colour brushed his cheeks. 'The bet was that I could make you develop a *tendre* for me. And steal a kiss.' His eyes didn't quite meet hers.

'I see.' Her fingers knotted themselves together again. 'Why?'

He shrugged. She realised with some amazement that he was embarrassed. He paced towards the window and finally turned to look at her. 'I suppose it was because you seemed impervious to my reputed charm. And then I saw how you looked at Poyton and it became a challenge to make you regard me in the same way. And I was drunk at the time.'

'How very flattering.' Claire focused on a spot near his head. 'So, you thought it would be amusing to trifle with a young girl's affections?'

'I am not excusing my behaviour,' he said quietly. 'If it is any consolation, I came to hold you in higher regard than any woman of my acquaintance. The night I kissed you, I had not set out to do so. But when I did the wager was the last thing on my mind.'

'Oh.'

'I was more than willing to marry you.'

'It was hardly necessary.' She should have been gratified by his words. Instead, a cold pit of disappointment swallowed her. What had she expected him to say? He wanted her for herself? He was in love with her? Ever since her parents' deaths, she had felt she was nothing more than an unwanted parcel, a burden that must be accommodated. Jane had always loved her and made her welcome, but she was aware that Edward regarded her as a duty.

'You chose to marry Ellison. Why did you?'

Why? Because she had been so hurt by Jack, she had wanted nothing more to do with him. Because she hadn't much cared what happened to her.

'He offered for me, and Edward gave me no choice.'

'You had a choice. You could have wed me.'

'I thought that at least Marcus *wanted* me.'

His face had closed down again. 'I am asking you again. Were you happy with Ellison?'

'I do not think one marries for happiness.'

'That's not an answer. Were you?'

She twisted her hands. 'I don't wish to speak of my marriage. It is hardly your concern.'

'Like hell it isn't!' He made a move towards her, then stopped. 'I have my answer,' he said, his voice harsh.

She felt almost frightened. The air was charged with the tension between them. She had no idea why he looked so cold and angry, although she sensed his anger was not directed at her.

She made a helpless gesture. 'Perhaps you should leave.'

'I never meant to hurt you.'

'I suppose not.' She looked away again, not quite sure of what she felt. 'I think I would rather not talk any more about this.'

'Very well.' For a brief moment, his expression held vulnerability, then it passed. His eyes were on her face. 'I would like us to be friends again.'

'I…I don't know.'

'I think it might be possible.' He moved towards her. 'Let me show you London. Something besides the inside of a ballroom. There is St Paul's, the menagerie at the Tower, the Royal Academy.'

'The Royal Academy?' Her mind was blank. His nearness, the strong planes of his face, the remembrance of the hard strength of his body seemed to be interfering with her comprehension.

'Yes. Do you remember? You once told me you wanted to see more of London than just balls and routs.'

'Did I?' She had a sudden recollection of sitting next to him at a picnic while he described such sights of London as the Tower, the vast parks, and the pleasure gardens. She had eagerly listened, fascinated by his descriptions.

She coloured a little. 'I once thought I would.'

'Now is your chance.'

'I…' She could feel herself weakening. Perhaps it was because he looked almost as eager as he had as a youth.

'If you come with me, I will return your fan.'

'My fan?'

A hint of a smile touched his mouth. 'Yes, your fan. If you recall, I still have it.'

'I think it is very unchivalrous of you to keep it.' Although, in truth, she had nearly forgotten he had it.

'Most unchivalrous. I've been saving it for just such an occasion. A leverage of sorts to promote my purposes.'

'I believe it is called blackmail.'

'Not quite. A fair exchange of goods. You will have your fan and I will have your company. So, where do you want to go?'

He was making her feel reckless again. As if she wanted to do something out of character from her usual staid self. 'Vauxhall, if you please.'

'Vauxhall?' He looked startled and then frowned. 'Vauxhall is hardly the sort of place I wish to take you.'

'But why? I think it must be fascinating. I have always wanted to see the cascades and the walks and the grottoes.'

'It is unsuitable for you. The men who frequent the place engage in wild behaviour, and the women are hardly respectable.'

He sounded as pompous as Edward, which had the unfortunate effect of making her feel rebellious. 'It cannot be all that unsuitable. Thea told us that two of her friends visited Vauxhall only the other evening. They are from quite respectable families. And the Prince Regent himself frequents the gardens.' She restrained herself from pointing out to him that he himself had told her of its delights and had obviously visited the pleasure gardens quite often. He'd certainly never mentioned any wild behaviour.

'If the Prince Regent attends, then there certainly must be no objection,' he said dryly. He considered her for a moment. 'Very well, we will go to Vauxhall. I will ask my grandmother to accompany us. For some reason, she still delights in the place.'

'That would be splendid!' She smiled at him as an unexpected surge of anticipation hit her. It was a feeling she had not experienced for years.

An odd expression crossed his face. Her smile faded. 'Will it really be so dreadful?'

'No,' he said softly. 'I would take you to the devil and back if you wished, just to see you smile like that.'

'Oh.' That strange breathlessness hit her again as her eyes met his. 'I…I don't think I would be that unreasonable.'

He laughed a little. 'I know. So, we will go to Vauxhall tonight.'

'Tonight? But that is too soon!'

'Very well; the day after tomorrow. The place is only open three nights each week.'

'Could we go next week?'

'No. I don't want you tempted to change your mind.' He picked up his gloves from the side-table. He gave her a quick smile. 'Don't look so worried. I promise you, you won't regret it.'

But, after he left, she wondered if she already did.

Chapter Six

Jane's rout could only be considered a success. Every room was filled with fashionably dressed guests, making one's way across the room was a feat in itself, and Lucy Gardner had already swooned in the drawing-room and had to be carried out by her flustered husband.

The unseasonably warm weather hardly contributed to the overall comfort of the guests. The servants had already thrown open the sashes to the drawing-room. Claire stood near one of them, fan in hand. Her satin slippers had begun to feel too small an hour ago. She shifted and wished it were possible to remove them.

'I wondered where I might find you.' Jack's voice startled her. He stood in front of her.

'I was rather warm.' She had wondered if he was coming, and now that he was here she felt tongue-tied and nervous.

'I imagine almost everyone is.' His eyes were on her, and he seemed to have no more idea of what he said than she did.

His eyes travelled over her in a slow, appraising manner. 'You look lovely tonight.'

'Th-thank you.' She wore a new gown of shimmery

white silk, the sleeves and hem embroidered in gold thread with a pattern of scrolls and leaves.

The warmth of his gaze told her he was sincere. She flushed a little. 'I didn't see you arrive.'

'I was unavoidably detained.' His mouth curved in a slow smile. 'So, Claire, does that mean you were awaiting my arrival?'

He was flirting with her. She frowned at him. 'I fear you read too much into my words, my lord. I meant exactly what I said. I did not see you arrive.'

'You do not need to address me as "my lord". My given name will suffice.'

'It is hardly proper to use your given name.'

'You did before.'

'It was not proper of me then. I should not have done so.'

'Why not?'

She sighed. 'Because it results in a sense of familiarity which leads to more unseemly behaviour.'

His brow inched up. 'I see. So, if you use my given name you'll be on the path to wanton behaviour?'

'Of course not!'

'Then what is your objection?'

'I…' She stopped, wondering if they were speaking different languages. 'Using one's given name implies a…a degree of intimacy we do not share.'

'What degree of intimacy is that?' He had folded his arms over his chest and regarded her with an interested look.

She restrained the impulse to glower at him. 'You are being difficult again.'

'Not at all. I merely want to know the ramifications of your addressing me by my Christian name.'

'Perhaps we could speak on another topic.'

'We could.' He grinned at her in his old way and she felt her resistance beginning to melt. 'You are very charming even when you're angry.'

He was doing the same thing he had done six years ago, flirting with her and making the most outrageous personal remarks that both flustered and pleased her all at once. And she felt no more sophisticated than she had then. She tried to give him her most quelling look. 'That is not the topic I had in mind.'

'Very well. My grandmother is more than delighted to accompany us to Vauxhall tomorrow.'

'That will be—' Claire began.

'Mrs Ellison, I had hoped to find you!' Lady Rotham's cool voice cut into their conversation.

Her brow rose as her amused glance went from one to the other. 'My dear Rotham, I know you wish to be seen together to still the gossip, but standing alone with Mrs Ellison, engaged in such exclusive conversation, is hardly the way to do so!'

'Since there must be upwards of three dozen people in the room, we're hardly alone,' Jack said.

'You quite know what I mean!' She turned her gaze on Claire. 'Mrs Ellison, I had hoped we might have a little tête-à-tête. Perhaps you would not object to walking with me for a moment.'

'That would be very nice,' Claire said untruthfully. Lady Rotham was not someone Claire wished to have a private conversation with. She had no idea how to politely refuse her invitation.

'But I object,' Jack said coolly.

'You have monopolised her quite enough. Come Mrs Ellison.'

A swift frown crossed Jack's face. 'I have something more I wish to say to Claire.'

'Mrs Ellison, do you always allow him to be so possessive? I think you must come with me just to teach him a lesson.' She firmly grasped Claire's arm.

Claire knew her face must be a fiery red by now. She wanted to sink with humiliation over Lady Rotham's arch comments. And how dared Jack stand there and glare as if he were fighting over her?

She allowed Lady Rotham to lead her away without a backward glance at Jack. Not that they advanced very quickly, for the crowd in the drawing-room appeared to have increased by another two dozen people.

Lady Rotham manoeuvred around a small group of women and managed to find a vacant spot near the mantelpiece. She fanned herself, her eyes drifting over the crowd. 'Such a crush tonight, and everyone is here! I saw Lady Jersey earlier. Jane must be delighted.'

'I am certain she is,' Claire responded politely, wondering how she could escape. She suspected Lady Rotham's motive for seeking her out had nothing to do with any fond feelings for her.

'I was pleased I could steal you away from Rotham for a minute. I have wanted to speak with you ever since that unfortunate ball.' She turned the full force of her charming smile upon Claire. Unfortunately, the lack of warmth in her eyes ruined the effect. 'You have become quite lovely, you know. Last time I saw you, you were pretty enough, but a trifle plump. Although some men might find that to their taste.'

Claire stared at her, too stunned to speak. Lady Rotham went on. 'Of course that was six years ago and you are much improved, although not in Rotham's usual style. Perhaps that is the attraction you hold for him.' She smiled again. 'I can see I have embarrassed you by my frankness.'

'He is hardly attracted to me.'

'But he is.' Her smile was filled with incredulity. 'Surely you are not all that innocent as not to recognise the signs? Although I wonder how much of it has to do with the need for a little revenge on his part.' She paused. 'A man with his pride does not like to be turned down.'

'I really do not see why this conversation is necessary.' Claire struggled to keep Lady Rotham from seeing her dismay. She looked desperately around, hoping for an avenue of escape.

'But it is.' Lady Rotham put a restraining hand on Claire's arm. 'You see, Rotham is to marry my ward.'

When Claire looked at her blankly, she added, 'Miss Snowden. I fear having him take another mistress at this time is a trifle awkward.'

'He doesn't want me for his mistress.' Where ever did Lady Rotham come up with that idea?

Lady Rotham's expression held complete disbelief. 'Of course he does. Why else would he pursue you in this fashion? He watches for you to come into a room, he is jealous if another man, such as Mr Devlin, speaks to you, he shows up at affairs such as this, which he never attends. I am not the only one with such speculations, you know, my dear.'

Claire's hands tightened around her fan. 'Even if I thought it were true, I would never think of becoming his mistress!'

'Perhaps not, but he can be very persuasive.'

'But I am not very persuadable. You have no need to worry that I will interfere with your plans. If you will pardon me, Lady Rotham.' Too angry and humiliated to say more, Claire turned away. This time, Lady Rotham made no move to stop her.

* * *

It was nearly three in the morning before the last guests left, and Claire tumbled into bed. But sleep eluded her. Lady Rotham's words rang in her mind. Claire finally rolled onto her back and stared up at the canopy. She had been too busy avoiding Jack and making polite conversation with the rest of the guests to mull over Lady Rotham's words.

But now, in the quiet of her bedchamber, they returned with full force. Was it true? That not only Lady Rotham, but others as well, thought Jack wanted her for his mistress? She cringed at the idea. Perhaps Lady Rotham only wanted to warn Claire away. Harry had said it was rumoured Lady Rotham wanted a match between her ward and Jack. But why would Lady Rotham even find Claire a threat to her plans? Certainly Jack did not want her as a mistress, or in any other way.

Or did he? Jane thought he was in love with her. And his manner towards her… Despite the tensions between them, there were times, such as last evening, when he looked at her and she could see the admiration in his eyes.

And there was his insistence on seeking her company. Surely offering to show her London was hardly necessary to prove they were not quarrelling?

None of it made sense. He couldn't possibly desire her. The thought made her tremble. Marcus had wanted her, too, and she had quickly learned a man's desire could be brutal and humiliating. But Jack's touch had never been anything but gentle; even his kiss so long ago had not frightened her.

Vauxhall. She was to go to Vauxhall with him tomorrow. At least the Duchess of Arundel would be there, but still she would be seen in his company in a place that was not quite respectable. What would Lady Rotham think? And everyone else?

She stifled a groan and flopped back onto her side. And the worst part of this whole affair was that she had no idea if she was more afraid of Jack or of herself.

Claire arose early the next morning. Still tired after a night of tossing and restless dreams, she staggered to her writing desk and pulled out a sheet of paper and a pen. She crumpled two sheets of paper before she finally composed a satisfactory note.

> *Lord Rotham,*
> *I regret to inform you that, after careful reflection, I feel it would be unwise of me to accompany you to Vauxhall Gardens this evening. I thank you for your kind invitation. I would be very much obliged if you would return my fan forthwith.*
> *Mrs Ellison*

She sighed and rested her chin on her hand. She supposed it would have to do. At least it was short and unemotional, which seemed the best tone to adopt. She sealed the note and when the maid entered with her chocolate and toast sent it off with her before she changed her mind.

Claire had just returned from a walk in Green Park with Thea when his response arrived by footman. She waited until she'd reached her room before breaking the seal.

> *My Dear Mrs Ellison,*
> *I regret to inform you that unless you are on the brink of death or waiting for me at our appointed*

time this evening I will be obligated to forcibly
carry you to Vauxhall. Your fan will be returned
forthwith as soon as you fulfil your part of our
agreement.
　Rotham

'How could he?' She read the note again, her temper
rising with each word. She had never heard of anything
so arrogant. Then she thought of the eagerness in his
voice when he'd asked her in the library and she felt
confused all over again.

How had everything become so complicated?

'Claire?' Jane poked her head into Claire's bedchamber and then stepped inside. She was dressed in a gown
of pale lavender silk. She and Thea were to attend another private concert.

'You look very charming, Claire, but are you certain
you must wear the neckerchief? It is evening, you
know.'

Claire looked down at the soft muslin she had tucked
into the neck of her bodice. It turned the cream gown
with its pattern of delicate flowers into a very modest
garment. 'What is wrong with it?'

Jane bit her lip. 'It is only—well, it is exactly the sort
of thing Aunt does. She must always tuck a bit of lace
or a kerchief in all her gowns as if she thinks someone
will be looking in that direction!'

'Does she?' Claire hadn't particularly noticed, but
now that she thought about it Lady Billingsley always
did swathe herself in clothing up to her neck. She re-
sembled a very full-breasted pigeon. 'Do you suppose
she has had problems in that way?' Claire tried to imag-

ine a gentleman attempting to leer at Lady Billingsley's ample bosom.

'Oh, Claire! I am certain she has not—that is, I have heard her described as handsome, but…' Jane shook her head. 'Claire, you are distracting me. What I wish to say is there is no need for you to do the same. You would look much nicer if you removed the neckerchief.'

Claire shook her head. 'I prefer to wear it.'

'You are no longer married to Marcus, dear.' Jane's voice was gentle.

Claire turned away and picked up her gloves. 'No.' Had Jane guessed that Marcus had forbidden Claire to ever wear anything designed to reveal the wearer's charms? As if such a gown would bring out the wanton nature he was certain lurked in Claire's person.

She turned back to Jane. 'Are you certain you and Thea would not like to come with us?'

'He did not invite us, dear.'

'I really do not think Edward would like this. Don't you think you should put your foot down and forbid me to go?' Claire asked hopefully. Jane's reaction to this whole affair had been extremely peculiar, almost as if she wished to push Claire into Jack's arms.

'No, I do not. You are widowed, and I am certain you're quite safe in Lord Rotham's care. And the Duchess will be there. But if you really don't want to go with him, why did you agree?'

'He blackmailed me. He still has my fan.'

'I see.' A ghost of a smile hovered around Jane's lips. 'How distressing.' But she didn't look as if she thought that at all.

Claire finally finished dressing and reluctantly went to the drawing-room. Jack stood near the sofa, idly inspecting a Dresden shepherdess on a side-table. He turned at their footsteps. Claire wished her heart wouldn't thud in such an annoying way. It never had six years ago. But then, Jack had been a friend, almost like Harry or Caroline, only not quite as comfortable. It had been Mr Poyton whose tall, spare figure and serious smile had made her stomach flutter and her hands tremble. At least at first. And then she had begun to notice Jack's changeable grey eyes and the way his mouth quirked when he was amused, and how he listened to what she said with such seriousness. At least the times when he wasn't teasing her.

She realised he had turned to her. 'Shall we depart?'

'I…why, yes.' A glance at his cool face made her shiver. 'Where is your grandmother?'

'She will join us at the embankment.'

'Oh.' She had at least counted on the Duchess's presence to prevent any sort of uncomfortable conversation.

They bid Jane and Thea goodbye. He settled her into his coach, then, after instructing the coachman, took the seat across from her. The coach suddenly seemed far too small for both of them. Her mind was blank. The silence seemed to stretch between them as the coach rolled through the streets. Claire finally pulled her eyes away from the window and stole a look at him.

He raised a dark brow. 'Should we make a stab at some sort of conversation or do you plan to maintain an icy, martyrish silence the entire time?' His voice dripped with chill sarcasm.

Claire stared at him. What did he want from her now? 'I fear I am not very good at idle conversation, my lord. If you wanted that you should have asked another lady.'

'I didn't want another lady. I wanted you.'

If he hadn't sounded so impatient, she would have

found his words oddly provocative. 'I have no idea why. You are snarling at me again.'

'Hardly.'

'You are. You sound as if my company is nothing but a form of torture.'

'What the devil did Celeste say to you last night?'

The abrupt change of topic startled her. 'I beg your pardon?'

'My stepmother. After she dragged you away, you spent the rest of the evening avoiding my company and then I received your polite, cool little message. I assume she said something unpleasant.'

'It was nothing to signify.'

'Indeed?' His brow inched up. 'I find that hard to believe. She rarely says anything that is insignificant.'

Claire bit her lip and then looked at him. His arms were folded and he'd leaned back in his corner with that stubborn, impatient look. Resisting him would prove futile. Besides, Claire was becoming tired of all the subterfuge. 'She wished to warn me of the improper designs you have upon my person.'

He looked startled and then suddenly laughed. 'Was that it?'

'Yes.' Claire felt irritated by his amusement. As if he found the idea improbable. Then she was irritated with herself for even thinking that way.

'So, you decided to decline my invitation for fear I planned to ravish you at Vauxhall?'

'Of course not! Particularly with your grandmother present. I merely did not want any speculations about our relationship.'

'Our relationship? I am still trying to determine what it is.'

She glared at him. 'Well, I certainly have no idea!' she snapped.

The carriage rumbled to a halt. With some surprise, Claire realised they had reached the embankment at the Thames. The footman opened the doors and Jack leapt out. He held out his hand to assist Claire.

She stepped down into the soft summer evening, careful to avoid his eyes. She glanced around and saw there were a number of other carriages already there, but none she recognised as the Duchess's.

She was surprised when Jack pulled her around to face him. Puzzled, she looked into his face.

A slight smile lifted the corners of his mouth, but his eyes were serious. 'There is no need to worry, Claire; I promise my intentions are not dishonourable.'

'I...I never thought they were.'

'And I apologise for snarling at you,' he said softly. 'And I don't find it torture to be in your company. Quite the contrary.'

'Oh,' she said again. The blood rushed to her face, making her feel light-headed. His grey eyes, smiling into hers, made it impossible to tear her gaze away from him.

He reached out and touched her cheek, causing awareness to flood through her. 'So, is my company torture for you, Claire?'

'I don't know,' she whispered.

He stepped closer. 'Don't you?' he asked, and she had the insane thought that he was about to kiss her.

The cough behind them broke the spell. They jerked apart, Claire's face crimson, when she saw the boatman.

'What is it?' Jack asked brusquely. He straightened the sleeves of his coat.

'Milady asked me to deliver this message.' The boatman held out a folded paper.

Jack took it, a hint of colour still apparent on his cheekbones. He quickly scanned the contents, then looked at Claire, a slight frown on his face. 'My grandmother arrived earlier and decided to cross without us. We're to meet her in the supper box.'

'Oh.' Claire tried to keep the dismay from her voice. Whatever was wrong with her? Jack surely hadn't been planning to kiss her. But why did he look as flustered as she felt? Perhaps he was as eager as she was to have his grandmother act as a shield from the odd tension that lately seemed to rise between them.

The boatman cleared his throat again. 'The boat is ready, milord, if you'll be wanting it.'

'Boat? Of course.' Jack started, then turned towards Claire. 'Shall we leave?'

He held out his arm. She placed her fingers on his coat sleeve, trying to recover her sanity as they headed towards the water.

'Claire, we're here.' He caught her arm, pulling her to a halt as she continued forward.

She blinked and realised another dozen steps would have put her in the river. 'Oh.'

'Daydreaming again?'

'I was merely thinking.'

He helped her into one of the boats, then took his place across from her. 'Most visitors to Vauxhall prefer to take the bridge but I thought you might like the sculls instead,' he said.

'It is lovely.' She gave him a swift smile, beginning to relax a little. A light breeze brushed her cheek. The mellow rays of the evening sun shimmered on the peaceful river. Another scull had pushed off, occupied by a noisy family who clearly intended to enjoy themselves.

He smiled back at her and this time she didn't avert her eyes.

The harmony was broken as the boatman pushed off. Startled, Claire grabbed the side of the boat.

Jack noticed her apprehension. 'There's no need to worry. I promise you we won't overturn.' Then his eyes danced in the old way she remembered. 'And if we should happen to I'm here to rescue you.'

'You would?'

'Of course, my sweet. In fact, I think I might quite enjoy it. A chance to hold you in my arms, have you at my mercy.' He grinned wickedly.

Claire stole a glance at the boatman, her face flushed. Despite the fact that the man seemed oblivious, she was certain he listened to every word. 'Jack, stop it!' Then her face heated when she realised his name had slipped out.

His grin broadened. 'Jack? Does this mean you've finally forgiven me?'

'It means nothing at all.'

'I think it does.' The smug look of male satisfaction made her want to wipe the grin from his face. Perhaps she should tip the boat into the water after all. She lifted her chin and looked away without answering.

'So our truce is in effect?'

She turned to look at him. 'What truce?'

'The one we declared. In your drawing-room. Do you remember? We sealed it with a kiss.'

'I did not kiss you!'

'But I kissed you—at least your hand.' His voice held a low, sensuous quality that made a chaste kiss on the hand sound as intimate as if he'd actually kissed her mouth.

Another boat glided by, followed by a second boat

filled with a boisterous, noisy party of men. By the time the noise settled, they had reached the grounds of Vauxhall. Jack helped her out, his hand lingering far too long on her waist.

He paid the boatman and then took her arm. He refused to release his grip as they slowly made their way from the river towards the entrance of the pleasure gardens.

Claire finally spoke. 'Really, must you hold my arm so tightly? I am not a prisoner you are leading to the Tower.'

'No. But you are my prisoner for the night.'

She looked up at him. 'I am not a prisoner.'

He lifted a dark brow. 'I got the impression you consider yourself here under duress. So that makes you a prisoner of sorts.'

'Do you always find it necessary to blackmail women into coming to Vauxhall with you?' Claire was desperately trying to find some way of pushing him back into the cool, remote lord he'd been since the lottery. The wicked gleam in his eyes and the sensuous way they roamed over her were doing peculiar things to her.

'No, not always. Just on occasion. But they usually find that being in my power is quite pleasurable.'

'Do they? I dare say they are all rattlebrains or you… you drugged them.'

He stopped then and turned to look down at her. 'I always choose very intelligent women, and I never resort to very foul methods,' he said softly. Apparently oblivious to the fact they were not quite alone, he ran a hand down her cheek, coming to cup her chin, tilting her face towards him. His dark eyes seemed to mesmerise her, and she had the mad desire to close her eyes and sway against him.

She backed away, horrified by her reaction. 'Don't! Please don't!'

Jack dropped his hand, staring at her. 'Claire? What the devil's wrong?'

She backed away from him. 'No…nothing. I don't like being touched like that!'

Something flickered in his eyes. His expression cooled. 'I may have the devil of a reputation, but I assure you I don't ravish unwilling women, my dear. You are quite safe.'

She looked at him helplessly. She had somehow managed to offend him again. 'Oh, no! I really did not mean—I know you will not hurt me.'

'Then you merely find my touch repulsive.'

Without thinking, she touched his arm, then drew back when he flinched. 'No, that is not it! I don't want any…any man to touch me like that.' She averted her gaze, afraid to see the derision that would certainly be in his face.

He said nothing for a moment, and when she finally stole a glance at him she was stunned to see anger in his face. She stepped back instinctively, a ripple of fear coursing through her.

Instantly, his face changed. 'My sweet, there's no need to look like that. I vow I won't harm you.'

'I…I was only thinking of something else,' she stammered. Of course he would not harm her; she somehow knew that. 'Perhaps we should go.'

'You are right.' He took her arm, his touch light on the long muslin sleeve of her dress.

Jack was relieved to see his grandmother seated quite composedly in the supper box, sipping a cup of tea. She gave them a pleased smile when she saw them.

'I decided I would come ahead on my own. Such a pleasant evening, don't you think? I have quite enjoyed sitting here by myself and watching the astounding assortment of guests. Although I must admit the overall quality of the crowd has declined from my youth.'

Jack seated Claire in the box next to his grandmother and took a seat across from them before turning a frown on the Duchess. 'You should not have come across by yourself. It is hardly proper.'

'I came with Francis, of course. I have sent him away to enjoy himself,' the Duchess said. She took another sip of tea. 'At my age, I am quite safe. No one has paid me the least heed.'

'An elderly major-domo is hardly adequate. And there is Claire to consider.'

A sudden twinkle appeared in his grandmother's blue eyes. 'I quite see—it is not my reputation but Claire's you are worried about. Well, once you are seen with me, no one will dare say a thing.'

'Unfortunately, no one has yet had that opportunity.' It wasn't only for Claire's reputation that he needed a chaperon; it was for himself. It had taken all his willpower to keep from tasting her generous soft mouth before they'd entered the pleasure gardens. Only her frightened look had stopped him.

'I dare say no harm has been done,' the Duchess said complacently. 'And if it has you only need to marry Claire to set things right.'

Claire looked as if she'd just been stabbed. Her face was white, her expression stunned. He stifled a curse. What the hell was his grandmother up to now? Did she actually hope he'd compromise Claire and they'd be forced into marriage?

'I am certain that will not be necessary and even if it

was I…I would never agree,' Claire said, sounding desperate. She avoided his eyes, keeping her gaze fixed on the painting of dancing fairies at the back of the box.

So, she planned to nobly refuse him, leaving him with the bitter knowledge that he'd ruined her again. He scowled. 'You would marry me, even if I had to force you to the altar.'

'That is quite ridiculous!' Claire snapped, and then shot a mortified look at the Duchess. Pink colour stained her cheeks. 'I do beg your pardon, your Grace.'

The Duchess covered Claire's hand with her own. 'My dear, I quite understand. However, I must assure you my grandson would make an exemplary husband. He can be quite stubborn and does have that dreadful scowl when displeased, but he has a good heart. I think the right wife would…'

'I am certain Claire has no desire to hear my matrimonial qualifications.' Jack gave his grandmother his most quelling look. Next, she'd be offering Claire his hand in marriage.

He stole a look at Claire and was surprised to see a little smile tugging at the corners of her mouth. Almost as if she was amused by the whole thing. His brow shot up. 'I suppose you find the notion I might make a satisfactory husband ridiculous?'

She started. 'No. That is, I think you might make a…a very nice husband.' A slight flush crept into her cheeks.

Did she really think that? The idea she might think him a nice husband was unexpectedly arousing. He stared at her, wondering what the devil she was doing to him. His gaze fell to her mouth, which had always fascinated him with its generous curve, and which looked so soft and kissable.

He jerked his gaze away when he realised his grandmother was eyeing him with a curious little half-smile. He felt the heat rise to his own cheeks. He was practically ogling Claire with his grandmother watching. He stood abruptly. 'I believe I will see to the supper.'

His footmen were just staggering in with the hamper of food he had ordered. Jack directed them to set the hamper near the table. The footmen left, only to be followed by a waiter who brought plates of ham, and salad, and chicken.

'I can see I am just in time.' Harry's cheerful voice caused Jack to mentally groan. He shot Harry a dark look, which was completely ignored.

Harry stepped into the box and grinned. 'Didn't know you were planning a party or I'd have invited myself along earlier.'

'How nice to see you, Mr Devlin,' the Duchess said warmly. 'We will be delighted to have you join us.'

So much for his plans for a tête-à-tête—not that it would have been possible with his grandmother. But Harry could be counted on to monopolise the conversation, and Claire.

Claire didn't appear overjoyed to see Harry. She contributed little to the conversation as they ate, leaving the Duchess and Harry to carry most of it.

Jack looked at her nearly full plate. 'You're not eating much, Claire.'

'I am not particularly hungry.' She gave him an apologetic little smile. 'But the food is very good.'

'No need to exaggerate, Claire,' Harry broke in. 'Food's a cheat for what you pay.'

She frowned at him. 'That is hardly a polite thing to say, particularly when you invited yourself.'

Harry started. Jack could not quite keep the smile from his lips. So, she wasn't all that pleased to have

Harry join them. And in a roundabout way had come to Jack's defence.

'Perhaps you'd care for some fruit, then. There are strawberries in the hamper,' Jack said.

'That would be very nice.' She rose. 'Let me fetch the fruit.' She knelt next to the hamper and lifted the lid. Then she shrieked and jumped back.

'What the devil…?' Jack pushed his chair out and dashed to her side.

'I am so sorry! 'Tis nothing. Only there is a mouse in the hamper.' Her hand was clasped to her breast.

'Good God!' Jack lifted the lid. The small grey creature huddled in one corner, its little nose trembling.

'Is it hurt?' Claire knelt back down beside him.

'What? The mouse or the tarts?' He glanced at her. 'The mouse should be fine; he's been dining on our dessert.'

'Oh, dear, of course.' She flushed. 'It is only he's so small and scared.'

She was concerned about a mouse? Incredulous, he stared at her and then laughed.

'Shall I lift it out, then?'

She turned even pinker. 'Yes, if you please.'

'Then what will you do with it?' Harry asked. He was watching the proceedings with great interest, and Jack suddenly knew exactly how the mouse had come to be in the hamper.

'Save it for the next time one wishes to pull a prank,' he replied. Harry merely grinned. Jack reached in and grabbed the mouse, hoping the creature didn't take it into his head to bite him. He lifted a brow at Claire. 'Now what?'

She looked at him with a peculiar expression. 'I…I

suppose we should release it somewhere. Perhaps in the trees.'

'What a coincidence! Our box is next to yours!' His stepmother's voice came from behind them.

She and Alicia appeared, Frederick Brenton in their wake. Celeste wagged a finger at Jack. 'How uncivil of you not to invite us!'

'It is a private party,' Jack snapped. The mouse twitched in his hand.

'Really?' Her gaze narrowed as it fell on Claire, who appeared to have turned to stone. Then she looked more closely at him. 'Whatever do you have in your hand?'

'A mouse.' He kept his voice bland.

Lady Rotham stepped back. 'A mouse! You cannot be serious.'

'I am. If you will pardon me.' He started to move, and the mouse nipped him on his finger. He swore, dropping the creature. It scurried towards Lady Rotham. She screamed and jumped back, knocking into the table. The claret toppled and spilled across the white cloth. Harry jumped up with a curse. Alicia shrieked and stumbled, and crashed into Harry who was attempting to wipe claret from his coat. He fell back onto his chair, Alicia on his lap. The Duchess merely sat and watched, her expression interested, as if she were at a play.

Claire wished she could disappear as easily as the mouse. The disaster was all her doing. And he'd been bitten! She turned to him, only to find his shoulders shaking. Bewildered, she saw he was laughing. He saw her face, and caught her hand. 'Let's leave. I am certain Harry will manage.' He pulled her out of the box.

They heard Lady Rotham say, 'Frederick, you must do something! There is a mouse loose in the box!'

Jack finally stopped near a fountain and looked down at her. He'd sobered up, but his eyes still danced with laughter. 'My dear, there's no need to look so concerned.'

'Should we not have stayed?' Claire clasped her hands, mortified. 'I fear it was entirely my fault for insisting you rescue the mouse. I am certain Lady Rotham will be very angry, and I cannot blame her. And Alicia! She fell on…on Harry!'

Jack laughed. 'I dare say it will be quite good for both of them.'

'But how? I don't think she likes him!'

His lips twitched. 'We will only hope Harry won't take advantage of the situation.'

Claire felt heat rush to her face. 'What a horrid thing to say.'

'I didn't mean to shock you.' He lightly touched her cheek, causing her to tremble. 'I suspect my grandmother will join us shortly. Do you wish to see the rotunda or explore one of the walks?'

'The rotunda.' It sounded infinitely safer than a walk with him. Even with his grandmother along. Then she remembered his hand. 'Are you hurt?'

'Hurt?'

'Your hand. The mouse bit you.'

He shrugged. 'It is nothing.'

'Let me see.' Could a mouse bite lead to infection?

'Claire, this is ridiculous.' But he gave her his hand nonetheless.

His hand was strong and lean. A scar ran across one finger where he had probably once cut it. She gently turned his hand over and looked at the injured finger. There was only a tiny red mark, and the skin had not been broken. His breath caught, and he stiffened. 'Claire,

I'm fine.' His voice was husky. He snatched his hand out of her grasp. 'My grandmother is coming.'

Claire's own face heated. What madness had possessed her to insist on holding his hand in such a public spot? Perhaps he was right; Vauxhall was dangerous, a place which could lead to all sorts of improper behaviour.

The Duchess bustled up. 'Thank goodness you managed to escape! I was forced to soothe Celeste's ruffled sensibilities before I could leave her safely in Frederick's care. The poor little mouse did manage to escape without harm, although for a moment I thought Alicia was about to deliberately step on it. I must admit she is a rather odd child at times.' She fanned herself, then beamed at them. 'Where shall we go now? I think the rotunda.'

They strolled through the rotunda—a huge circular building filled with columns and paintings and statues. An enormous chandelier, lit with hundreds of lamps, hung from the vast ceiling. The building was crowded, and Claire had never seen such an assortment of people from all classes mixing together in one spot.

Unfortunately, her pure enjoyment of a place she had always longed to see was disrupted by Jack's presence. Not that he was behaving with anything but the utmost propriety. He was quite engrossed in explaining the subject of each of the paintings, drawing her attention to the orchestra, and pointing out various other items of interest. And Claire was engrossed in Jack. Instead of paying proper attention, she found herself admiring the way his dark hair curled at the back of his neck, staring at his lean, blunt fingers, and thinking that the slight shadow of his beard around his mouth gave him a rather dashing aura. Several times, she found herself merely staring at him when he asked her a question. And then she was forced to come up with a sensible reply.

By the time they had left the rotunda and returned to the garden, Claire doubted if she could remember much about the room except its size. She only prayed Jack had not noticed her regard. Or the Duchess. How humiliating it would be if the Duchess thought Claire had a *tendre* for Jack. It was not true, of course, but still it would make things even more awkward.

By now, the sun had set and the garden was lit with hundreds of lamps. They stopped for a moment to listen to a trio of singers, and then the Duchess announced she wished to take one of the walks.

Jack looked at Claire. 'Do you wish to do so?' His voice wasn't particularly enthusiastic.

'That would be nice.' The Duchess looked so eager, Claire didn't have the heart to decline. She was beginning to feel tired. A quick glance at Jack's face showed he also looked strained, as if he wished the evening to end. He probably regretted offering to show her London.

'Splendid!' The Duchess apparently didn't notice their lack of enthusiasm. 'You take Claire's arm and I will follow. I cannot walk quite as fast as I once did.'

Jack held out his arm, and Claire gingerly placed her hand on his sleeve. He flinched at the slight touch, almost as if she'd burned him. Claire bit her lip, wondering how they were ever to make it through the rest of the evening.

Jack said little as they started down the well-lit walk. Claire tried her best to keep from touching more than his sleeve. He seemed to be doing the same thing, holding his body stiffly away from her.

The Duchess trailed behind. They were forced to stop several times and wait for her to join them. She finally spotted a stone bench and announced she wanted to sit. 'But you must go on ahead without me. I will soon catch up.'

'I don't think…' Jack began.

'Of course we will wait,' Claire said at the same time.

He glanced at Claire, a slight smile lifting his mouth. 'I think we are in agreement that we'll wait.'

'It is not necessary,' the Duchess said firmly. 'I insist you go on. I would like a bit of privacy for a few moments.'

'Privacy?' Jack stared at her. 'You will hardly find it here.'

'You are being quite obstinate.' She gave them a beatific smile. 'Now, go on and I will join you shortly. I wish a few moments to myself so that I may enjoy this lovely evening in silence.'

A trio of giggling ladies sauntered by. Jack gave Claire a helpless look and shrugged. 'Very well. Claire?'

'I suppose it will be nice.' Oh, dear. The last thing she wanted was more time alone with Jack. They could walk very, very slowly and hope the Duchess would soon catch up.

'Go along, then.' The Duchess waved them away.

They started away, but not before they heard her say, 'I have always thought this would be the perfect place for an offer of marriage.'

Jack started and Claire turned crimson. When they were out of earshot, he pulled her to the side of the path next to a stand of shrubs. 'Claire,' he began.

Several youths staggered by. One of them called out, 'You've got a fine bit of muslin, my lord!'

Jack turned an icy stare on the youths. 'You are quite mistaken.'

The young man visibly shrank. 'Er, beg pardon. No

offence, mi-milady.' One of his companions yanked his arm, and he nearly tripped before they scurried away.

Jack looked down at Claire. 'Shall I put a bullet through him?'

'No, I wish you would not! It is not that important.'

'Claire, I am sorry.' He ran a hand through his hair, looking more out of countenance than she'd ever seen him.

''Tis no matter. I…I haven't often been mistaken for a bit of muslin.'

'I hope not. Damn! I should never have brought you here.'

'I insisted so you cannot blame yourself. And I…I have quite enjoyed myself.'

'There's no need to spare my feelings.' He gave a slight laugh. 'Besides the mouse and the amusing little diversion that followed, there is my grandmother. She was to provide a proper chaperon. Instead, she seems determined to get us to the altar together.'

'I…I can't imagine why.' Her face must be a thousand shades of red.

She realised he was staring at her. 'Would it be such a bad idea, Claire?'

His eyes had that dark intensity that made her tremble and feel as if her body was about to catch on exquisite fire. She bit her lip. 'I…I am certain it would not be…be wise.'

'Why not?'

'I…'

'My lord! How could you?'

Claire and Jack jerked apart at the sound of the dismayed feminine voice.

'What?' Jack snarled.

The woman was short and plump and gaudily dressed

in a striped gown that revealed a great amount of ample breast. Even in the dim light, Claire could see her face was heavily painted.

The woman clutched Jack's arm. 'How could you? When last night you were with me and now…now I find you with this creature!'

He shook her arm off. 'What the devil are you talking about?'

She gave a loud sniff. Tears gleamed in her eyes. 'All the promises you made me! Do they mean nothing, my lord?'

'I have no idea who you are. I fear you are mad or drunk.'

'Oh, no! Dear Rotham! How can you be so cruel?' She flung herself at him and then appeared to collapse in a swoon. He caught her as she slid down his front. She opened her eyes and clutched at the lace on the front of his shirt. 'I knew you would not leave me.' Her eyelids fluttered shut.

Claire stared at them, her mind numb. She backed away. Jack, his arms full of flesh and silk, looked as if he'd been struck.

'I…I'd best go,' Claire said.

'No, wait! Damn it!' He struggled to pry the woman's hands from his shoulders.

'Oh, dear!' The Duchess suddenly appeared behind Claire. 'Now what has gone wrong?'

Chapter Seven

Jack had just finished dressing when his footman appeared. 'A message for you, my lord.'

Jack took the note and quickly scanned the contents. A scowl appeared on his brow. 'I have a call to pay.'

'My lord, I believe Lady Rotham and Miss Snowden are to arrive shortly,' Hobbes said. He brushed a fleck of dust from the sleeve of Jack's morning coat.

'They can occupy themselves until I return.' Jack strode to his dressing-table and retrieved Claire's fan before leaving the room.

Twenty minutes later he was shown into Lady Dunford's drawing-room. Claire and Lady Dunford sat together on a sofa, a copy of a periodical opened on a table in front of them.

Claire's eyes widened in surprise as he entered the room. She looked fresh and lovely in a soft pink gown, a locket hanging from a ribbon about her neck.

Jane rose from the sofa, a smile of welcome on her face. 'Lord Rotham, how kind of you to call.'

He bowed over her hand. 'Thank you.'

'Will you be seated? We have just received a new *La Belle Assemblée*. There are some delightful new fashions. Do you not think Claire would look well in a gown of sea-green crêpe?'

He glanced over at Claire, who looked as if she wanted to vanish. His mouth curved in a slow smile. 'Most charming, although she looks lovely in anything she wears.'

He was delighted to see her flush, despite the angry look she shot him.

He turned back to Jane, who watched them with a pleased little smile on her face. 'I cannot stay long, but I wondered if I might speak to Mrs Ellison alone? I have some business to discuss with her.'

Jane's blue eyes widened slightly. 'Why, of course.' She suddenly beamed at him and left the room.

He watched her go, hit by the surprising revelation that Lady Dunford actually thought he planned to make Claire an offer. More astounding, she actually approved.

'My lord, is there something you wished to speak to me about?' Claire had risen from the sofa and was standing near him. Even if he had planned to propose marriage, her frosty expression would have given any sane man pause.

'Your note.' He raised a sardonic brow at her expression. 'You did command me to return your fan, I believe.'

'Yes, but I thought you would send it back.'

Her cool voice had the effect of irritating him. He'd no doubt she intended to retrieve her fan and then never see him again. He folded his arms across his chest. 'And I thought I would deliver it in person. Particularly since you discourteously ran off with Devlin.'

A faint blush rose to her cheeks. She lifted her chin. 'I did not run off with him. He offered to take me home and the Duchess agreed. Under the circumstances, I could not see what else I was to do. You were occupied with that…that…'

'Doxy? Trollop? I assure you I have never seen the woman in my life.'

Claire sniffed. 'She certainly seemed to know you.'

'She claimed to know me. There is a difference.'

'Then why were you embracing her?'

He scowled. 'I was hardly embracing her. After nearly strangling me, she fainted in my arms. Trying to disengage her was worse than an attack by a litter of kittens.' He gave a short laugh. 'Do you really think I would come from her bed to you?'

'I…I don't know.'

'As soon as you were out of sight, she made an amazing recovery and scampered off.'

'Oh.' Claire wrinkled her brow. 'But why would she do that?'

'You might ask Devlin.'

'Harry? But why?'

'Never mind.' His mouth quirked. 'Do you believe me, Claire? That I did not know the woman?'

'I suppose.' She still looked doubtful.

'It is true.' He smiled at her, his humour restored. She was beginning to look less haughty and rather adorably confused. 'Should we try another outing? Perhaps to someplace more staid such as St Paul's.'

A smile touched her lips. 'I would hope nothing so peculiar would happen there.' Her face sobered. 'But I would like my fan, if you please. It was my mother's.'

His eyes strayed over her soft mouth. Almost without thinking he said, 'Of course. But since our evening ended so abruptly last night I have one more condition.'

'One more condition? What?'

He moved towards her. 'A kiss.'

She stood very still, her face growing pale. 'No! That is not fair!'

'It was hardly fair of you to deprive me of your company last night.'

'But I had a reason for doing so!' She backed away from him, then was brought up short by the sofa.

'Perhaps.' He came to stand in front of her. 'But still, I was forced to make my way home alone. And think of the mouse bite. It does hurt; I could hardly sleep because of the throbbing in my thumb.'

Her gaze flew to his hand, and then she looked back at him. 'I think you are exaggerating, my lord.'

'Only a little.' He looked into her face, which was filled with apprehension. If he was any sort of gentleman, he would back off, but there were advantages in forgetting he was one. And he was determined she would discover his kisses were nothing like Ellison's.

'You may kiss me,' he said. 'Then you'll be in control.'

Her expression wavered. Seeing victory at hand, he pushed ahead. 'It won't be too painful, I promise. And then I'll return your fan.'

She took a deep breath as if she were about to do something distasteful. 'Very well.' She knotted her hands. 'I am not very good at this.'

'That doesn't matter.' He reached towards her, and she flinched. He dropped his hand. 'I won't hurt you.' He felt as if he was trying to approach a nervous filly.

He restrained the impulse to crush her to him as she approached. She stood on her tiptoes, and he bent his head. Then her soft lips, as light as butterfly wings, brushed his cheek. He could not stop the groan that escaped him.

She stepped back. 'Is something wrong?' Her eyes were puzzled.

'No,' he said shortly. Nothing except he was hot and hard with desire. 'No.'

She bit her lip. 'I really don't know how to kiss properly.'

'There was nothing wrong with your kiss.'

'Oh.' She looked vulnerable and embarrassed.

'Would you like to try again?' he asked. 'Or perhaps I could kiss you and you could tell me what you think of my kiss.'

She flushed. 'I am certain you are very good.'

He shrugged. 'I don't know. I think I would like you to decide for yourself.'

She did not resist as he pulled her to him, careful not to alarm her. His lips brushed over her sweet, cool mouth, and he used every bit of will-power in his possession to keep from ravishing her lips. Her body felt soft and fragile in his arms. Her scent of lavender filled his senses. Caught in her spell and his own rising passion, his kiss deepened. Her lips parted and he heard her small gasp as his tongue invaded her mouth.

He returned to his senses with a thud. Dazed, he released his hold on her. His gaze focused on her flushed face and the equally confused look in her eyes.

Finally he spoke. 'What did you think?' His voice came out more husky than he'd intended.

'I imagine you have had a lot of practice.' Her voice was shaky.

'That doesn't tell me anything. Did you like my kiss?'

'I…I don't know,' she whispered. She looked completely stunned. 'Perhaps I should go.'

'I believe I'm the one who should leave,' he said automatically, and then could have cursed himself for his stupidity. What had happened to the cool, sophisticated address he was known for?

But she was backing out of the drawing-room door, leaving him staring after her.

And it wasn't until he reached his house that he remembered he'd forgotten to return her fan.

Claire shut the door to her bedchamber and leaned against it. She closed her eyes and groaned. Whatever had possessed her to let him kiss her? No, she had let him force her to kiss him. No, even that was hardly fair of her. She could not lie to herself. She had wanted to touch him, feel his cheek with its hint of beard that always seemed to be there no matter how well shaven he was.

Perhaps she really was the Jezebel Marcus had thought her, filled with base desires. Brushing her lips across his cheek had made her want to do more. And when he'd offered to kiss her she had put up no resistance at all.

Harry called a few days later right on the heels of Lady Billingsley, who had arrived only minutes before. He bowed to the ladies and even managed to elicit a fluttery smile from Lady Billingsley when he addressed her. 'How charming you look. Puce is a most becoming colour with your complexion.'

'Really, Mr Devlin! Flattery is useless on me!'

'But I never flatter.'

'Well, I must own this is my favourite colour. I have had a number of compliments on it.'

'I can quite see why.'

Lady Billingsley actually looked flustered. Her hand went up to touch the kerchief stuffed into her round neckline. 'I was just telling Jane that she was very remiss in letting Claire go to Vauxhall with Lord Rotham alone! She refuses to believe his purposes are of the most unscrupulous!'

'Aunt! She was with the Duchess.' Jane looked exasperated.

Lady Billingsley paid no heed. 'You cannot imagine the vile things that are being spread about!' Ever since Jack had insulted her at the Hawkes' ball, she had missed no opportunity to abuse his character.

Harry looked shocked. 'But I can. Which is why I felt obliged to add my services as well as the Duchess's. Do not fear, Lady Billingsley, Claire was well protected at Vauxhall.'

'I really did not need your services, Harry,' Claire snapped. She yanked her needle through the embroidery she held in her hand. He should be defending Jack, not participating in Lady Billingsley's ridiculous speculations.

Harry raised a brow. 'Didn't you? You seem to be in a poor mood. Do you have the headache?'

'Perhaps we can discuss something else.' Claire jabbed viciously at the silk cloth and managed to prick her finger with the needle. She felt out of sorts. Perhaps it was the rain that seemed to be coming down in sheets, running down the windows in dismal rivulets. And Lady Billingsley's lecture on her accompanying Jack to Vauxhall and hints of his wicked intentions had made her feel even more cross. She wished everyone would go away and leave her.

Harry seated himself on the satinwood armchair near Thea. 'Very well. I am to attend a masquerade tomorrow night.'

'A masquerade! How delightful! I have always

wanted to go to one,' Thea exclaimed. 'Will you dress in costume?'

'I rather think I will dress as a Turkish sultan.'

'You will look splendid! Is it a public or private event?'

'Private. Mrs Robards holds one every year. I would offer to escort you, but I fear this one is not quite suited to young ladies.'

Mrs Robards? Jack's lovely friend? So, Jack would most likely be there—not that Claire cared a bit. She had not seen him since the morning he'd kissed her and she was quite grateful.

'Masquerades are never suitable for young ladies.' Lady Billingsley sniffed.

'I think Mrs Robards is quite lovely,' Thea said. 'And she has nice, smiling eyes.'

Lady Billingsley gave a little gasp. 'Dorothea!'

'And how would you know that, minx?' Harry asked.

'I nearly ran into her once at the theatre. She smiled quite kindly at me.'

'Oh, dear child, you must never speak to such…such a creature.'

'But when I run into someone I always pardon myself.'

'You should not even notice such a person!' Lady Billingsley's chin wobbled as it did when she was about to launch into another tirade.

The conversation came to a halt when the butler appeared. 'Lord Rotham.'

Claire's hand jerked up, and she managed to prick herself again. Her heart leapt to her throat as Jack appeared in the doorway. He stopped abruptly when he saw Harry, then came into the room. His face was expressionless. Claire sat very still, the embroidery frozen in her hand.

Jane rose and held out her hand. 'Lord Rotham, how nice to see you.'

Lady Billingsley abruptly stood. 'I fear that I will be obligated to leave if you intend to receive him! I cannot stay in the same house with a…a libertine!' She gave Jack a cold glare, then stared at Jane as if challenging her to choose sides.

Claire shot to her feet, her face heated with angry colour. 'How can you say such an insulting and hurtful thing? And in front of him, as if he were not even here!'

Lady Billingsley gasped. 'How…how dare you speak to me in such a way? You are a wicked girl!'

Jane rose, her own face pale. 'I cannot have you talk to Claire in that fashion or insult my guests. I must ask you to leave, Aunt.'

Lady Billingsley's face turned an angry red. She clamped her lips together for a moment, then spoke. 'Very well. If that is what you wish, Jane. I will wash my hands of this whole affair.' She gathered up her reticule, her face distorted with fury, and stalked out of the drawing-room without a backward glance.

There was an uncomfortable silence. Harry recovered first. He rose with a lazy movement. 'An interesting lady. I must be off, although I should enjoy watching the rest of the little drama.' He bowed towards the ladies. 'Servant, Rotham. Will I see you at White's?'

'Perhaps.' Jack's face was even more expressionless, if possible, and there was a tinge of colour in his cheeks. He waited until Harry's footsteps could be heard clattering down the stairs, then turned towards Jane, Claire and Thea who stood in stricken silence. 'I had only called to return Mrs Ellison's fan. I will not trouble you further.' He started to lay the fan on the table.

Claire, who had had every intention of treating him with icy politeness the next time she saw him, dashed forward to catch his coat sleeve. 'Oh, please don't!' The remote look on his face was almost more than she could bear.

He stared down at her. She was scarcely aware of Thea and Jane slipping quietly from the room. She realised she was still clutching his coat sleeve. Flushing, she drew her hand away. 'I…I wish you would not go. I am very sorry for Lady Billingsley's words. She was quite upset I went with you to Vauxhall and somehow she has the most erroneous notion you wish to…to compromise me.'

His mouth quirked sardonically. 'And so you risked Lady Billingsley's wrath to defend me.'

Claire dropped her gaze before the intensity of his. 'I don't like to see people attacked.'

'I know. It is one of the things I have always admired about you.'

'Is it?' She looked up into his dark face, feeling rather dizzy.

'Yes.' He placed the fan in her hand. Then he was gone.

She sank against the door, wanting to cry. For some reason, she had the unhappy premonition she would never see him again.

Chapter Eight

The next evening, Claire stood in her brother's library, staring down at a note just delivered by a footman. She crumpled it with a furious hand. How could Harry do such a thing? He'd always had a streak of mischief, but to involve Thea was going much too far! Even if no one discovered she had been at Mrs Robards's masquerade, the harm would be done in the very deceit.

And what if some harm did come of it? Claire dreaded to think of the consequences. It would make her own indiscretions pale in comparison. Young, unmarried girls had very little latitude in behaviour; the smallest breach of propriety could bring a reputation into question.

Thea had spent the day with a friend and her family, and then was to have gone to the theatre with them. Jane had been in bed most of the day with the migraine. And Claire had just settled down in the library for a quiet evening at home.

No matter that Harry assured her he would stay right by Thea's side and no one would ever recognise her. She supposed she should be grateful he'd at least sent a note. But she still wanted to strangle Harry for this. And she certainly could not spend the evening worrying about Thea.

She must go and retrieve Thea herself.

A half-hour later, Claire was seated in the carriage, a black domino over her gown. The little maid, Sally, sat in the corner of the carriage, her eyes wide with a mixture of apprehension and excitement.

Claire wore a half-mask she'd managed to locate. She had left a vaguely worded message with the servants, and prayed Jane would not enquire about her whereabouts. She hoped she would be back with Thea before anyone noticed her absence.

Her stomach churned as the carriage approached Mrs Robards's house. The street in front of the imposing town house was crowded, voices and laughter carrying on the clear night air.

Claire stepped down, clutching the domino around her, grateful for the anonymity of her mask. After instructing the coachman to wait for her, she climbed up the steps of the town house behind a group of unusually boisterous women. But when the footman asked to see their invitations one of the women spoke in decidedly masculine tones, which he quickly transformed into a falsetto. He pinched the footman's cheek while his companions laughed.

Claire slipped around them, hoping the stony-faced footman would be too occupied to notice. Already, the laughter and noise and the strangeness of seeing nothing but masked faces gave her a feeling of unreality.

Music seemed to be coming from the top of the circular staircase. She climbed the stairs, holding up the folds of the domino that must be her brother's for it was far too long. She was jostled first by a Spanish lady and then by a priest. By the time she reached the top, she wanted nothing more than the safety of her brother's library.

Then she thought of Thea in this noisy, peculiar crowd and her resolution stiffened. She stepped inside the ballroom. The dancers were performing the steps of a minuet, but the costumes made it almost a parody of the elegant dance. How was she ever to locate Harry and Thea? The only Turkish sultans she'd ever seen had been between the pages of a book. She vaguely recalled a ferocious-looking man in a turban and strange baggy breeches.

Finally, she spotted a man in a blue turban who was about Harry's height and build. She started through the crowd after him. Someone grabbed her arm. She gasped and turned.

'And where are you going, my pretty maid?' The man's voice was raspy as if he was taking great pains to disguise it. It was the priest she'd seen on the staircase.

'I am to meet someone.' She tried to shake him off, but his grip only tightened.

'Surely you have something you must confess?'

'Nothing. Let me go.'

She finally managed to jerk her arm away and escape. But by the time she made it to the spot where the turbaned man had been he'd disappeared.

Now what to do? She felt alone and more than a little afraid by her encounter with the priest. The dancers had dispersed. She saw a lady in a pink domino, who could be about Thea's height. Her hopes were crushed when a harlequin minced up to the lady and kissed her fully on the lips. The lady squealed.

Discouraged, Claire turned away. She made her way

around the ballroom but each time she spotted a woman who might resemble Thea her hopes were dashed as soon as she neared the person. And there seemed to be an assortment of men dressed in oriental garb.

Finally she caught a glimpse of the man in the blue turban as he left through the terrace doors. She pushed her way past a pirate and a devil and followed him out. At least the terrace was well lit, although the garden below was dark. She glanced around and finally spotted the man heading down the steps towards the garden. Claire dashed after him, as fast as a gown and a silk domino would permit.

The garden was not large, but the dark bushes and trees made it ideal for privacy. Her sultan was heading towards a clump of shrubbery in one corner. She stumbled after him, tripping more than once over the awkward domino. And then she gasped as a pair of strong arms circled her waist.

'I've caught you at last, my elusive one!' The priest's raspy voice sounded in her ear. His hand brushed over her breast in a very unholy manner.

Claire struggled as he turned her to face him. 'Let me go! I am not what you think!'

'You are what I have been waiting for. Come, release me from my vows of celibacy!' Her attacker managed to plant a wet kiss on her cheek, barely missing her mouth.

'No!' Claire tried to shove against his chest. He pinned her to him and yanked her into the bushes. His hand came up to remove her mask. She yanked one hand free and clawed at his face.

He released her and yelped. 'Vixen! You shall pay!'

She started to run, only to trip over the folds of the domino. She tumbled to the ground, the breath knocked from her. Her mask fell to one side. She tried to rise, only to find herself tangled in the garment. Tears of fear and frustration filled her eyes. Her attacker laughed triumphantly, then exclaimed, 'What the hell are you doing?'

'We do not allow rape here,' a woman's cool voice said. 'Hamilton, please oblige me by removing him from the premises.'

Claire slowly made it to her knees, her whole body trembling. Her stomach felt as if she'd been punched. Her vision cleared in time to see a burly man forcibly hauling the priest away accompanied by a volley of curses.

'Are you all right, my dear?'

Claire looked up into the unmasked face of Sylvia Robards.

Claire could not miss the startled look that flashed in the other woman's eyes. 'Mrs Ellison?' She quickly knelt by Claire's side, not an easy task in her voluminous Elizabethan costume. She picked up Claire's mask. 'Let me help you put this on, and then you must tell me why you are here.'

Her fingers deftly tied Claire's mask, and then she helped Claire to her feet. Claire took a tentative step and gasped at the excruciating pain that shot through her right foot. Instantly, Mrs Robards took her arm. 'Can you walk at all?'

'I…I think.' But her second step proved equally painful.

'I must take you to my room.' Sylvia made a motion and the same man who'd escorted the priest away came to her side. 'Our guest has hurt her foot. I should like her taken to my chamber with as little fanfare as possible.'

'Aye.' Before Claire could protest, he'd swept her into his strong, muscular arms.

'I…I am fine. If you could take me to my coach?' Claire suggested tentatively.

Mrs Robards smiled at her with sympathy. 'We must look at your foot first. Do not worry; I shall see no harm will come to you.'

Her voice was kind. Claire said no more as she was carried through some sort of side entrance and up a stair-case. They entered a large bedchamber. Claire had an impression of soft candlelight and luxurious golden hangings before Hamilton laid her on the bed. 'Will we be needing some water and cloths for the lass?' he en-quired.

'Yes, that would be splendid.' Mrs Robards seated herself on the bed next to Claire. 'Would you feel com-fortable removing your mask now?'

'Yes.' Claire pulled it off, glad to be free from it. She struggled to sit up against the pillows. 'I really must go home. This is very kind, but I…I don't want to impose on you.'

'I fear Jack would have my neck if he knew I sent you home without seeing to you properly.'

'Jack?' Claire's heart lurched.

'Yes.' She smiled at Claire and then rose in a graceful movement. 'I must remove your slipper.' She moved to Claire's feet. Claire bit her lip and tried not to gasp as Sylvia gently eased the satin slipper from her foot. 'To properly wrap your foot, I must remove your stocking also.' She completed the task and looked back at Claire. 'Does Jack know you are here?'

'Oh, no.' Claire could feel heat rising to her cheeks. Mrs Robards probably not only considered Claire a per-son who stole into private parties, but one who came for clandestine meetings as well. 'I am very sorry…I know I have no invitation, but I received a note saying that my niece would be here. With Harry Devlin. I wanted to stop them, but I…I could not find them. Harry was to be a sultan and when I saw a man in a turban I followed him into the garden. And then that man, he…' Her voice trailed off. She was mortified she had got herself into such a horrid situation.

'I see.' Mrs Robards gently probed Claire's sore foot. 'I fear there is some swelling. You may have a sprain.' She looked up as a maid entered with cloths and a basin of water. She waited until the maid left and then, with great efficiency, wrapped Claire's ankle. After that, she wiped the dirt from Claire's hands and face. 'I saw Mr Devlin very briefly tonight, and then he left early. I saw no sign of a young lady with him. I rather suspect your niece was not here.' She sat back. 'You look much better. Who sent you the note?'

'Harry. He said he had persuaded Thea to accompany him, and I was not to worry, as he would keep her very safe. She was to go to the theatre with some friends,' Claire said, worried. What had happened to Thea? Claire prayed she had changed her mind and was safe in Lady Buxstead's care.

'Certainly I will ask my servants, but I don't think you need to worry about Miss Dunford.' Mrs Robards rose from the bed. 'I will, however, send Jack to you.'

'He is here?'

'Yes, although he does not particularly seem to be enjoying himself. He has something else on his mind, I fear. But perhaps after he sees you…'

'Please don't send him here. I just want to go home.' Claire felt panicked by the thought.

'But, my dear, he will be furious if I do not.' An amused smile lifted her lips.

'But he'll be even more furious with me if you do.' How could she ever explain this to him? 'I dare say you might find me strangled,' Claire finished despairingly.

Mrs Robards gave a gurgle of laughter and Claire saw what Thea meant by smiling eyes. 'I doubt it.' She paused by the door. 'Just remember to treat him kindly. He is not used to being in love.'

Claire stared after the closed door in shock. Surely Mrs Robards had not been implying Jack was in love with her? He could not be. Claire sank back on the pillows. She could dismiss Jane's romantic speculations, but for Mrs Robards to hint the same thing was another matter entirely.

And now what was she to do? Trapped in Mrs Robards's richly decorated bedchamber, she felt as if she was awaiting a lover.

This was ridiculous.

Claire gingerly swung her feet over the side of the bed, trying not to brush her sore foot against the covers. But putting the least weight on her foot nearly made her yelp. Limping from the bedchamber to her coach was impossible. Besides, she would most likely get lost in the unfamiliar house.

She finally lay back against the pillows, tired and frustrated, and extremely apprehensive.

Jack threw down his hand, caring little that he'd lost again. Lord Ashton grinned as Jack shoved his vowels toward him. He was dressed as Puck. 'Another round, Rotham? At this rate, I'll recover the entire amount I've lost to you over the past few years.'

Jack downed his glass of brandy. 'Later.' He rose, too

restless to sit for another hand. The small room used for card games was crowded and hot. An air of unreality hung over it, rather like a vision of hell, with no one quite what they seemed.

'My lord.' He turned to find a footman standing next to him. Or at least he thought he recognised the man as one of Sylvia's servants. Since members of the upper classes enjoyed masquerading as servants, he couldn't quite be sure.

'Mrs Robards wishes to speak with you.'

Jack followed him out of the card room. He was surprised and more than a little puzzled when the man led him up the ornate winding staircase and towards Sylvia's own private apartments.

Sylvia came from her small saloon, a little smile on her face, although she looked rather worried.

'What is it?' he asked, taking her hand. They had briefly been lovers, but now were good friends, and he still cared about her welfare.

''Tis nothing to do with me. But I fear Mrs Ellison is here and has—'

'Claire is here?' He stared at her, his mind hardly taking it in. 'Impossible!'

'She is in my bedchamber.' Her hand gripped his. 'Listen to me; I am certain she has sprained her foot. She is here because she thought her niece came with Harry Devlin and Mrs Ellison wanted to rescue her.'

None of it made sense to him. Only that Claire was hurt. 'What happened?'

He waited until Sylvia finished, his anger and concern growing.

'I want to see her,' he said grimly. He shook off Sylvia's hand.

'Of course.' She touched his sleeve. 'But only if you

promise not to scold her too much. She fears you mean to strangle her.'

'Does she?' A slight smile lifted his lips. 'I might.'

Sylvia opened the door to her chamber, allowing Jack to precede her in.

His heart leapt to his throat when he saw Claire's pale, wide-eyed face. He stared at her for a moment, scarcely noticing when Sylvia left the room. Then he stalked towards the bed.

Claire watched him with an odd mixture of relief and apprehension. It took all her will-power to keep from shrinking back in the bed. He looked grim, as if he'd caught her doing something improper. But surely attending a masquerade wasn't all that horrid. Maybe he'd been interrupted in something. A vision of the couples she'd spotted stealing kisses flashed through her mind. Certainly he was not quite dressed. He had removed his evening coat and his white linen shirt was open at the neck under a white embroidered waistcoat. He looked slightly rumpled, but it only emphasised his dangerous masculine aura.

Her mouth went dry as he came to stand next to the bed. He hovered over her, his arms crossed. 'What the hell are you doing here, Claire?'

She gazed up at him, not certain if she could speak. She swallowed and lightly licked her lips. The gesture only made his eyes darken to a smoky grey. 'I...I came to find Thea,' she managed to croak.

He raised a disbelieving brow. 'Thea? Why would you expect to find her here?'

'I...I received a note from Harry. He said he was bringing her.' Why must he stare at her like that? She felt vulnerable and exposed, lying on the bed. She restrained the urge to pull a cover over herself, which would prove awkward anyway, since she was lying on the top of the brocade bedcover.

He looked even more sceptical. 'Indeed? Harry was here for a few brief moments, but I assure you Thea was not with him.'

'Oh.'

'And even if she had been with him you had no business coming here by yourself without an escort.' He scowled. 'Sylvia told me what happened. You were damned lucky Sylvia keeps servants posted to watch out for those sorts of things. Or you might have been raped.'

How dared he lecture her? She had no idea where Thea was, she'd been frightened, her foot hurt, and she felt like weeping. She tried to glare at him. 'If you are only here to scold me, I…I wish you would le-leave.' Her voice shook. She turned her head away so he wouldn't see the tear trailing down her cheek.

'Damn it, Claire.' His voice was rough, but the hand that pushed the hair from her forehead was gentle. 'Don't cry, my sweet. Look at me.'

'No. Go away. I want to go home.' She closed her eyes, willing him to leave.

She felt his weight settle on the bed as he sat next to her. 'I'll take you.'

She finally turned her head to look at him. The grimness had left his eyes only to be replaced by tenderness. It scared her more than his anger had. 'I have my coach,' she told him. 'Please leave; I am certain you were occupied with other activities.'

'Nothing of importance, I assure you.'

His face so close, a stray lock of hair tumbling over his forehead, was making her dizzy. She searched for anything to put distance between them. 'Then why are you not dressed?' she blurted out.

'I was playing cards. I prefer to play without my coat.' Then comprehension dawned in his eyes. His lips curved in a wicked smile. 'I see. You thought I was engaged in activities of a more amorous sort.'

Claire felt heat course through her cheeks. 'I really give very little thought to what you do.'

'Really?' His smile was decidedly dangerous. 'I should hate for you to think I was in the arms of another while renewing my acquaintance with you.'

'Is…is that what you are doing?'

'Yes.' He bent over her, his hands on either side of her head on the pillows. He smelled of brandy and a scent she'd know anywhere as his own. His eyes glinted down at her. 'How could I think of another woman when there's you?'

'I wish you would.'

'Even after the kiss we shared?'

'Yes! We should not be sharing kisses or anything else.' She attempted to shove him away, but he caught her hands, easily imprisoning them in his own above her head. And then he kissed her.

This time his kiss was urgent and demanding. She closed her eyes with every intention of resisting him. He released her hands, and then his hand briefly cupped her cheek before moving to the soft curve of her breast. His weight settled half-across her, his mouth coaxing a response. Of their own accord, her lips parted beneath his insistent pressure, allowing him entry into her mouth. His tongue touched hers, and instead of the revulsion she'd felt with Marcus she eagerly returned its thrust, finding the taste and feel of him intriguing.

A small sound of protest escaped her as his mouth

lifted from hers. He left a trail of kisses down her neck as if he meant to taste her, and then his hands fumbled with the strings of her domino. He pushed it aside, so his lips could caress the soft skin above the mound of her breast. All the while his hands moved on the side of her breast in slow, languorous circles.

She knew she should push him away. But his weight was strangely pleasurable, and her body tingled with awareness. And when he finally freed her breasts, his tongue licking an exposed nipple, she gasped as her stomach contracted. She clutched at his arms, feeling the taut, hard muscles beneath her hands.

All too soon, he moved back to her mouth, his tongue seeking entrance. This time she welcomed him. He shifted his weight more firmly on her, and then she gasped again, this time in genuine pain as his foot brushed hers.

Instantly, he lifted his head. His eyes were dark and heavy with passion. 'Claire?'

'My foot,' she whispered.

He stared at her for a moment. 'Damn,' he said softly. He rolled off her. 'Let me look.'

'No!' Sanity was rapidly returning along with the throbbing in her foot. 'It is fine.' She tugged at her bodice and yanked the domino closed, her hands trembling.

But he was already by her feet. He gently touched her sore foot and she whimpered. He looked up at her, his eyes narrowed. 'I had no idea you'd hurt it this badly. Why didn't you tell me?'

'You gave me no chance to do so.'

'No. I did not.'

'I want to go home.'

He came to stand by the bed. 'Of course.'

'In my own coach.'

'You will go in mine.' Before she knew what he meant to do, he had scooped her up in his arms.

Outside the door, they met Mrs Robards. She looked at them with a slight smile. 'Leaving? A wise idea, but I think masks would be in order.' She held two in her hand.

She helped Claire on with hers and then slipped one over Jack's face.

'Will you be all right, my dear?' she asked Claire.

'I hope so. Thank you. I am sorry to be so much trouble,' Claire said shyly.

'It was my pleasure.' Her smile was kind.

'Now that the courtesies have been observed, perhaps I should take her home. She's hardly a feather,' Jack broke in. He sounded impatient and irritable.

'I never asked you to do so,' Claire said. She was horrified to find her voice trembled instead of sounding cold and haughty. She was angry, and humiliated and hurt. First he tried to seduce her, then insisted he must take her home, and now he sounded as if she was nothing more than a troublesome burden. And heavy at that.

'I think the servants' entrance would be best. We don't want the other guests to think abduction is now acceptable.' Mrs Robards's voice was amused.

Hamilton led them through the same back staircase used earlier. Claire shut her eyes, her foot throbbing, her emotions in turmoil. They finally reached the night air. She scarcely heard as Jack said goodnight to the servant.

Unfortunately, it was not so easy to avoid others out in front of the house. They were the object of more than one ribald comment. Claire buried herself in his chest despite the mask she wore. He finally paused, and gave instructions to the coachman.

'Claire, are you awake?' His breath wafted over her cheek.

'Yes, of course.' Only humiliated to her very bones.

'I wasn't certain. I'm going to help you into the coach. I did not want you to start awake and hit your head.'

He carefully helped her in and arranged her across one of the seats. Then he stepped out. She heard his voice and then he entered, sitting across from her.

'Are you comfortable?' he asked politely as the carriage moved forward.

'Yes.' She had no intention of telling him otherwise.

'You can safely remove your mask.' He had already removed his. His expression was impossible to see in the shadows of the coach.

Claire fumbled with the strings, wishing she could keep it on. She had the lowering feeling if she insisted it would only lead to another argument. She was too tired to argue. Then, she straightened. 'My coach!' Oh, no! She had already kept her brother's elderly coachman standing far too long. And Sally probably thought she'd been kidnapped.

'I've already sent one of my servants to tell your coachman I am escorting you home.'

'Thank you.'

He said little else after that, except to ask again if she was comfortable. They finally arrived at her home. Jack sprang out and then helped her from the carriage. 'I can walk, if you will only support me,' she told him. She had no desire to have him stride into the house with her in his arms. Perhaps Jane would not be up and she could sneak to her room without anyone the wiser. She could come up with a plausible explanation of why her foot was injured.

He ignored her. He swept her up in his arms and carried her up the steps. His coachman had already rapped on the door.

Claire cringed when she saw the amazed and then concerned expression of the butler. And then wished she could faint when she saw Jane followed by Thea behind him, their faces filled with worry.

Chapter Nine

Jack located Harry at White's the next morning. From Harry's elegant rumpled waistcoat and red eyes, Jack guessed he'd been up the entire night at play.

Harry leaned negligently back in his chair. Across from him were Lord Richard Peyton and the Honourable Charles Byers. Byers was slumped back in his chair, his cravat awry. Lord Richard raised a languid hand in greeting.

'I want to speak to you,' Jack told Harry. He resisted the urge to yank his friend up by the collar and knock him down.

Harry attempted to raise a brow. 'Can this not wait? As you can see, I am a trifle foxed. Not in any condition for a confrontation as I suspect you want.' Harry's speech always became uncharacteristically elegant when he'd been drinking.

'I want this matter settled now,' Jack snarled.

Byers came to life. 'Lay odds on Rotham.'

Harry rose. 'Since I do not desire a disagreeable scene, I shall be happy to oblige.' He lurched up from his chair and made a lopsided bow. 'Gentlemen.'

Jack found an unoccupied niche in one of the saloons.

He waited until Harry had slumped down into a chair before speaking.

'What the hell do you mean by sending Claire a message saying you were taking Dorothea to the masquerade?'

Harry looked surprised. 'I did not want her to worry. Thea changed her mind at any rate. There was no harm done.'

Jack leaned over him. 'No harm done? Claire took it upon herself to rescue Thea and showed up at Sylvia's. She was attacked and ended up with a sprained ankle.'

Harry stared at him. 'Good God!'

'Yes.'

'I never thought…' Harry seemed to be sobering up rapidly. 'Whatever possessed her to do such a damnably stupid thing?'

'Undoubtedly to save Thea from whatever debauchery she imagined you planned to lead her into.' Jack glared at him. 'I ought to call you out.'

'I'd hardly fault you.' Harry looked unusually serious. 'Was she harmed?'

'No, thank God. Sylvia watches for that sort of thing. Unfortunately, they did not determine the identity of her attacker. He'd have a sword through him by now.'

'He'd have two,' Harry said grimly. He stood, albeit somewhat shakily. 'Who stopped him?'

'Hamilton. Sylvia found me.' Jack looked at him. The contrition in Harry's voice was the only thing that stopped him from planting his fist in Harry's face. 'One more thing.'

'What?'

'The bet is off.'

'*What?*'

'The bet's off. I'm forfeiting. I'll deliver Satan and the money at your convenience.'

Harry looked at him as if he'd lost his mind. 'You can't do that! The devil, Jack! At least wait until after your race. I thought…' He paused. 'What about Claire?'

'I intend to marry her,' Jack told him, then stalked off.

Jane smiled fondly at Claire. 'Really, Claire, I am sorry about your poor foot, but I must admit it was rather romantic to see Lord Rotham striding into the house with you in his arms. He looked very dashing without his coat, his hair mussed and that grim look on his face.' She was sitting on the edge of Claire's bed. She looked lovely and fresh and not at all as if she'd spent the prior day in bed with a miserable headache.

Claire scowled. 'There was nothing at all romantic about any of it. He acted as if I was nothing but an inconvenient sack of flour he was forced to haul about.' Except when he'd been kissing her with such passion. She had barely slept between the pain in her foot and the remembrance of his embrace. After giving up on sleeping, she had finally decided he had drunk too much brandy and had scarcely known what he was about. Except there had been nothing clumsy about his expert caresses. Even now, she felt a blush rise to her cheeks.

To her chagrin, she realised Jane was watching her with great interest. 'Oh, Claire. There is nothing to be ashamed about. I think it was quite daring of you to steal from the house in such a clandestine fashion to meet him at the masquerade. I promise I will say nothing to Edward.'

Claire's mouth dropped open. 'Steal from the house to meet *him*? Is that what he said?'

'Yes. Well, he wanted to assure us you had been quite safe all along. I dare say he felt we needed some explanation about your foot. What a shame you had to trip on the staircase there.'

'I did not…' Claire stopped. She could not tell Jane why she'd really gone. She had taken one look at Thea's guilty face and known there had been some plan to go to the masquerade. For some reason, Thea had changed her mind and gone to the theatre after all.

Jane patted her hand. 'I shall send Briggs in to help you dress. Perhaps you would like to come down and sit in the front drawing-room.' She rose. 'I do hope you enjoyed yourself while you were there.'

'You are not shocked?'

'No, although I suppose I should be. I know that Lord Rotham would never let any harm come to you.' She looked at Claire, a small smile touching her lips. 'I know he cares for you.'

'Jane! He doesn't…that is, not in that…that way!'

'But he does. And furthermore I don't think his intentions are at all dishonourable.' She left the room, leaving Claire to look after her in dismay.

Claire tried to feel more cheerful after one of the footmen carried her down to the drawing-room. The day was unusually fine; the sunlight streaming through the windows brightened the pale peach walls of the drawing-room. Thea had provided her with a copy of *Clarissa*.

An hour later, Jane and Thea announced they were leaving to pay their morning calls. Claire finally gave up on *Clarissa* and leaned back against the cushions with a heavy sigh.

Jack. No matter how she tried, she could think of nothing but his kiss. And her response.

She had suffered Marcus's kisses and lovemaking. His kisses had been brutal, the intimacies of the marriage bed brief and humiliating. There had been no tenderness, and she'd soon learned he wanted no response from her except passive submission. She had learned to drift away in her mind, caring little what happened to her body.

But not last night. Her body had come alive under Jack's skilful hands and mouth. She had been aware only of him, the scent and taste of him, the feel of his muscles under her hands. She had been shocked by the intensity of her response and more than a little afraid.

She closed her eyes with a groan. Unfortunately, if she were forced to spend too many days idle like this she would have far too much time on her hands to brood.

'Lord Rotham.'

Her eyes jerked open at the sound of the butler's voice. She hardly had time to respond before the subject of her thoughts strode into the drawing-room. He carried a large bouquet of flowers in one hand.

'I...I am not receiving,' Claire stammered. Her heart was thudding much too loud, and her hands felt clammy.

He came to stand in front of her. 'So I was informed. However, I have some business with you.' He looked down at her, his face rather grim as if the business was not particularly pleasant.

'Oh.' Nothing else sprang to mind.

He handed her the bouquet. It was a lovely mix of roses and pink dianthus and Queen Anne's lace. The spicy scent of the pinks blended with the sweet, heavy fragrance of the roses.

'I hope your foot is better,' he said.

Claire inhaled the scent of the flowers and glanced up into his face. 'Yes, thank you. The flowers are beautiful,' she added rather shyly. Why did he look so stiff?

She was even more confused when he tugged at his cravat as if he was nervous. He picked up a figurine from the table near the sofa, then put it down, clearing his throat.

'Is there something wrong?' Claire asked. He looked very peculiar.

'No.' He frowned at her. 'Will you marry me?' he asked abruptly.

Claire stared at him, the blood draining from her face. Surely she had misheard. 'I beg your pardon?'

'I asked if you would marry me.' A tinge of red washed over his cheekbones. His voice was cool and stiff. Exactly as it had been six years ago when he'd asked her the very same question.

Claire's hands tightened around the bouquet. Her head spun, her mouth was dry. 'But why? Surely it…it cannot be because of last night?' Did he again think he was obligated to marry her to save her reputation?

'No.' His mouth relaxed a little. 'Perhaps. If only because you need a protector. You have a propensity for getting into trouble.'

'Really?' Claire's voice shook despite her attempts to remain calm. 'Is that the only reason? I assure you the last thing I need is a husband to protect me.'

'No, that's not the only reason.' He clasped his hands behind his back and paced towards the mantelpiece, then turned to face her. 'I need a wife. My relations have brought it to my attention that it is time I marry.'

A wave of disappointment washed over her. 'I am certain there are many women who would be pleased to oblige them.' Claire stared down at the bouquet, praying she would not cry.

'That may be true. However, I wish to marry you.'

The impersonal, cool tone stiffened her spine. As if

he had looked over a selection of eligible women and decided she would most suit his requirements. She gave him a cool look. 'I can't imagine why. We do nothing but quarrel.'

His gaze swept over her face and then down to her lips. A slight smile lifted his mouth. 'Not all the time,' he said softly.

She blushed in spite of herself. 'I must thank you for your flattering offer, but I do not want another husband.'

'Why not?'

His blunt words caught her off guard. 'Because I do not wish to give up my independence ever again.'

He looked at her for a moment. 'I see. Very well, as my wife you will be free to do as you wish within certain bounds.'

'Certain bounds? And what are those, my lord?' Claire was beginning to become indignant. He sounded as if it was a settled matter.

His look was direct. 'I would expect you to remain faithful to me.'

As men always did while they pursued their own amorous interests. 'Really? And I do not suppose you would put the same limitations on yourself.'

'I would.'

Taken aback, she dropped her gaze to the bouquet, her blood pounding in her ears. He would be faithful to her? But he would expect her to perform her wifely duties, warming his bed. The thought of lying in his arms was making her dizzy and more than a little afraid.

And he had said nothing of love.

'Well?'

She looked up to find him watching her very closely. 'I…I cannot accept your offer.'

'I intend to see you will.'

She gasped. 'What are you talking about? You cannot force me to marry you.'

He stalked towards her, a determined look in his eyes. She made an attempt to swing her legs over the edge of the sofa, but the movement only made her foot hurt. She shrank behind the bouquet, her eyes wide as he came to loom over her. The brief thought that he planned to abduct her crossed her mind.

'Jack, don't!' she pleaded in a breathless voice as he leaned towards her.

But he only plucked the bouquet from her hands and laid it on the table near the sofa. He came back to her, bracing his hands on each of her shoulders so she was forced to look into his face. 'Why don't you want to marry me?' he asked softly.

'I…I…' Claire licked her lips, her gaze fastened on his face. His eyes were dark, and the sight of his lips so close only reminded her of last night. It was an effort to keep her thoughts focused. 'We are not suited.'

'Nonsense. Give me another reason.'

'I…I did not like being married. I hated it!' She closed her eyes, humiliated and ashamed at telling him, of all people, how she had detested it.

She heard his sharp intake of breath, and then felt him rise. She prayed he would leave her in peace.

But he didn't. The next thing she knew, he was sitting next to her. 'Claire,' he said softly.

'Please just go away.'

'No.' He gently touched her cheek. 'I have no intention of going away. Not this time.' His hand dropped to catch hers, and he lifted it to his lips for a brief moment. 'There's no need for you to be afraid. I will not be the same sort of husband as Ellison.'

No. She finally looked into his serious, compelling

eyes and knew for certain he would be very different from Marcus. And it frightened her. Whether he loved her or not, she had no doubt he would expect her to share his bed and he would want more from her than passivity. And even if she were mad enough to accept his proposal he would find her most disappointing.

She took a deep breath. 'You don't understand. I did not like being a wife.'

He was silent for a moment, his eyes on her face. She could not tell what he thought. He finally spoke. 'I am willing to offer you a marriage of convenience until you are ready to share my bed.' His eyes fell to her lips. 'Although I do not think you find my touch entirely repulsive.'

A flush stole over her face. 'No, but…'

'But what?' His hand strayed to brush a lock of hair from her face.

'A few kisses are different from the…the other thing.'

His hand stroked her cheek. 'Are they? Usually, under the right circumstances, one leads naturally to the other.'

His touch was hypnotic. She was finding it difficult to both think and breathe at the same time. 'Does it?'

'Yes.' He leaned towards her. She made a feeble effort to shift away, but he caught her chin. His kiss was leisurely and undemanding, completely unlike last night's. When he finally lifted his head, she was shocked to discover she wanted more.

'I think that is enough for today.' His voice was oddly husky. He moved away from her, leaving her feeling strangely bereft. 'I will leave you for now. But be assured I don't intend to give up so easily this time.'

Chapter Ten

Claire sat on a sofa in one corner of the Duchess of Arundel's elegant saloon. Her eyes were on Thea, fresh and lovely in a white gown of silk gauze shot with silver threads, her hair tumbling to her shoulders in golden curls. Thea stood with the Duchess and Jane near the door, receiving guests. The Duchess had insisted on holding a reception in honour of Thea's presentation at Court yesterday.

It was only to be a small reception. 'I know, dear Jane, that you and Edward decided to hold a ball after his return, but I wanted to do this. 'Tis a most important event in any young lady's life, so I think a small celebration shall be in order.'

However, it was more than a small gathering. And somehow, on such notice, the Duchess had hired a small group of musicians and the affair had all the signs of turning into a ball.

Claire watched Harry enter, and then stiffened when she saw Jack come in behind him. She quickly looked away, her hands trembling around her fan. He'd come to call yesterday, but she'd been resting in her bedchamber. He had left another bouquet of flowers, this one of fragrant pink roses, and a basket of strawberries. Thea had teased her unmercifully, and Jane had smiled in an irritatingly knowing manner. Claire had felt increasingly confused.

Did he really want to marry her? She had thought of little else in the six days that had passed since he'd offered her marriage. He'd called on her three times, but only very briefly, as a proper suitor should. Twice, Harry had been there at the same time as Jack, so there had been no chance for private conversation. She had felt disappointed and relieved all at once.

In spite of her best resolution, her eyes were drawn to him as he bowed over Thea's hand. The sight of his broad shoulders beneath his dark green coat and his strong, muscular legs encased in tight drab breeches made her shaky, almost as if her body remembered the feel of him.

As she watched, Lady Rotham approached him, her protégée at her side. He bowed over Alicia's hand, and she gave him one of her poised, cool smiles. She recalled Lady Rotham's words that Jack was to marry Alicia. He would hardly have offered marriage to Claire if it were true, so she must have only wanted to warn Claire away. Claire had no doubt if she were rash enough to accept Jack's offer Lady Rotham would be most displeased.

Of course, she had no intention of marrying again. Certainly not Jack. She was not in love with him nor was he in love with her. This odd attraction he had for her was no basis for a marriage. And she never wanted to be at the complete mercy of a man again.

'Brooding, my dear? We can't allow it.'

Harry's amused voice startled her out of her reverie. She looked up and managed to smile. 'No, I was only thinking.'

'Dangerous.'

'Perhaps for you.'

He raised a lazy brow. 'A trifle out of sorts, I see.'

Claire sighed. She was in no mood for Harry's careless banter. Despite his apology, she hadn't quite made up her mind to forgive him for attempting to lure Thea to a ruinous evening. She observed his elegantly cut coat, and carefully dishevelled blond locks. 'You look quite splendid.'

He pretended to preen himself. 'I was rather satisfied myself.' He ran an expert eye over her face and gown. 'I must say you look exceedingly lovely yourself tonight. The role of languishing invalid quite becomes you.'

''Tis not a role I particularly enjoy.'

'I imagine not. If I recall, when you broke your arm, you were out two days later trying to climb the same tree.'

'Well, I assure you I have no intention of attempting to attend another masquerade.'

'Not even if Jack is there to rescue you?'

'No, most certainly not!' Claire felt a blush creep up her face. 'Besides, he did not rescue me. I was managing quite well on my own.'

'Of course,' Harry said blandly. 'However, I believe your gallant knight is heading our way. Undoubtedly to rescue you from my dastardly clutches.'

Claire half rose from the sofa, then gasped as she stepped on her injured foot. She clutched at Harry's arm for support. 'Please don't leave me.'

He looked down at her hand, one eyebrow cocked. 'Must you wrinkle my coat?'

'Harry!'

'Really, my dear. What precisely do you think he intends? This is his grandmother's drawing-room after all.'

She didn't need to turn to know Jack was standing at her side. Her entire body tingled with awareness. Her fingers tightened around her fan.

'Claire.'

She forced herself to meet his eyes. 'Good evening, Lord Rotham.'

His gaze flickered over her face. 'Good evening, Claire.' His voice was low and caressing, as if they were alone.

She looked at Harry who promptly took her arm. 'I was just about to take Claire to the ballroom.'

'I will be more than happy to take your place. In fact, I insist on doing so,' Jack drawled.

'Claire?' Harry glanced at her, his eyes full of amusement.

'That is very kind, but I…I have something to discuss with Harry,' Claire said. Her face coloured at the fib, but the thought of having to converse with Jack, even in this crowded assembly, made her want to run.

His eyes narrowed. 'Do you? I am certain it can wait until later.'

'It is important.' She felt even more disconcerted when he visibly stiffened, his eyes losing all expression.

'Very well.' He bowed and turned on his heel.

Instead of feeling relief, Claire wanted to weep, an all-too-common emotion lately. Why had she been so rude? It was only because she had suddenly felt so vulnerable and nervous at the sight of him. She hardly remembered Harry until he cleared his throat. 'Shall we proceed to the ballroom?'

'What?' She stared at him blankly. 'I…yes, that would be nice.'

His expression was not unsympathetic. He picked up the cane she was using and handed it to her. He took her other arm, and they slowly proceeded to the ball-room.

Harry beckoned a footman and had him fetch a chair. He placed it in a corner and Claire sat down. Harry glanced down at her. 'What is it you wanted to discuss? A topic of prime importance, I gather.'

'I've forgotten.'

'I see.' His lips twitched and he glanced out towards the floor where the dancers were performing a cotillion. He brought his eyes back to her. 'Jack will ride his black in a race tomorrow. A cross-country race,' he said casually.

'A race?' Claire's head jerked up. 'He never said anything.'

'I dare say he has other things on his mind when he's with you.'

'A cross-country race sounds so dangerous.' A vivid memory of Jack racing across a field on a large bay colt flashed through her mind. He had jumped a hedge on a dare, a hedge no one had ever attempted before. He'd landed on the other side, his dark hair shining in the sun, and Claire's heart had leapt to her throat.

He'd pulled the dancing colt to a halt and looked down at her, his eyes laughing and triumphant. 'So, my lovely Claire, I have won my wager. What do I get from you?'

'A scolding. How dare you do such a reckless thing?'

'I was in no danger.' He patted the still prancing horse on the neck. 'I had no doubt he'd do it.' He grinned at her. 'Could it be you were worried about me?'

'I...no, of course not.' Claire turned away and marched off, angry with herself for caring that he might fall and break his neck. He was the worst flirt she'd ever met and why he persisted in forcing his attentions on her was beyond her comprehension.

Claire jerked her mind back to the present. She realised Harry was watching her with a slight smile. She flushed. 'I suppose he will do very well,' she said, trying to keep her voice indifferent.

'Probably. I am betting he'll win.' Harry looked back towards the dancers. 'Shall I fetch you a lemonade?' He started off. 'And I do hope, my dear Claire, that you can be a little bit kind to Jack. I should hate to see him driven into Alicia's all-too-willing arms.'

He sauntered off. Claire glanced at the dancers, and her gaze froze. Jack was moving through the steps of the dance with Alicia. They looked lovely together, graceful and elegant. Only a few inches shorter than Jack, Alicia seemed to complement him perfectly.

Of course, it would be wonderful if he decided to fall in love with Alicia. Then he would no longer be so insistent upon marrying Claire. Perhaps he'd realised his proposal had been precipitous, an impulsive act brought on by some chivalrous notion he should marry her after the masquerade. The thought was horribly depressing. If he really wanted to marry her, he would have insisted on dragging her away from Harry in his usual arrogant manner. Instead, he had walked off and was now with Alicia.

Perhaps the injury to her foot had affected her reason. She wanted him to leave her be, didn't she? Whatever was wrong with her? It hardly mattered to her what he did, or whether he was now pursuing another woman.

She stood, no longer wanting to watch the painful spectacle of Jack and Alicia. She grabbed her cane, and hobbled towards a small connecting saloon. It was not crowded. Claire found a seat near one of the windows.

She groaned as she remembered Harry was fetching her a lemonade. Well, she hadn't asked him for one anyway.

Despite her attempts to think of something else, she found herself straining to hear when the last strains of the music finally died away. Her whole body seemed to tense and she realised she half hoped Jack would seek her out. And then she would try to make up for her rudeness.

Instead, Alicia's cool voice cut through her thoughts. 'Is your foot giving you much pain?'

Claire looked up to find the girl standing in front of her, her lips turned up in what Claire supposed might be a sympathetic smile. Tall and graceful and lovely in a net tunic of pale blue stain, she made Claire feel awkward.

'A little.'

'May I sit?' Without waiting for Claire's answer, she seated herself next to Claire, carefully arranging her skirts so as to minimise the wrinkles. 'I had hoped to speak with you, but it seems we are always in company.'

Claire never would have guessed. When they had chanced to meet, Alicia had seemed to do nothing but look at Claire with a cold expression.

'One rarely has a chance to converse at such affairs,' Claire said politely.

'Yes. How true.' Alicia toyed with her fan, a little smile on her face. 'But tonight I particularly wanted to see you. I…I have some news I wanted to tell you.'

'Oh?'

'Yes.' She looked down at her lap, and then raised her eyes to Claire's. 'In fact, you are the first person I wanted to tell. Lord Rotham has asked me to marry him.'

Claire felt the blood drain from her face. She managed

to fix her lips in some semblance of a smile. 'Has he? How…how nice.'

'Yes.' Alicia dropped her eyes modestly for a brief instant before looking back up. 'I have told no one but you. I know you are a very particular friend of his. The wedding will be soon, as he must marry in order to inherit Blydon Castle.' She looked at Claire's face. 'He didn't tell you that?'

'He said nothing.'

'It was part of his great-uncle's will. He has six weeks to find a suitable bride. I will expect you to give him up.'

'To give him up?'

'I do not want him coming from your bed to mine.'

'I beg your pardon?'

'Are you not his mistress?'

Claire stared at her. 'No. We are only acquaintances,' Claire said automatically. She felt disembodied, as if she were someone else speaking.

'But that is not what everyone thinks.' Alicia looked almost pleased by the shock on Claire's face. For a moment, Claire felt she was looking at Lady Rotham, but the impression quickly vanished. 'I am so glad you are only good friends. I would not mind an occasional dalliance later on, but I would prefer not to begin my marriage with a mistress underfoot.'

'I would hope not.' Claire had no idea how she managed to keep her voice level.

'Are you well? You look rather pale,' Alicia enquired with false solicitude.

''Tis rather warm in here. And my foot hurts.' She hardly knew what she said. So, Jack hadn't really wanted her at all. He had said he needed a wife, but apparently any wife would do in order to get his castle.

With overwhelming relief, she saw Harry across the room. He was smiling down at a vivacious blonde in rose silk. Claire rose awkwardly to her feet. 'If you will excuse me, I…I must speak with Harry.'

'Harry?' Her gaze followed Claire's. 'Oh, yes. Mr Devlin. He is most charming. You are also good friends?'

'Yes.' Harry had glanced over at them. He kissed the lady's hand and then headed their way. 'He is a good friend.' At this moment he seemed her only friend.

'I see.' Alicia smiled in an arch manner. 'So, perhaps we might expect an interesting announcement?'

What was she talking about? Claire stared at her, then realised what she was hinting at. About to deny it, Claire changed her mind. Recklessly, she said, 'Perhaps, but I am not saying.'

Still smiling, Alicia said, 'How unkind of you not to confide in me, particularly after I confided in you.'

'But then, I am not worried Harry has another *good* friend.'

At least she managed to make Alicia's perfect smile fade and her eyes narrow.

Harry appeared at her side, executing a small bow in Alicia's direction. 'Good evening, Miss Snowden.'

'Good evening, Mr Devlin.'

He turned to Claire. 'First I am forced to fight my way back with a full glass of lemonade in one hand, am jostled by a very ungainly female, spill a drop on my coat, and then I find you gone.'

Claire laid her hand on his arm with a proprietorial air. She gave him her sweetest smile. 'Dear Harry, I am so very sorry to cause you so much trouble. But perhaps you would take me back to the ballroom and sit out with me.'

He stared at her. 'Er, certainly.'

Claire smiled at Alicia, feeling as if her face was about to crack. 'You will excuse us, will you not?'

Alicia blinked and then smiled back. 'Of course. I am certain you would like a tête-à-tête.' She rose and drifted off.

Harry gave her a quizzical look as he removed her fingers from his arm. 'I fear you will leave a bruise. My coat is already wrinkled beyond hope. Now, perhaps you will tell me why the charming Alicia thinks we need a tête-à-tête?'

Claire bit her lip. 'I really do not know.'

'Don't you?' He took a pinch of snuff. 'What is wrong, Claire? Have you quarrelled with Jack again?'

'No!' She glared at him. 'I hope I might never speak to him again!'

'I see we're in for another interesting time,' Harry remarked.

Jack hardly heard a word his grandmother said. His mind was too occupied with the couple sitting on chairs at the side of the ballroom. It was all he could do to keep from stalking across the room, hauling Harry up by his cravat and smashing him into one of the Corinthian columns. What the hell did he mean by hanging all over Claire as if he were her *cicisbeo*?

And why the devil was she encouraging him? She was fluttering her fan and gazing up at him with a smile on her face, as if he was the most fascinating man in the world. A look she'd never yet bestowed on Jack. And not once had she glanced his way.

In fact she had made it obvious she hadn't wanted to see him this evening. Which was why he had walked off instead of dragging her away from Harry at the beginning.

What had he expected? After threatening her with marriage she would fall into his arms? She needed to be gently persuaded that marriage to him would be nothing like the hell she must have experienced with Ellison. But every time he saw her his resolutions flew out of the window. He only wanted to take her in his arms and make love to her.

'Perhaps you should speak to Claire instead of glaring at her.' His grandmother's dry voice broke into his thoughts.

'I beg your pardon. What were you saying, ma'am?' He felt a slight flush creep over his cheekbones at the knowing look in her eyes.

'Have you and Claire quarrelled?'

He scowled. 'You would do better to ask if we haven't quarrelled. We can hardly be in each other's company for more than two minutes without an argument.' Except when they were kissing.

The Duchess smiled slightly. 'I do think I will host a small house party now that the season is nearly over. I shall persuade Claire to come.' She glanced over at Harry. 'I believe I shall ask Mr Devlin if he will escort me to supper. I hope you will not mind escorting Claire.'

She drifted away. Jack was about to follow when his stepmother appeared next to him. By the time he managed to escape her, Claire had vanished.

She was not in the supper room. Harry was there with his grandmother. Jack was amused in a grim way. It was obvious that at least his grandmother had no objections to his marrying Claire.

He finally found Claire in his grandmother's private drawing-room. She sat in a Chippendale chair, her hands clasped on her lap, the light from the lamp casting a dim shadow across her face. She looked lovely and very melancholy. 'Claire.'

She started and looked up at him. He was stunned to see a bleak look in her eyes before her face became shuttered. 'What are you doing here?'

He stepped into the room. 'Looking for you.'

'I can't imagine why. We have nothing to say to each other.' Her voice was cold and distant.

He frowned, his instincts telling him something had happened since yesterday. 'What's wrong?'

'There is nothing wrong.'

He came to stand in front of her. 'There is. What is it?'

She raised cold eyes to his face. 'You no longer have any need to pry into my life. I pray you will leave me.'

'Not until you tell me what has happened.' He stared down at her. 'Claire, my sweet girl, what has upset you?'

He was taken aback at the blaze of fury in her eyes. 'I am not your sweet girl. I don't know what you want from me, but I have nothing to say to you.'

'Don't you?' He retreated into his own cool shell. 'Perhaps, then, you will at least have the courtesy to tell me what I've done to offend you. Was it my offer of marriage? I meant no insult, but perhaps the idea of marriage to me is repugnant enough so you took it as one.'

She rose unsteadily to her feet and glared at him. 'How dare you speak to me of marriage now? I wouldn't marry you if you were the…the last man on this earth!'

He advanced towards her, a cold smile lifting his mouth. 'Not very original, are you, my dear? How about I wouldn't marry you if it meant I'd be forced to spend the rest of my life in Newgate? Or I'd rather die a horrid death than marry you?' He came to stand so close, their bodies were nearly touching. He could almost feel the rise and fall of her chest.

She moistened her lips. 'Wh-what are you doing?'

He cupped her cheek. She trembled like a nervous filly under his hand. 'You haven't yet answered my question,' he said softly. 'Never mind, I'll ask in another way.'

'My lord—Jack, don't.' The coldness left her eyes, and she looked vulnerable and a little scared. Her eyes pleaded with him, her lips parted, soft and inviting.

With a groan, he possessed her mouth, hard and swift. She attempted to push him away, but he crushed her to him, pinning her arms between their chests. She made a soft sound in her throat and sagged against him. His tongue teased her lips, coaxing, until she opened them to him, shyly responding to his thrusts. He finally released her, shocked at his violent desire to take her on his grandmother's sofa.

He stared at her. Her mouth was swollen and vulnerable from his kiss, her eyes huge and dazed. She looked as shaken as he felt.

He smiled grimly. 'I think you want me more than you care to admit.'

'No.' She looked stricken. 'Please…oh, how could you? How could I?' she whispered. Her hands went to her cheeks as if she was distressed beyond reason.

Something very peculiar was going on. 'Claire, there is no need for you to be so upset. It was only a kiss.' He reached out to touch her cheek.

She flinched and looked up at him. He dropped his hand. 'What is it?'

She took a deep breath. 'I…I should not be kissing you. You see, I…I am in love with someone else.'

Chapter Eleven

Claire sat up in her bed, brushing the hair from her eyes. Relieved, she heard the sounds of a London morning—a pedlar calling out his wares, the rattle of a carriage, the barking of a dog. Her dreams had been filled with images of Marcus, his face cold and taunting, and even in her dream she'd felt the fear and humiliation she had lived with.

She felt the same relief mixed with guilt that she always did after such a dream. Relief she was away for ever, guilt she should feel such an emotion at knowing she'd never again see the man who had been her husband.

Husband. With a jolt, the events of last night flooded her consciousness.

She could still see Jack's face after she'd told him she was in love with someone else.

He'd gone quite still, his hands dropping to his sides. In the lamplight, she'd watched his face pale, the expression wiped from it. 'I don't believe it,' he said, his voice flat.

Claire gulped and looked away. 'It is true.'

He laughed in an odd way. 'Is it? Harry, I presume.'

She looked back at him, unable to make a response.

He bowed. 'Then I will leave you, ma'am. Forgive me if I don't wish you happiness.' Then he strode away, closing the door quietly behind him.

With a horrible sinking feeling, Claire knew she had made an unforgivable mistake.

Now, Claire folded her arms around her bent knees, hugging them to her chest. She had never felt such misery, such hopelessness. She'd been so hurt and angry at the thought that he'd turned around and offered Alicia marriage after making her—Claire—an offer. She had no idea why he had kissed her, only that it was an insult. She had wanted to wound him as badly as he had wounded her.

And she had. His face had told her that. And then she'd known: Alicia had lied.

She had to see him. She would call on him as soon as she was dressed. Then she remembered his race was today. She sank back on her pillows, her heart even more heavy. She had no idea even where the race was held or the time it was to start. Her attempt to appear indifferent had prevented her from asking Harry.

She had no choice but to wait.

Harry was shown into the study where Claire sat staring out of the window at absolutely nothing, a pile of correspondence in front of her on the desk. She looked up, half-dazed, and then started at the sight of his black eye and bruised cheek. She shot up. 'Oh, Harry! What has happened? Did someone hit you?'

He gave a short laugh which made him flinch. 'Jack.'

'Jack?' Claire's hand went to her throat. 'But why?'

'He did not precisely say. I had hopes you might enlighten me. He merely called me a traitor and then hit me. This was with his uninjured hand. I'd hate to think what would have happened if he'd had full use of both.'

The blood drained from her head. 'Jack was injured? When?'

'He fell going over a hedge. There is no need to look so fearful. He has an injured wrist, but nothing very serious. I, on the other hand, am in much worse shape.'

Claire was instantly ashamed. 'Oh, Harry, I am sorry…it is just…'

'There is no need to explain. Which brings me to the point of my visit. Perhaps you can tell me why he found it necessary to plant his fist in my face before informing me he had no intention of wishing me well in my future nuptials.'

'Oh, dear heavens, I…I never thought…' Her voice trailed away and then she forced herself to go on. 'It was something I said. I am afraid I…I told him I was in love with someone else.' She looked away, unable to meet Harry's eyes.

He was silent for a moment. 'So he concluded it was me. Tell me, my dear, was there a particular reason why you hinted such a thing? Trying to make him jealous or merely rid yourself of him?'

Even more chagrined, Claire knotted her hands together. 'Neither. Miss…someone said he was betrothed to Alicia Snowden.'

'And what reliable source told you that?'

There was no point in lying to Harry. 'Miss Snowden. Last night. She said it was a secret, but he had just made her an offer.'

Harry stared at her. 'What the devil would make him do such a thing? He wants to marry you.'

'How do you know that?'

'He told me. Then what happened?'

'He…he kissed me and that was when I…I told him I was in love with someone else.'

'Damn it, Claire, how can you be such an idiot? The man is more than half in love with you whether he'll admit it or not!'

She looked at him, his words adding to her misery. 'Oh, Harry! As soon as I saw his face, I knew I was wrong. But she said he must marry to inherit a castle, and I told him I wouldn't marry him when he asked me after the masquerade so I thought he had decided to offer for her.'

'He asked you to marry him?'

'Yes, but I really didn't want to be married again.' She sniffed, trying to keep the tears at bay. 'I am so sorry! Now I have ruined your friendship as well.'

Harry stepped forward. 'Hang it all, Claire, please don't look like that!' He patted her shoulder with an awkward movement. 'All is not lost. He'll probably come around once he realises we aren't to be married.' He didn't sound very confident.

She gave him a weak smile. 'It probably is, but I promise I'll try to set things right.'

He eyed her with some apprehension. 'Don't do anything rash. Besides, he is to leave London tomorrow.'

'Tomorrow?' She hadn't much time. She looked at Harry's face, pale beneath the bruises, and knew she couldn't let things stay as they were. She touched his sleeve. 'You must go. You look terrible.'

He frowned—a movement that made him flinch—then gave her a brief hug. 'Don't look so despairing, my dear. He'll come around, but he needs time.' He touched her cheek. 'And no more lies.'

Jack picked up the decanter of brandy, ready to pour himself another glass. He set the bottle down in disgust.

Getting thoroughly drunk was not the answer to his sprained wrist. Nor would a headache in the morning do a thing to ease the emptiness he felt in his soul.

Even connecting with Harry's face had brought nothing more than temporary relief.

'Hell!' He slammed his fist on the table. He scarcely noted the pain that seared through him as his sore hand hit the wood.

'My lord.' His butler's voice recalled him to his senses. He spun around, a frown on his brow. 'What is it?'

'It is Mrs Ellison, my lord. She wishes to see you.'

Claire? What the devil was she doing calling on him this late? It was nearly ten in the evening. He scowled. 'I am in no condition to receive visitors. Tell her that.'

'She seems rather distressed.' Simms allowed a note of reproach to enter his voice.

He should send her away. All logic told him so. But his body, his desires told him something different. He wanted to see her one last time. 'Very well.'

He stood by his desk, waiting for her, his face in the shadows. She hesitantly entered, still limping slightly. She looked around, apparently not seeing him at first.

He stepped forward. 'What brings you here? I usually don't receive visitors this late at night. Particularly ladies—unless, of course, the business is purely for pleasure. I doubt you're here in that capacity.'

She flinched. A twinge of conscience pricked him, making him even surlier. 'Well?'

'I know you are leaving London tomorrow, so I had to come tonight. I came to apologise.'

He stared at her. 'Apologise? What for?'

She knotted her hands together, suddenly reminding him of the girl she had been.

'For lying to you.'

'I have no idea what you're talking about. When did you lie to me?'

She took a deep breath. 'Last night. When I…I told you I was in love with someone. And then I let you think it was Harry. It was so wrong of me. It has ruined your friendship with Harry. I…I have made a horrid botch of everything.'

'So if you are not in love with Harry you love someone else?' he asked carefully.

'No, there is no one.'

He should have been glad, but he felt only anger and a strange hurt, almost as if it were six years ago. 'I obviously owe you an apology, then. I had no idea my attentions were so unwelcome that you felt you must lie in order to escape them.'

'No, it was not that—'

He interrupted her. 'And I have not been honest with you either. For, you see, there was another wager. A dare of sorts. I was to marry the lady whose fan I pulled in the fan lottery. The fan I pulled was yours.'

She went very still. 'I see,' she finally said.

And then she turned and left the room. He heard her footsteps recede, heard Simms's voice and her softer one.

And then she was gone.

And he felt as if part of his soul had gone as well.

Edward arrived two days later. Claire had barely finished packing when Thea dashed into her room. 'Claire! You must come down!'

Claire straightened, a mismatched pair of gloves in

her hand. 'Is something wrong?' Thea looked rather distraught. For an odd, heart-thumping moment, Claire wondered if Jack had returned.

'Yes. No. I don't know! Papa is here. He wants to see you immediately.'

'Oh, drat!' Claire bit her tongue from uttering a much stronger epithet. In the past two days, she'd felt cross and snappish, wanting to be left alone. She had no idea if she was angry or depressed or indifferent. Not even after the disaster six years ago had she felt so horribly empty.

She laid the gloves on top of a flowered muslin dress and followed Thea down the stairs to Edward's library. Certainly a bad sign. He always used the library for unpleasant business with his family.

He stood near his mahogany desk, tall and upright, in a dark blue coat and buff pantaloons. His greatcoat lay draped across a mahogany chair and from the creases in his usually impeccable attire it was apparent he had not bothered to change.

He was a handsome man with a pair of piercing grey eyes, which were now fixed on Claire with a disapproving expression.

Jane stood near him, looking exasperated. 'Really, Edward, I think a cup of tea would be in order first.'

'I wish to speak with my sister. I did not come from Brussels merely to take tea. Please be seated, Claire.'

'I never thought you would believe such malicious gossip.' Jane came as close to glaring at him as Claire had ever seen.

Edward's jaw moved in the way it did when he was straining to keep his temper. 'And I never thought you would defy my orders by allowing that man to cross my threshold.'

'That man? He happens to be my godmother's grandson, and I would never insult her by treating him so rudely. He has behaved at all times in the most gentlemanly way! And this happens to be my threshold also. Unless you mean to tell me I have no say in my own home.' Without giving him time to utter another word, Jane stalked from the room.

'So? Would you explain yourself?' Edward nearly snarled as he turned to Claire who remained standing near the desk.

'Explain what? How can you be so beastly to Jane?' Her suspicions that the entire male sex was beyond insufferable were rapidly being confirmed.

'She has encouraged and condoned your relationship with a man who ruined you six years ago. She knows how I feel about him.' He took a pace around the side of the desk.

'I had asked her to keep an eye on you, perhaps look for a suitable husband. Instead, I find you repeating the same foolish errors you made before.'

'Find me a suitable husband? I have no intention of ever marrying again! Nor do I have the least idea what you are talking about.'

'I am certain you do.' When she continued to stare at him, he said, 'Very well, I'll spell it out. Rotham. You have been in his company. Do you deny it?'

'No.'

'Has he seduced you?'

'That is really none of your concern. I'm no longer a young innocent girl and am quite old enough to know my own mind.'

'He has.' He took a step towards her, then halted, fury in every muscle of his face. 'I will call him out for touching you.'

'This is ridiculous!' Claire could scarcely believe her ears. Had he run mad? 'He hasn't seduced me! And even if he had I…I would never cross your doorstep again if you called him out!' Claire began to wonder if she'd run mad herself. She'd never stood up to Edward before. No, that wasn't right. She'd stood up to him six years ago when he'd tried to force her to marry Jack. 'And wherever did you hear this information?'

Without a word, he held out a sheet of paper. She took it and recognised Lady Billingsley's precise, spidery handwriting. Claire read it, her anger growing as Lady Billingsley described in great detail Jack's persistent licentious attentions to Claire with the aim of seducing her, Claire's scandalous encouragement and Jane's foolish complicity in the whole affair.

Disgusted, Claire's hand fell to her side. 'How dare she? This was none of her business!'

'She was concerned for your well-being. She had every right to report the situation to me,' Edward said coldly.

'But this is completely wrong! He was not trying to seduce me! How could you believe this?' She moved towards him, waving the paper in his face.

He stepped back. 'I, too, was concerned with your welfare. I did not want to see you hurt again, as I knew you would be if he was allowed near you.'

'You don't know anything,' Claire said, fighting to keep the despair from her voice. Her brother was right, Jack had hurt her, but she'd never let Edward know that. She was equally angry with Edward for always wanting to arrange her life, imposing his will on her no matter what she felt.

'Claire…'

'If you must know, it is quite unlikely I will ever see

Jack again. He has already left town. And I am leaving London as well. Tomorrow!'

Edward favoured her with one of his most imposing frowns. 'I forbid it. You will leave London with the rest of us.'

'You cannot dictate to me.'

'Claire, you are unreasonable. There is no need for you to quit town now Rotham is gone. You will stay until the season has finished. There is Jane to consider, and Thea. You will upset them by leaving now.'

Looking at his implacable expression, Claire realised there was no arguing with him. And, with the tension already caused by her seeing Rotham, her departure would only add to it. So, she would stay, if only for Jane's sake.

Jack stared out of the tall window of his library at Grenville Hall. The rolling lawn spread before him, a cluster of trees at its edges, and in the distance a small hill crowned by a temple. The sky was a pure cerulean-blue, but the contrast between it and his morose thoughts only served to irritate him.

'John?'

He spun around. Alicia stood near the table behind him. She was dressed in a pale blue gown, a broad-brimmed hat in her hand.

'What are you doing here?' He realised his tone bordered on rude. 'I thought you were out on a picnic.' He attempted to sound more civil, although the last thing he wanted was company. Unfortunately, his stepmother and Alicia had unexpectedly shown up at Grenville Hall two days after his own arrival.

'I was, but I pleaded a headache.' She gave him a little smile.

'Then you should be resting.'

'I don't really have a headache. It was the only way I could be certain of getting you alone.'

'Is something wrong?'

She smiled again, her eyes fixed on his face. 'No. Yes. There is something, actually.'

Jack stifled a groan as a feeling of foreboding washed over him. She had seemed to be constantly underfoot the last few days. 'Alicia, if there is a problem…you should be speaking to Celeste. I doubt I can help you.'

'I love you.'

He stepped back as if he'd been slapped. His mind refused to work for a moment, before snapping back into focus. 'Alicia, you cannot know what you're saying.'

The flash of passion that lit her usually cool eyes stunned him. 'But I do! I have loved you for ever! Since I first saw you. Oh, I know you do not love me. Not yet! But I know…that if only you would let me I could make you care for me!'

'Alicia, please…' He had no idea what to say. He'd sometimes suspected she might have a schoolgirl crush on him, but in the past year he'd assumed she'd outgrown it—if indeed it had ever existed. 'Of course, I care for you, but…'

'Oh, do not tell me only as a sister! I won't have it!' She came closer, so he was backed up against the window.

He held out his hands, trying to ward her off. 'Alicia…'

'I know you must marry, and soon. And now that Claire will never marry you you have very little choice. I…'

He stared at her. 'How do you know Claire will never marry me?'

Alicia stopped, looking taken aback for a moment, then gave him a pleased little smile. 'Oh, she told me she was in love with Mr Devlin.'

Claire told her that? He couldn't imagine Claire confiding in Alicia. The two barely spoke, and he sensed Alicia thoroughly disliked Claire. He frowned. 'When?'

'The night of Dorothea's assembly,' she said blithely. She held out her hands. 'What does it matter? I know you want Blydon Castle and you must marry to keep it.' Her voice had lost its passionate tone. She sounded quite sure of herself.

He frowned. 'How did you find that out?'

'I... Celeste told me.' She gave him a sweet smile. 'So you see you must marry me. I know I will make you a good wife.'

Looking down into her upturned face, he found the thought of taking her to his bed repulsed him. She was lovely, but there was something unpleasant about her. 'Alicia, I cannot marry you. It would not be right. I do not have the feelings for you that would make you happy. You deserve a man that will truly love you.'

She must have seen some of his feelings in his face. She backed away, her face looking hard and cold and very angry. 'You don't want me. Not even for your castle.'

She stared at him. 'But if you think there's a chance of marrying Claire Ellison you are quite wrong.' Her laugh was harsh. 'I've fixed it so she'll never marry you. Not after what I've told her!'

She turned on her heel. Jack stood rooted to the spot as he watched her go. Then he moved, his face grim. He was going back to London.

Two nights later, Jack entered White's and found Harry playing at one of the tables. Harry looked up, threw his hand down and rose. 'Excuse me, gentlemen.'

He followed Jack to one side of the room. 'I trust the expression on your face doesn't mean you intend to run me through?'

'What did Alicia tell Claire?' Jack demanded.

Harry raised a brow. 'What makes you think I should know?'

'The damnable fact that Claire suddenly decides to pretend she's in love with you.'

'How do you know she's not?'

'She told me so. I've no doubt she told you why.'

Harry dropped his drawling manner. 'Alicia told Claire you were betrothed the night before your race. This was before you kissed Claire.'

Jack briefly closed his eyes. It was all he could do to keep from smashing his fist into the wall. It all fell into place. No wonder she wanted to do anything to escape him. And then he'd deliberately hurt her in the worst way possible when she'd come to him.

'She's still in London, but whether she'll see you or not is debatable.'

'She will if I have to abduct her,' Jack said grimly. 'The least I can do is apologise.'

Harry's mouth tilted in a sudden grin. 'Good luck. I suspect you'll need every bit you can get.'

Jack raised a brow. 'Particularly after your interference. I've half a mind to challenge you after all.'

'I fear it would do little to further your cause.'

'But it would give me great satisfaction,' Jack said. He turned and left Harry, wanting to escape before he did something regrettable.

A light misty rain was falling as he stepped out into

St James's Street. He moved aside to let two gentlemen enter. Lord Alverstoke nodded. 'Back so soon, Rotham?'

'Yes.' He nodded towards Alverstoke's companion and then stiffened when he met the icy grey eyes of Edward Dunford.

Chapter Twelve

Claire smiled at the innkeeper's plump, pink-cheeked daughter. 'I have everything, thank you.'

The girl finally gave up trying to ask Claire questions and, after a quick curtsey, left the room. Claire sighed and propped her chin on her hand, staring down at the plate of food. It looked well prepared, but she had little appetite. The sound of heavy rain pattered on the window of the private parlour in which she sat.

She supposed she should count herself fortunate a parlour had been available. Due to an unexpectedly heavy rainstorm, the inn was crowded. The innkeeper had given her this small room which at least had an adequate fire. She had no idea why she was even here. For some reason, last night, Edward had suddenly announced she was going to Hartfield Hall after all. So, this morning he'd practically hustled her into his coach with one of the maids. By coach, the trip usually took a good ten hours of jostling over the roads, and if one left early enough it was almost possible to make the trip in a long day.

But nothing had gone right. First, the maid had developed the toothache and was moaning so badly, Claire had stopped at the first posting house and sent her back to London. Then they'd been delayed due to an accident between a farm wagon and a phaeton. The latest disaster had been rain so heavy the roads were nearly impassable. The coach had lost a wheel in the mud, and she had been forced to walk a quarter mile to the inn, her ankle aching. At least the innkeeper, taking one look at her mud-spattered gown and undoubtedly forlorn expression, had taken pity on her and been kind.

She took a bite of the roast beef and then was startled when the door opened. She heard the innkeeper's voice and then she stiffened in shock. Dear God, it couldn't be!

'I will ask the lady myself.'

'But, my lord…' the innkeeper protested.

Claire half rose in panic. Unless she dived under the table, there was no escape. With a kind of horror, she watched as Jack stepped into the room. His gaze swept the room and then fell on her.

Without removing his eyes from her face he said, 'Mrs Ellison and I are acquainted. I am certain she will not object to my sharing the parlour.'

He closed the door firmly behind him.

'Wh-what are you doing here?' Claire managed to ask. The room seemed to spin. She clutched the top of the chair and prayed she would not faint.

'I came to see you.' He didn't move from the door. His hair glistened with droplets of water, his caped greatcoat was soaked.

'Why? How…how did you know I was here?'

'Thea told me.'

'Thea?' Whatever was he talking about? Her mind refused to work in any coherent manner.

'She didn't precisely tell me. She said you'd left London. I presumed you were going to Hartfield Hall.'

'But why are you here?'

'I want to talk to you.' His eyes remained on her face.

'I can't imagine why. Last time we met you made it quite clear you despised me.' At least her voice now sounded quite normal.

'I want to apologise to you for my words.'

'I wish you would not. I assume you were not lying when you said you had made a wager to…to wed me.' She pulled her shawl more tightly around her shoulders and looked away from him. 'I…I wish you would go.'

He came across the room towards her. 'No. Not until I speak to you, explain to you why I behaved so abominably. Then you may send me away if you wish.'

She looked back up at him. His eyes were dark and intense, pleading with her to listen. She'd never seen him so passionate about anything.

'Very well. I suppose that is the only way I'll escape your company.' He coloured at her words, and she suddenly felt ashamed of herself.

He gestured towards the small sofa. 'At least come and sit with me. I cannot talk to you across a table with a half-eaten dinner.'

'I would prefer to stand.' And keep the table between them. He looked so tired and defeated she feared her resolve to keep him away would dissolve.

He stepped back. 'Almost before you left my study, I regretted my words. It is true, I did make a wager I'd court and marry the woman whose fan I pulled in the lottery. You have no idea how I felt when you stepped up to dance with me. You had been on my mind for six years; I had never thought to see you again.' He looked at her. 'I tried to tell myself I planned to marry you because of the wager, but I realised I was lying to myself. I wished to marry you because I wanted you. I called the wager off.'

Claire stared at him, bewildered, not really comprehending what he was saying. 'Who was the wager with?' she finally asked.

'Didn't you know? Harry.'

Harry? 'But how could both of you? How could you both do this to me again?' She felt like crying, the cold anger rapidly disappearing before the hurt and betrayal she felt.

'Claire! I am so sorry.' He came around the table then. He pulled her into his arms, drawing her against his chest. She stayed for a moment, then pushed him away.

He reached for her. 'Claire, don't. Please let me hold you.'

'You're…you're wet.'

'Oh, hell!' He shrugged out of his greatcoat, dropping it to the ground. 'Come back here.'

Claire shook her head. 'No. I…I don't think it is such a good idea. I don't think I want to forgive you.'

He came up behind her, putting his hands on her shoulders. Their coolness penetrated the wool of her shawl. She shivered. 'Now you're damp and cold,' he said. His hand travelled down her arm to catch her hand. 'Let's at least stand by the fire.' He drew her over to the fireplace, then turned her gently by the shoulders to face him.

'I am sorry,' he said quietly. 'I thought by now you knew Harry was part of the wager. Or at least guessed.'

She gave him a direct look. 'If I had consented to marry you, by some remote chance, did you ever plan to tell me about this?'

'Yes.' His laugh was short. 'I suppose I had hoped by

then it would not have mattered. I justified myself by forfeiting the wager with Harry, the day after the masquerade.'

'What did you forfeit?' A sum of money that was probably trifling to a man of his wealth.

He hesitated. 'My horse. Satan. He has been Harry's horse for more than a week.'

'But how could you wager him?' Claire was horrified. She knew how much he loved his colt. The horse seemed a part of him. And then for him to forfeit the wager before he'd even known he would lose for certain…

He shrugged. 'At the time I made the wager I was angry and more than a little drunk. I needed a wife, and I was indifferent as to how I obtained one.'

'To inherit your castle.'

'How did you know?' His voice held surprise.

'Alicia told me.'

His smile was humourless. 'That was probably the only true thing she said to you. As a condition of inheriting Blydon Castle, I must marry within six weeks from the date the will was read. Otherwise, the estate is to be sold and the proceeds to go to a charity. I am not allowed to purchase it.'

Six weeks? Well over a month had passed since the lottery. Claire clasped her hands together. 'How long do you have before you must wed?'

'About five days, I believe.'

'You do not have much time.' She suddenly felt sad. She remembered how he had talked of the romantic old castle, and his eccentric uncle of whom he'd obviously been fond. How could his uncle have made such ridiculous conditions? 'Isn't there someone…?'

'No.' She looked up to find a sardonic smile curving his lips. 'There's no one at this late hour. At any rate,

I've discovered one thing I don't want is a marriage merely to secure a property.'

'I see.' He no longer wanted her. Wasn't that what she'd desired all along? She'd never expected the wave of disappointment that washed over her.

She realised he was speaking. 'So perhaps we could try another truce. A second one. Our first did not work out very well.' He hesitated. 'I would like us to be friends, if at all possible.'

Friends. 'That would be very nice.' Her voice was polite, as if she were accepting a second cup of tea.

'Well…' He held out his hand. 'Shall we shake on it?'

She laid her hand in his, the touch of his now warm skin sending a jolt of awareness through her. She pulled her hand away, her cheeks hot with colour.

He backed away from her, passing a hand over his hair. He looked flustered. 'I could do with some food.'

'You're welcome to mine, but I'm afraid it's probably cold.'

'I'll ring for the proprietor.' He strode towards the door.

They ate in silence, or rather Jack ate as Claire had no appetite. Instead, she found herself watching him across the table. His hair was still damp and a lock fell over his forehead, making him look rather vulnerable. Her hand ached with the need to smooth it back from his brow.

He finally looked up and frowned at her. 'You're not eating,' he said.

'I'm not very hungry.' She shoved a few peas aside, feeling unaccountably depressed. She felt as if they were taking their last meal together. If she had any sense, she would leave the table and go up to bed. He would go tomorrow, and so would she. If she rose early enough, perhaps she could leave without seeing him.

'So, your brother decided to send you to Hartfield. Is that what you wanted?' he suddenly asked.

'I was tired of London, so I had no objections. I wanted to be by myself for a while.'

'Do you plan to stay there?'

'Perhaps.' This stilted polite conversation was worse than their quarrels. 'Are you returning to Grenville Hall?' She wanted no more questions about her plans.

'I will go abroad for a while. We have a small estate in Italy that has been rather neglected. I may go to Greece after that.'

'That sounds very fascinating.' And rather lonely. She had a sudden image of him viewing the wonders of Greece, but quite alone. He didn't look as if it pleased him much. In fact, he looked very tired; lines of fatigue showed on his face and the shadow of his beard was beginning to show.

'Yes.' He stood abruptly. 'You should go to bed. You look all done in.'

She rose also. 'So do you.' She held out her hand, not quite knowing what to say. 'Thank you.'

He took it, lifted it to his lips for a brief moment. 'Thank you.' He dropped her hand and hesitated. 'My room is near yours if I can be of any further service to you. Otherwise, I will bid you goodbye. I plan to leave as early as possible tomorrow.'

'Yes. Goodbye, then.' She turned away quickly so he wouldn't see the tears that threatened to spill over. And then she left the room.

This time she was in a carriage. She saw nothing but mist, but the carriage was moving faster and faster. Her baby was beginning to cry, and she pleaded for the coachman to stop. And then she was rolling and rolling. The baby flew out of her hands. She screamed…

The knock echoed the pounding of her heart. She sat up, disoriented and shaking. 'Claire! Claire! Open the damned door!'

She automatically stumbled towards the door, and them remembered she was in the inn. Fingers trembling, she managed to unlock it.

Jack stood in the doorway. He wore a dark robe, and his hair was tousled. Claire blinked, trying to clear the fog from her mind. 'Jack?'

'What's wrong? I heard you scream.'

'I…I had a bad dream.' She shivered, the tears she always felt after the dream springing to her eyes.

He stepped into the room and shut the door. 'My God! I thought you'd been attacked. You don't know…' He touched her wet cheek. 'Claire? You're crying.'

She shook her head. 'No…'

'And you're trembling. Claire, don't, my sweet.' His arms came around her, drawing her against his chest for the second time that night.

'My…my baby,' she whispered.

'Baby?'

'He…he killed him. M-Marcus.' She began to cry, silent shaking sobs she couldn't seem to stop.

His arms tightened around her, one hand stroking her hair until her sobs subsided. Then he drew her towards the bed and sat down, still cradling her against his chest. His robe had fallen open and his skin was rough and warm against her cheek. He held her tight until she ceased shaking, and she lay against his chest, eyes closed, completely spent.

'What happened?' he asked gently.

Claire pulled away from him and took a deep shuddering breath. 'I was…was with child. I…I thought Marcus would be pleased, but he only seemed angry. And one night we…we had gone to a dinner at some neighbours'. It was winter. Marcus was angry; I could see it. And in the carriage he…he said I was flirting with the unmarried son. He accused me of being unfaithful.' The details were vivid in her mind. His hateful, venomous words, her cowering in the corner, afraid he would strike her as he had many times before. But he hadn't. 'He…he said he could hardly bear to sit in the same coach with me. He told the coachman to drive faster and faster so he would be rid of my company. And we overturned.'

Jack was very still. She had no idea what he thought, only that she must go on. 'I…I lost the baby. He…he was born too soon; he lived only a few hours. And…and Marcus said it was a good thing as he…he wasn't his son.' She looked at Jack, the anguish and pain still fresh in her heart. 'How could he say that? How could someone say that about an innocent baby?'

'I don't know.' In the moonlight, his face was pale, his eyes dark with some emotion she did not understand.

'I…I was never unfaithful,' she whispered.

'I know.'

'He…he was my baby. I wanted him.'

'I know.' He reached for her again, pulling her back against his chest. 'Claire, I am so very sorry. For all of this.'

'I…I didn't want to live. He…he hated me, Jack.'

His arms tightened around her, as if he meant to never let her go. His chin rested against her head. She curled up against him like a small child, feeling more comforted and warm than she had felt for ages. They sat like that for a long while, the moonlight bathing the room in a soft silver light.

Claire finally stirred, her eyelids half-closed with drowsiness. 'I...I should let you go to bed,' she whispered. She didn't really want him to go; he felt too good.

'Very well.' He stood with her in his arms, letting her slide down the length of him, still holding her against him. 'Which side do you prefer?'

'Side?'

'Of the bed. I'm staying with you.' His voice was firm, brooking no argument.

Her face flamed. 'Jack, no. I don't think...'

'I'm not going to seduce you,' he said softly into her hair. 'But you're not sleeping by yourself. I want to be there if you have more bad dreams.'

He felt so warm and solid. And very, very masculine. She should shove him away. 'I like the left side of the bed.'

She felt the soft rumble of his laughter. 'And I like the right. This will work out very well.' He scooped her up and gently laid her on the bed. She watched, alarmed to see him remove his robe. She was relieved to see he wore breeches. But nothing else. She closed her eyes, the sight of his broad, muscular chest covered with a mat of dark hair making her blood quicken. Then the mattress sank as he settled in beside her, his body coming to rest against hers.

Claire lay on her back, her body rigid. He shifted and then his arm curved under her head, drawing her to his chest. 'This is better,' he murmured. 'These beds weren't made to accommodate two people.' His hand stroked her hair. 'Comfortable?'

'I think so.' Despite the oddness of being held in a man's arms, she felt amazingly nice. His heart beat steadily under her ear and the rhythmic rise and fall of his chest was soothing. She was beginning to feel drowsy. Her eyes fluttered shut.

Jack let his hand rest on Claire's silky hair and listened to her soft, even breathing. He shifted uncomfortably and stifled a groan. It was going to be a long night. He was so damned hard he feared he would burst through his breeches. He'd often dreamed of holding her in his arms just like this, but after a night of passionate lovemaking when they'd both been satiated. And if he did want her again he would first caress one of the soft breasts pressing into his chest, and then kiss her awake, his hands moving down…

'Hell.' Better to think of something else. Like how he'd take great pleasure in running Ellison through. Cold fury filled him every time he thought of what Claire had endured at the man's hand. And then to lose her child. Jack shut his eyes, his hand tightening on the nape of Claire's neck. He'd felt such pain as she told him. The child should have been his. Now he felt a kind of helplessness and guilt and a desire to protect her from any more such anguish.

But what was he to do? Force her to marry him? She'd made it clear she wanted to say goodbye. She was in his arms now, but certainly it was not out of any great desire for him. His mouth twisted. He would do best to go abroad and try to let her become a memory. Something he'd not succeeded with before despite several lovely mistresses.

She stirred in his arms, her small hand moving across his chest. The innocent movement only made the heat in his loins flare. He gently eased her from him, and turned her on her side, her body soft and pliable under his hands. He then arranged himself around her, his arm curved over her body. He shut his eyes. Eternity would feel like a heartbeat compared to this night.

Claire awakened, confused to find an arm draped around her body, a hand resting on her stomach. A heavy weight she identified as a leg was wedged between her own legs. Her eyes flew open, and then she remembered.

Oh, heavens! What in the world was she doing in Jack's arms as if they were lovers? Last night it had somehow seemed the most natural thing in the world to drift asleep on his chest, but in the cold light of early dawn she was thoroughly mortified.

To make matters worse, she realised her cotton night-dress was riding up around her upper thigh so her bare flesh was in contact with the cloth of his breeches.

She struggled a little to try and free her leg. The only thing that happened was he pulled her closer to him. His hand shifted to cup her breast, the touch sending a peculiar shudder through her body. She stiffened, both wanting to push away from him and press herself as close as possible to him at the same time. It was as if her body was on exquisite fire. She moved again.

This time he murmured her name, sounding as if he was still half-asleep. He pressed himself against her, and she felt his hardness against her buttocks. Instead of the revulsion she'd felt when Marcus had done the same, she felt a contraction in her gut. Instinctively, she rubbed against him.

His hand jerked away from her as if he'd been scalded. He sat up. The sudden loss of his warmth made her feel as if she'd been doused with cold water.

'Claire?'

'I'm still here.' She closed her eyes, awash with embarrassment. What if he'd been awake enough to notice how she'd responded to him?

He slid down and leaned over her, his breath warm on her ear. 'I'm glad. I'd hate to wake up and find you'd slipped from the room. You don't sleepwalk by any chance?'

The slight amusement in his voice made her relax. 'No. Only scream.'

He laughed softly. 'Not too often, I hope.' His hand brushed against the nape of her neck.

'Only when I have that dream.'

She felt him move down beside her. Then he pulled her around to face him, cradling her head in his arm. 'Do you have it often?' he asked quietly.

'Not any more. I used to have it all the time. Or others. I…I don't know why I did last night. I am sorry for disturbing you.'

His face hovered over hers. 'I'm not. I wish I had been there for you all the other times.' He gave a bitter laugh. 'If it weren't for me, there would have been no reason for you to have such dreams. Nor to lose your child. An apology is damn little to offer you at this point. I'm surprised you even deign to look at me.'

She stared into his dark face; his eyes were filled with self-loathing. Months ago she had wanted to throw the same things at him, make him see what he'd done to her, but now she only felt for the pain he had. 'It was not your fault. I chose to marry Marcus.'

'You chose him because I had humiliated you. You were too young to know the sort of man he was. If I hadn't made the damnable bet, none of this would have happened.'

'But I might have easily married another man who was no better.' She reached up and touched his face.

'Please, don't do this. I don't think I could bear knowing you blame yourself for all of this. You did nothing to me that night.'

'I ruined you and was not man enough to insist you marry me. I should have forced your brother into giving you to me. By the time I discovered you were to marry Ellison, it was too late. Your brother refused to let me see you, saying you never wanted to lay eyes on me again. You had made your choice.'

She stiffened. 'You saw Edward again?'

'Yes, the day before your wedding. I was determined to talk some sort of sense into you. I planned to promise you anything—a marriage where you'd only need lay eyes on me for the ceremony if that's what you wanted.'

'He never told me. I…I thought you had left for Italy.' And that was when she had decided to accept Marcus.

'I should have suspected something like that. I should have abducted you before you reached the church.'

'We…we were married at home. It wouldn't have worked.'

'From your bedchamber, then.'

The expression in his eyes was making her dizzy. 'There's a very prickly rosebush outside. You would have had to be very careful.'

'A few scratches would have been worth it.' His eyes were intense. 'So you really forgive me?'

'Yes.' She could not help it. Her hand crept up to touch his face, the growth of beard rough under her hand.

He caught her hand, planting a kiss on her palm. 'Thank you,' he said simply.

He dropped her hand, his eyes still on her face. 'Do you know how beautiful you are?' he whispered. 'I have often dreamed of holding you in my arms as I did last night.'

'I…I think it is still night.' What was she saying? Her breathing was hard, and she felt as if every nerve in her body was alert, waiting.

'Almost dawn,' he corrected her. His eyes were still fixed on her. 'Did you sleep at all?'

'A little. I have never slept with a man before. I…I mean, not like this,' she blurted out.

'And I've never slept with a woman before. Not like this.'

'Haven't you?' The thought pleased her, even if it had been platonic. But there was nothing platonic about what he was doing to her now.

'No.' He trailed a finger down her cheek. 'Claire, I am very close to seducing you.'

'I've never been seduced before either.'

'What do you think about the idea?'

'I suppose you're very good at it.' She knew she should shove him away, jump from the bed. Instead, she waited, her pulse thudding in anticipation.

'Possibly. I don't know.' He suddenly pulled away from her, running an agitated hand through his hair. 'You must think I am totally depraved.'

'Depraved? Why?' Now what was he talking about? All she could think about was touching his face, and then his dark, silky hair.

'For suggesting such a thing. After all that has passed between us. Forgive me.' His voice was stiff. He'd half turned away from her, so she only saw his profile. He looked virile and dangerous and oddly vulnerable all at once.

Her heart went out to him. She sat up, the sheet falling away from her. She touched his arm. 'Jack, don't! There is no need to apologise for…for wanting me. I am honoured. Besides, I…I find you very…very attractive also.'

He looked at her, his mouth quirked wryly. 'Do you?'

'Yes. I always have, even when I thought I was madly in love with Mr Poyton. I…I noticed your shoulders.'

The distant look was beginning to fade. 'Really?'

'Mr Poyton's were very disappointing in comparison.'

He laughed. 'Was that all you noticed?'

'There was more, but I don't want your head to swell.'

He gave her a wicked grin. 'Particularly as there's another part that's swollen enough as it is.'

Heat suffused her face. 'I…I am sorry.'

'There's no need to be. A mere compliment to your charms, and the torture of lying next to you all night. Of course, if you wished there were something you could do to alleviate the condition…'

'I…' She hardly knew where to look. Her body felt languid and heated at the thought.

He rose from the bed. 'I am teasing you, my sweet Claire. I'd best return to my room and see if I've been robbed during the night. I don't believe I locked my door. Then we'd better see about sending you on your way to Hartfield.'

He leaned over and lifted her chin, then planted a kiss on her lips. He tasted familiar and heady, and she was thoroughly bereft when he lifted his head.

Chapter Thirteen

Leaving proved impossible. Not only did it still rain; her coach wheel could not be repaired because it was impossible to send for a blacksmith in the foul weather.

Claire stood in the window of the parlour, watching the rain pour down the windowpane, and felt extremely sorry for herself. A cheery fire burned in the grate and pink-cheeked Molly had already provided her with a steaming pot of tea. Jack had gone out to check on her coach and had come back with the news, then left again to check on his horse.

There was no reason for him to stay. He could make it back to London on horseback today if he left now. She wanted him to go, for she didn't think she could bear another farewell.

She turned from the window and gave a little shriek to find him right behind her.

He raised a brow. 'I thought you only screamed when you were asleep.' He was dripping wet, water running from the brim of his hat.

'And when people sneak up on me like that! Couldn't you at least announce your presence?' She was so happy to see him, she spoke more irritably than she'd meant to. 'I didn't expect you. Aren't you leaving for London?'

'In this weather? Unless you're hoping I'll catch a chill.'

'Oh, no! It's only I expected you would want to leave as soon as possible. Of course I wouldn't want you to become ill. You must remove your coat and come stand by the fire.' She probably sounded completely inane.

He shrugged out of his coat and draped it over one of the wood chairs near the fire. His waistcoat and shirt were damp, as were his breeches. 'Don't you have a change of clothes?' she asked.

He slanted her a half-smile as he went to stand in front of the fire. 'Yes, but they're not in much better condition. They're still damp from last night.'

'I hope you don't become ill,' she said anxiously. 'Would you like a cup of tea or something stronger?'

'Tea will be fine.' He turned to look at her. 'There's no need to fuss over me. I've been wetter and for much longer.'

'You wouldn't be stranded in an inn in the middle of nowhere if it weren't for me.' Claire felt even more guilty when he sneezed.

'Do you suppose we could spend an hour together without one of us apologising for something?' he asked.

'I am sorry,' she said, and clapped a hand over her mouth.

He suddenly smiled at her. 'That proves my point.'

She poured him a cup of tea, somehow recalling he liked it with a large spoon of sugar and no milk. She brought it to him, his hand brushing hers as he took it. The contact sent a shiver down her spine. As she watched him hold the cup and saucer in his hand, she had a sudden memory of his hand cupping her breast.

She watched him take a sip from his cup. Certainly, she'd always noticed him, but until now she'd had no idea what her strange mixture of breathlessness and a peculiar awareness of him had meant. Now she knew. It was desire.

She'd never thought she would actually long for a man to touch her in her most intimate places. That she would want to touch him, run her hands over his face and down the strong, broad chest she had lain on last night. Perhaps even the final act of intimacy wouldn't be so repugnant if it was with a man she trusted and loved.

Loved? She couldn't possibly be in love with him. She looked up to find his eyes on her with a strange expression. 'Perhaps I should worry about *you* becoming ill. You look rather peculiar. Is something wrong?'

'Um, no.' She flashed him a nervous smile. 'Nothing at all.' She backed away from him. 'I think I'll go to my room and…and read.'

'Very well.' She couldn't tell if he was disappointed or not.

But as she left the parlour she was very aware that his eyes were on her.

Jack spent most of the day attempting to distract himself from thoughts of Claire. He played numerous games of cards with Mr Flynt, a merchant from Manchester, visited the stables twice, and tried to force himself to stay away from Claire's room. Worried she might be ill, he asked the innkeeper's daughter, Molly, to check up on her when she didn't come down for lunch. Molly bustled in to report she was quite fine, only a little tired. He tried to tell himself he was relieved when the rain lifted. Then he could leave the next day.

She came down to dinner, dressed in a soft cream gown, a shawl over her shoulders. Her hair hung loose, brushed and shining. He could almost feel its silky softness in his hand. Fortunately, Mr Flynt ate with them, keeping up most of the conversation, answering Claire's questions about his business. Jack could hardly keep his eyes off her—her soft, kissable mouth, the golden sheen of her hair in the candlelight, the way her slender fingers gripped the stem of her wineglass. She avoided looking at him, but the few times she did he saw the soft colour rise to her cheeks, almost as if she knew his lustful thoughts.

Finally, Mr Flynt excused himself. Jack shoved back his chair and stood. 'You should probably go to bed yourself, Claire.' His voice was abrupt and cool.

'Yes.' She stood also, gripping her hands together so tightly, they turned white. 'Are…are you retiring now?'

'Not for a while.' He planned to stay up and drink and try to keep himself from coming near her room until he was sure she was asleep. He frowned at her. 'Are you worried you'll have another bad dream?'

'No.' She still made no move to go. Her lips parted as if she wanted to speak.

'What is it, then?' he asked more gently. She looked young and vulnerable with her hair around her shoulders. He wanted to pull her to him, reassure her he would keep her safe, and then make passionate love to her. Which would hardly inspire trust in her.

'I…I was wondering if you would…' She stopped, looking mortified.

'If I would what? Claire?' He was appalled when she backed away from him and, with a stricken look on her face, fled from the parlour.

* * *

Claire shut the door behind her and leaned against it, briefly closing her eyes. What sort of madness had made her think she could possibly ask Jack to sleep with her again? She had spent the day working up her courage, knowing she would never see him again after today. She wanted to spend a night in his arms, this time as lovers. But somehow she couldn't bring herself to the point.

She slumped down on the bed. She'd never seen herself as seductive. She had no idea how one even went about doing such a thing. As wrong as it might be, she wanted him, wanted to please him, and experience what it would be like to have someone who wanted her only for herself, who cared about her, to make love to her. And her bed looked so lonely. After last night, it was full of memories.

She slowly reached down and removed her shoes. She had best go to bed. She started to peel off her stockings. The knock on her door startled her. She froze, her heart thudding in her chest. Every instinct she possessed told her it was Jack.

The knock came again. 'Claire? Open this door!' He sounded irritated.

No wonder. He probably thought she was completely irrational after this evening.

'Claire! If you don't open the door, I'll break the thing down.'

He was perfectly capable of doing it. Or at least trying and creating a dreadful scene. She padded to the door and turned the key, then opened the door just a crack. 'I am fine. Just rather tired.'

'You didn't sound fine. Let me in.' Without waiting for an answer, he shoved the door wider, forcing her to move back, and stepped inside. He closed the door behind him, leaning against it. His eyes roved over her face. 'What's wrong, Claire?' he asked gently.

'N-nothing.' To her consternation, tears filled her eyes. It was so humiliating; Edward had always made it known that feminine tears were a sign of manipulation and weakness.

'Why are you crying? Claire, don't…' With a groan he stepped forward and caught her in his arms. 'What is it?' he asked roughly. 'Tell me.'

She buried her face in the fine linen of his shirt. 'I…I wanted you to stay with me tonight,' she said into his chest.

She felt him stiffen, heard his sharp intake of breath. 'Do you know what you're saying?'

'Y-yes.' She hugged him tighter, afraid to look at him.

'If I do, I won't be able to keep away from you.'

'I know. I…I might not be able to keep away from you.'

His arm tightened. 'Claire, I am not certain you're thinking clearly.'

'I am. I…I don't expect anything from you. You don't need to act honourably or apologise or…' A thought struck her. 'If you don't want me…'

'Not want you? Oh, God!' He crushed her to him, knocking the breath from her. Her body was pressed to him and she felt how much he did desire her.

He loosened his grip and lifted her face towards him. His eyes danced in front of hers for a dizzy moment before his mouth crashed down on hers. She was descending into a dark, whirling void where there was only him. He suddenly released her, and she clung to him to keep from falling. 'Are you certain?' he asked thickly. His breath was coming in hard gasps as if he'd been running.

'Yes.' She reached up to stroke his jaw, marvelling at the strong masculine angle. 'Do you need to lock your door first?'

'What?' Then he laughed. 'No, it's done.' His hand trailed over her collarbone, lightly skimming over her breast and down the curve of her hip. 'Don't worry about anything.'

'I…I have no idea what you want me to do.' Despite her marriage, she had no idea what a man like Jack would expect. Marcus had merely wanted her to lie still and passive until he satisfied his need, collapsing on her with a harsh grunt.

'Nothing. That is, just let me love you. Although—' his eyes darkened '—a kiss might be nice.'

Shyly, she draped her arms around his neck and pulled his head towards her. He waited, not moving, letting her take the initiative while she moved over his lips in exploration. He opened his mouth, and she hesitantly thrust her tongue in. He tasted masculine and heady, and when his tongue touched hers she pressed closer to him, finding the dance they engaged in erotic beyond imagination.

He groaned and pulled away. 'Turn around,' he said in a thick whisper.

She obeyed and felt his fingers undoing the fastenings at the back of her gown. Her body trembled with a mix of apprehension and an odd excitement as he slipped the soft gown from her shoulders. His lips brushed the nape of her neck before he fumbled with the lacings of her stays. It fell to her feet, followed by her petticoat. She crossed her arms over her breasts, feeling shy and vulnerable, her defences falling away with each article of clothing. At least a sheet would provide some shield. 'Shouldn't we get into bed?' Her voice barely worked.

'No, not yet,' he murmured. His hands caught hers

from behind, gently pulling them to her sides. Then he pulled her against him, his hands caressing her breasts through her thin shift, while his mouth left a trail of hot, fiery sensation from the nape of her neck to her shoulders.

Her breasts hardened under his hands, aching for fulfilment. She made a little moaning sound in her throat as his hands left her breasts to slide down her hips and pull her more tightly against him. She felt his desire for her, hard against her buttocks. Her eyes closed as his hands spanned the soft flesh of her stomach and then moved in lazy, caressing circles. Her whole body was at once languid and heated and pliable as if she would go wherever he led.

He turned her in his arms. He started to push the short sleeves of her shift down. Claire's eyes snapped open. Her hands caught his. Was she to be completely naked in front of him? And he still wore everything except his coat and cravat.

'Jack… I…don't think…'

Despite the heavy-lidded passion in his eyes, he stopped. 'What is it, Claire?'

'Aren't you going to remove some of your clothes?' Then she could have bitten her tongue at his startled expression. 'That is…I have almost nothing on, and you are still dressed.' Perhaps it was customary for men to keep their clothes on while removing all of their mistress's. Of course, there was one necessary article that must come off.

He must have read her thoughts. His mouth suddenly curled in a slow, sensuous smile. 'Yes, I had planned on at least one item. But is there something else you had in mind?'

'What do you usually do?' This was not what she'd

expected at all. She had never thought of lovemaking as something one discussed, particularly in the process.

'Usually, I prefer nothing. That is, I wear nothing.' His eyes were laughing. 'But I didn't want to alarm you by tearing my clothes off.'

'Oh. So you just tore my clothes off instead?'

He laughed. 'Claire, do you know how delightful you are?' His voice was a caress. 'So what do you want me to remove?'

'Your waistcoat?'

'That's a start.' He obligingly shrugged out of his embroidered waistcoat and let it slide to the ground where it joined her stays. 'What next?'

She bit her lip. 'Your shirt.' It seemed a safe enough request. She studiously avoided looking anywhere past his waist.

'You do it. To even the score.'

She hesitantly fumbled with the first buttons of his shirt. He waited, standing completely still, head bent as he watched her. The desire to touch his naked chest increased with each button. Impatiently, she tugged his shirt from the band of his breeches, then spread it open. She ran her hands over the dark hair on his chest, feeling the hard muscles beneath.

He drew in a sharp breath. 'I think it's time to lie down,' he said hoarsely. He swooped down upon her and carried her the few steps to the bed and laid her gently on the mattress. He knelt with one knee on the bed and covered her mouth with his. His hand began to caress her breasts through her chemise. Her nipples peaked under his expert touch. She moaned in protest when he moved away. But it was only to slide the silk stockings down her legs. And then his hand slowly moved up her leg and paused to stroke the sensitive flesh of her inner thigh. She shuddered, a throbbing in her very centre craving a more intimate touch.

He shifted from the bed and stood. He bent down and took off his shoes and stockings, then straightened. He stripped off his shirt. Her gut contracted at the sight of his hard, muscular chest, the dark matted triangle of hair narrowing to a thin strip that disappeared into his breeches.

His eyes, now the grey of an approaching storm, were fastened on her face. His hands moved to the fastening of his breeches. Claire swallowed, feeling shy and shaky. She looked away, and then he was beside her, his warm, hard body against her, the hardness of his arousal pressing against her thigh. She stiffened, but he kissed her, long and slow, until she was lost in his caress.

'Now I have fewer clothes than you. Shall I make this more fair?' He was already tugging at the hem of her chemise. She obediently raised her hips so he could easily slip the garment over her head.

Jack felt her stiffen as he gazed at her lovely naked body for the first time. Her breasts were small, but perfectly rounded, her waist slender, her hips softly curved. His gaze followed the exquisite curve of her hip down her shapely legs and then came to rest on her face. 'You are perfect,' he whispered. Her expression was tinged with anxiety as well as desire.

As much as he wanted to move on top of her, push her legs apart and sink himself in her depths, he knew it would only frighten her. From the innocent way she kissed him, he knew she'd never been properly kissed, never been properly loved in her marriage bed.

He lowered himself next to her, and then slowly ran his hand over her ribcage, moving down to the soft flesh of her stomach. He stroked her there in slow, lazy circles, feeling her relax, before he moved lower. She closed her eyes. His hand tangled in the mound of curls, then moved down to part the soft hidden cleft. Her eyes opened in surprise. 'Jack…'

'Am I hurting you?'

'No.' She bit her lip, her eyes fastened on his face. 'It…it feels different.'

He slid two fingers inside. She was hot and wet. He stroked her until she arched against him with a little moan. His own desire was increasing to the point where he could no longer wait. He moved so he was over her. Her face was flushed with desire, her tawny hair spread around her shoulders in a filmy cloud, her eyes wide and trusting fixed on his face. Tenderness filled him. He wanted nothing more than to love her with his body. 'You're ready for me now.'

She nodded. He parted her thighs with his knee, the tip of his erection poised at her entrance.

Claire bit her lip again, waiting for the sharp pain that always happened. She was surprised by the swift tenderness that crossed his face. 'I promise I won't hurt you, my sweet.'

The feel of him against her swollen tissues threatened to send her mad. 'Please…' Her hips moved under him.

He thrust into her. She felt only a brief discomfort as she stretched to accommodate his unfamiliar presence. Then there was only a welcome fullness and a desire for movement to quell the aching throb inside her.

His slow strokes increased her throbbing need, pushing her towards a precipice. Instinctively, she found a rhythm to match his, her hips moving, meeting his ever-deepening thrusts. And then her world exploded in a burst of pleasure that racked her body and left her gasping. His own climax followed, and his seed spilled into her.

Soft butterfly kisses fluttered over her neck. Claire slowly opened her eyes to find Jack's face only inches away from hers. He smiled. 'Are you awake?'

Her hand curled around his neck, resting in his thick, silky hair. 'I am now. Is it morning?' she asked sleepily. Her body felt slow and languorous, the slight ache between her thighs reminding her of last night's activity.

His thumb caressed her cheek. 'Not quite.' His mouth curved in a wicked smile she could see even in the dim light. 'I can't sleep.'

'Oh.' She felt a blush cover her face. 'So you are waking me up to keep you company.'

His hand caressed her breast, then moved lower to stroke her stomach. Her womb contracted at the slight pressure. To her embarrassment, she felt herself grow wet.

He laughed softly, his hand drifting lower still. 'Not quite. I had hoped you might help me sleep.'

'Jack, you're not playing fair,' she said weakly. Even as she spoke, she was parting her thighs in wanton invitation, her body pressing against his hand.

'Never.' He rolled on top of her. His hands and mouth continued to do wicked things to her, until she begged for him, and for the third time that night she was lost in a world where there was only him.

Chapter Fourteen

Jack reached for Claire's warm, soft body and encountered a pillow. He opened his eyes and rolled onto his back. From the intensity of the light stealing through the cracks in the shutters and across the bed, he could see it was well into the morning. He sat up, the sheet falling away from his chest.

Claire stood near the window, her back to him, apparently lost in thought. She wore her shift, the outline of her softly curved body visible beneath the fabric. Her hair hung loose, a soft brown cloud tinged with gold against the cream shawl around her shoulders. He felt his loins harden and it was all he could do to keep himself from summoning her back to bed. However, he feared one more encounter and she'd barely able to walk.

He watched her for a minute, the same mix of desire and tenderness he'd experienced last night filling him. Would this have been how he'd have felt each morning if they had married six years ago? Except they'd most likely have a child or two by now. Or more. The thought of Claire with babies—his babies—was unexpectedly erotic. He frowned. Best to get his thoughts on another track before he pulled her back into his arms.

'Claire.'

She turned, clutching the sides of her shawl together. 'I didn't know you were awake. I hope I did not disturb you.'

Her voice was too polite. He frowned. 'No. What are you doing up?'

'I couldn't sleep.'

He raised his brow. 'You should have awakened me. After all, I had no compunction in doing so to you when I couldn't sleep.'

She flushed and looked away. 'I knew we both had long journeys today. I…I thought you probably needed your rest. Neither of us slept much.'

'No.' Something in her tone made him hold back the innuendo he was about to make. 'What is it?'

She didn't meet his eyes. 'What is what?'

'What is wrong? Are you having regrets already? If you recall, I didn't exactly force myself on you.'

'I know. If anything, I forced myself on you.' She looked extremely unhappy.

'Claire, come back to bed.' He held the covers open.

Her eyes widened, and she bit her lower lip in a nervous gesture. 'Jack, I don't think…'

'I don't want to make love. We need to talk.'

She crossed her arms, pulling nervously on the edges of her shawl. 'I can't think of what there is to say. If you are worried about last night, I did nothing I regretted and of course I have no intention of holding it over your head in any way. After all, we are both adults, and I knew perfectly well what I was doing. And after today it is unlikely we shall see each other again—'

She broke off, looking completely appalled as he

threw back the covers and rose from the bed. 'What are you doing?'

'I don't like carrying on conversations while I'm lying abed and the other person is doing their best to escape me. So I'm about to even the playing field.'

She backed up against the wall, her eyes fixed resolutely on his face. 'Shouldn't you at least put on some sort of clothing?' she asked, her voice almost squeaky.

He gave her a devilish smile. 'Should I?'

'I certainly think so. I cannot carry on a rational conversation with a…a naked man!'

'Perhaps I should remain undressed. I'm not certain I'm going to like your rational conversation,' he said dryly. Nevertheless, he walked around the side of the bed and reached for his breeches. He pulled them on, deliberately taking his time. When he finished fastening them, he found her still standing in the same spot, her eyes fastened on him as if frozen. This wasn't the response he elicited from most women after a night of passion. In fact, they were generally in bed as he dressed, hoping to lure him into one more passionate interlude.

Annoyed, he raised his brow in his most sardonic fashion. 'So, after having your way with me, you've decided we're not to meet again? Were you disappointed? If so, I'll be more than happy to provide a more satisfactory demonstration.'

'Why must you be so difficult? I was only trying to assure you I didn't mean to hold you to any sort of obligation! And I did not have my way with you! You make it sound as if I…I ravished you!'

At least her icy reserve was beginning to melt. 'Didn't you?'

'No!' She turned away, but not before he saw a tear trickle from her lid.

He strode to her side and caught her shoulders. 'Claire, I am sorry. My devilish temper. Please, turn around.'

She gave a little sniff that tugged at his heart. 'Claire, don't cry, please.'

'I don't know what you want from me,' she whispered.

He was floored. What did he want? All he knew was he didn't want to leave her yet. 'Come to Italy with me.'

She half turned. 'Italy?'

A sudden pounding on the door made them jump.

'Claire! Claire! Open this up.'

They stood dead still. 'Hell!' Jack said.

Claire's hand went to her throat. 'Edward! Oh, dear heaven.'

'Claire! Are you awake? Open the door!'

'The whole inn should be awake by now,' Jack said sarcastically.

Claire shot him a furious look. 'Yes. I…I am awake. Please give me a minute,' she called.

She turned to Jack, a beseeching look in her eyes. 'Please, can't you do something? Hide?'

'Where? Under the bed? I hate to guess what's beneath it. And I've no desire to leap from the window like a common thief.'

Her face was ashen. 'But he'll kill you!'

'I doubt it.' She was shaking so, he caught her hand. 'You'd best open the door. Don't worry, my dear; I can take care of myself.'

Bracing herself as if she were about to mount the gallows, she walked to the door and opened it a crack.

'Edward, what are you doing here? Shouldn't you be in London?'

Jack heard Edward's voice. 'Let me in, Claire. I can't converse with you in this hall.'

'But I'm really not dressed and...'

'He's with you, isn't he?' Edward's voice rose sharply. He started to shove the door open.

She tried to hold the door. 'Please, Edward.'

The door flew open with such force, Claire stumbled back, then steadied herself. Jack folded his arms across his chest, curbing his desire to knock Edward to the ground. Edward's eyes swept around the room, no doubt seeing the discarded clothing, before his eyes lit on Jack. Jack met his furious, disbelieving gaze with a dispassionate one of his own.

'You!' Edward's fist clenched. He took a step forward, his face turning an alarming red. 'I should kill you for this.'

'No!' Claire clutched her brother's arm. 'It is not his fault.'

Edward shook her off as if she were nothing more than an annoying fly. 'I knew as soon as Dorothea told me she'd spoken to you you'd come after Claire. Not only have you ruined my sister, you have seduced my daughter into deceit and complicity.'

'Edward...' Claire pleaded.

'I did not ask your daughter to inform me of Claire's whereabouts. I assure you, I sent her home with my housekeeper as soon as I realised she was in my house. However, I will not deny I used the information.'

'To seduce my sister out of some sort of revenge. I suppose you think I will willingly let you wed her now,' Edward snarled.

'I am starting to think I should call you out for insulting your sister as well as myself,' Jack said, his voice deadly soft.

Edward made a move towards him. 'Then name your weapon!'

Jack shrugged. 'It makes no difference to me.'

'Stop this! Both of you!' Claire shouted. She grabbed Edward's arm. Both men stared at her in surprise. She glared at her brother. 'This is the most stupid thing! If you must know, I...I seduced him!'

'What?' Edward exclaimed.

'Claire!' Jack said in a warning voice at the same time.

'I asked him to come to my bed.' Her voice was steady. 'So, you see, there is no reason to call him out. And if you do I...I will never forgive you!'

'Claire!' Jack snapped. 'I don't need your protection.'

Edward looked at her as if she'd sprouted two horns. He took two steps back as if she were something unclean. A muscle in his cheek worked.

'Get dressed!' he finally snapped. 'I'll speak with you in the parlour.'

Jack moved around the bed towards him. 'We'd best talk first, Dunford.'

'Very well.' Edward spun on his heel and left.

Chapter Fifteen

Claire watched her brother close the door, a sick feeling washing over her. Except for the location and the lack of a few other players, it could have been six years ago. And she could not suppress the horrid feeling the scene would play out to the same bitter end.

Without looking at Jack, she bent to pick up her wrinkled gown. No wonder Edward was so furious. Her gown and petticoat lay crumpled on the floor. Her stays and stockings peeked out from underneath Jack's shirt. Anyone entering the room would have had no doubts about last night's activities.

She straightened up, almost slamming into Jack who had come up behind her. She looked up at him, trying to keep her mouth from trembling. To her surprise, he looked quite calm. 'I am sorry. I never meant to cause you so much trouble,' she whispered.

'You didn't. I fear it was the other way around.' He brushed her cheek with the back of his hand. 'Don't look so stricken. I promise this won't hurt you.' He glanced down at the gown she held in her hand. 'It looks rather crumpled. Do you have something else to wear?'

'Yes.'

'Get it, then. I'll help you dress.'

Heat stained her cheeks. 'That is not necessary.'

'You are trembling too much. I fear you'll make a sorry mess of it.'

She went to her trunk, feeling more numb than ever. His matter-of-factness was worse than if he was furious with her. That she could deal with, but not this. How could he be so calm? Perhaps he'd been faced before with an angry brother, or, worse, an angry husband. The thought was hardly comforting.

She pulled out the first thing she could find—a morning gown in a pale yellow sprigged muslin. She turned with it in her hands. Jack had retrieved her petticoat and stood with it in his hand.

'I can manage. Don't you think you'd best dress?' she asked. The sight of his uncovered chest and muscled arms was unnerving. Not to mention the intimacy of seeing her undergarment in his strong masculine hand. Although how she could even be thinking of such things at this moment was beyond her.

'In a minute.' He brought her petticoat to her. 'Put this on, and I'll help with your other things.'

He turned his back and went to get his shirt. Claire removed her shawl, and managed to get the petticoat tangled in her shift in her haste. By the time she started over again and got it on, she felt as heated as if she'd been on a brisk walk.

She glanced over at Jack. At least he had his shirt on, although it was not buttoned. Her face coloured as a shaft of desire shot through her. And when he picked up her corset she felt as if she was on fire.

She practically snatched it from his hand. 'I think I will leave it off today.'

'As you wish. But you'll need help with your gown.' He retrieved it from the chest where she'd laid it.

She glanced at the item and wanted to groan at the sight of the small buttons down the back. Unfortunately, her rumpled gown was the only one she'd brought that she could fasten herself without the assistance of a maid.

She tried to think of anything else but him as he eased the gown over her head and then fumbled with the buttons at the back. The process seemed to take an eternity. She could not stop the reaction of her body as his fingers brushed her bare skin and swept aside the hair from the nape of her neck. She was too aware of his silence, and his breathing which was rather hard.

With more than a little relief, she finally stepped away from him.

'Thank you.' She avoided his eyes.

'I hope it's satisfactory.' His voice was rather choked.

She flushed. 'Quite. I suppose you've had a lot of experience in doing this.' Then she could have bitten her tongue.

'Hardly.' His voice was curt. She stole a look at his face and saw a slight flush on his own cheekbones. It suddenly occurred to her that, despite the cool look in his eye, he was not quite as calm as he presented himself. With his dark hair rumpled and his shirt unbuttoned, he looked like a ruffian, and in sore need of a valet.

'Do you need some help dressing?' she blurted out.

He backed away from her as if she'd offered to scorch him. 'No! That is, I'll manage.' He turned away. 'Go and brush your hair.'

Hurt by his abruptness, Claire turned away and went to pick up her hairbrush, almost running into the bed. She backed away and smashed into Jack.

'I beg your pardon.'

'Of course,' he said stiffly. He stepped away. 'I'll be on this side of the bed. Perhaps you could stay on the other.'

'Very well.' Her own voice was equally cool. She yanked the brush through her tangled locks, trying to still her sense of impending doom.

She carefully kept her eyes averted from his side of the room, although she could sense his every move as he dressed. He finally rose from the bed after pulling on his boots.

He moved to the door. 'I will see you shortly.'

'No.' Claire turned and put down her brush. 'I'm coming with you.'

Jack frowned. 'You'd best stay here until I deal with Edward first.'

'No. I will not have you two decide my fate while I sit here waiting to be summoned like a disobedient child! I am quite tired of being treated as if I was seventeen again!'

He looked at her for a moment. 'As long as you don't have some misbegotten idea of trying to convince your brother you seduced me.'

'Well, why not? It is the truth. If I hadn't so wantonly thrown myself at you, you would not be in this situation.'

He looked as if he wanted to strangle her. 'I've half a mind to lock you in the room if you continue on in this vein. I don't need you defending my honour.'

'I'm not defending your honour. I am merely telling the truth.'

'Hardly, my dear.' He held the door open.

Claire stalked past him, not wanting to let him see how furious and trapped she felt. The whole thing was too close to last time. The icy anger in her brother's eyes, the cool, remote expression on Jack's face, her feelings of being so very helpless and so horribly wrong. She would do anything this time to keep her fate from being the same.

Edward turned impatiently from the mantelpiece where he'd been staring at a portrait of an impossibly fat cow. His brows snapped together in his most ominous fashion when he saw Claire.

'What are you doing here? I told you to wait in your room.'

She met his gaze squarely. 'I am not a child. Anything you want to say can be said in front of me. Otherwise, I will consider the matter closed.'

She plopped down in the nearest chair, folded her hands in her lap and fixed Edward with a challenging stare.

He made an impatient sound. 'Then I suggest we discuss this matter outside, Rotham.'

'No. She is right; she's not a child. Anything we have to say should be said in front of her,' Jack said.

His defence surprised her. She felt unexpectedly grateful for this show of support despite his cool manner. Perhaps he wasn't utterly angry with her.

Edward's mouth worked. 'Very well. Then I'll get to the point.' He gave Jack a hard stare. 'I'm not letting you off again. I don't know what you said to her last time to dissuade her from marrying you, but by God you're not escaping again.'

Jack was lounging against the wall, arms folded across his chest. A peculiar look flashed across his face. 'I've no intention of "escaping", as you so elegantly put it. I'll procure the special licence tomorrow. We can be married the day after. Unless you'd prefer we go to the border.'

Claire shot up from her chair. 'This is utterly ridiculous! I will not marry you!'

Jack gave her a deadly smile. 'I hate to contradict you, my dear, but this time you will.'

She clutched the back of the chair. 'No! I am no longer an innocent girl who has been ruined. I am a widow and am allowed a certain amount of…of indiscretion.'

They both looked at her as if she were insane.

'I have no idea where you got such a foolish notion, but in case you've forgotten there is Dorothea to consider. For her sake, if not your own, you have a duty to mitigate the negative effects of your rash and inconsiderate behaviour. Her prospects will hardly be helped if her aunt is involved in scandal,' Edward said. 'Unless, of course, you agree to have no more contact with her.'

She felt dizzy, her mind trying to comprehend that Edward was actually threatening to cut off all communication with Dorothea if she didn't concede to his wishes. She couldn't bear to look at Jack. 'I can't imagine what scandal you refer to. No one need know we were here.'

'There is the risk you might be with child.'

Jack's child? Edward's tone implied she was in danger of contracting some horrible disease. She had scarcely thought that their night of passion might result in a child as her one pregnancy had come nearly a year and a half after marriage.

She hardly noticed when Jack came to her side until he spoke. 'Leave us, Dunford. I want to talk to her alone.' His voice was cool and commanding.

Edward stared at him for a moment, and then, with a curt nod, left the room.

Claire moved from the chair towards the window.

Sounds of the daily activities of the inn drifted through the window: the neighs and snorts of the horses, the rattle of harness and stomping of horses' hooves, two loud voices raised in argument. Ironically, the sun now shone brightly.

She felt him move up behind her. His hands lightly gripped her shoulders. 'Look at me, Claire.'

She shook her head. 'I don't want to marry you,' she said in a low voice.

She heard his sharp intake of breath. 'That may be, but you are going to.' He turned her towards him. His eyes were dark, his mouth set in a determined line. 'As soon as I get the licence.'

'Couldn't we at least take some time to think about this? When we are more rational?' Perhaps she could think of some way to escape this. It was the same nightmare all over again—her brother exerting his will over her, Jack facing her with grim determination. Except now he was no boy of twenty-one, but a man who would not be easily persuaded to leave.

'I am perfectly rational.'

'You cannot be or you would never consider this. I don't know why you must let Edward bully you into marrying me.'

His brows crashed together in the most deadly frown she'd ever seen. 'Is that what you think?' he asked, his voice deceptively soft. 'Edward is bullying me into this?'

She backed up until she was pressed against the windowpane. 'Of course. We had agreed to part amicably until he…he found us.'

'That was all on your side, my dear. I never agreed to any such thing. If you recall, I asked you to come to Italy with me.'

'But as your mistress,' she whispered. Oh, why was he doing this to her?

'I never said that either. I wanted you for my wife.'

'But why?' The room seemed much too hot. She hoped she wasn't about to faint—something she'd only done once before when her arm had been set for a broken bone.

'Because, despite your protestations, you have no idea how the game is played. And your brother is right—there may be a child.'

She coloured. 'It is unlikely. It was much too difficult the first time.'

'Nonetheless, I don't plan to take that risk. And no child of yours and mine is going to be illegitimate.'

'Then we can wait to see if that possibility arises. I…I really don't want to be married again.' And not another marriage like her first, where she was passed off as an inconvenient problem.

He stared at her hard, and then his expression slowly changed. 'Why not, Claire? After last night I would think marriage to me would not be too repulsive.'

She swallowed. 'That is not all that is important in marriage.'

'No, but it can make it much more pleasurable.' He slowly moved towards her. She sidestepped away from the window, but found herself backed up against the wall. He stopped so they were almost touching. She practically held her breath, trying to keep her chest from coming into contact with his, and flattened herself against the wall as much as she could.

'I…I don't suppose you could move away,' she said breathlessly.

'No.' His eyes were pools of ink. His hands came up on either side of her head. Then he lowered his head.

She braced herself for his assault. Instead, his mouth slanted across hers, warm and gentle and persuasive. She tried to remain stiff and unresponsive. But she could not hold out against the persistent coaxing of his mouth. He made no effort to pull her to him, but of its own will her body swayed against him, her lips opening to his. His tongue invaded the warmth of her mouth, lightly touching the tip of her tongue.

But when she felt the hardness of his arousal pressing against her belly sanity returned in full force. She opened her eyes, breaking the contact of his mouth. His own eyes jerked open—dark and dazed with confusion. He stared at her for a moment as if he was trying to regain his senses. Then he stepped back. 'I believe I proved my point.' His voice was husky.

'Yes. No.' She hardly knew what she was saying. 'That is, I am not certain what your point was.'

He frowned, shoving a lock of hair away that had fallen over his brow. 'I haven't a clue what it was, to own the truth.' He looked at her, his eyes sober. 'You must marry me, Claire. You have no choice.'

'Of course I have a choice.'

'No. Not unless you want your brother riding rough-shod over you again. He's already threatened to keep Dorothea away from you. I've no intention of finding out what else he plans to do.'

'I am certain he'll change his mind.'

'Will he?' He looked at her steadily, and she dropped her gaze. She knew perfectly well that Edward would carry out his threat despite Jane's pleading. And she could not meet them secretly and cause more friction.

'So, if I step out of the picture now, he'll be content to let you live your life in splendid isolation? I doubt it very much. He most likely will find you another worthy suitor. Is that what you want?'

'He couldn't force me to marry again. I am nearly four and twenty.' But her voice faltered.

'Yes.' His smile was grim. 'You do have a choice. You may choose to marry a man you at least know or step into the unknown. Or perhaps you might hold out against Edward and be rewarded with a measly pittance to live on and no hope of seeing your family.' He lounged against the sofa, watching her face carefully. 'And, if you recall, your brother made it quite clear he had no intention of letting me escape, as he so elegantly put it, this time. That means he most likely will call me out. Do you want the scandal of a duel between us attached to your name? Since you are the injured party, I would be obliged to let him shoot me. Of course, if you want me dead…'

'Don't!' The trap seemed to be closing in on her. She suspected he was exaggerating for the point of persuasion, but an image of him wounded, perhaps dying from a bullet, sprang to her mind. And all because of her. She knew Edward's haughty pride and his inability to ever back down. He'd no doubt call Jack out.

No. She couldn't let it go that far. She couldn't hurt Jane or Dorothea. Or risk Jack's life. And, despite her feeble attempts to defy him, Edward had neatly cornered her as he always had. And through her own foolishness.

'You are right. I have no choice.' She looked at him steadily. 'I will marry you.'

Chapter Sixteen

Claire stared out of the window of her bedchamber in Hartfield Hall. She supposed it would be considered, under ordinary circumstances, the perfect day for a wedding. The sun was bright, the rolling hills green and dotted with sheep. She let the curtain fall and sat down on her bed. Jack was due to arrive before noon. They were to be married in the yellow drawing-room.

At least that part would be different. Last time the wedding had been held in the chapel.

Of course there were other differences. Jane had been there, helping her into her fine silk wedding gown, trying to reassure her, despite the furrow of worry on her brow. And then Jane had pulled her down beside her on the bed and, turning pink with embarrassment, had explained to Claire the details of the marriage bed.

This time there would be no shocking, humiliating surprises in that area. Even now, the thought of lying in Jack's arms made her feel dizzy with remembered pleasure. Only she had no idea if he'd even want her.

Or, if he did, whether she'd be able to keep her heart from wanting him as well.

* * *

The Duchess of Arundel smiled across at Jack from her seat on the swaying carriage. 'There is no need to look so apprehensive. Everything will work out splendidly. You'll see.'

'Undoubtedly.' His bride was being coerced into marrying him. He'd spent the better part of the last two days travelling or cooling his heels waiting for an appointment with the archbishop for the special licence. His head hurt like the devil, and not only had he run into his grandmother, who had insisted on coming, but Jane and Dorothea and Lady Billingsley were following in another carriage. Dunford would probably have his head.

Jack scowled at the passing scenery. Trying to dissuade his grandmother was like trying to pry a barnacle off a ship's hull. Jane had come to the Duchess after Edward had gone after Claire, worried that Edward meant to do something drastic. The Duchess had assured her that Jack was well able to look after himself and Claire. Unfortunately for Jack, there had been no satisfactory explanation for why he'd needed to see the archbishop except the truth—he was going to marry Claire as he'd compromised her. The next thing he knew, his grandmother had insisted there was no way in the world she would let Claire face those two men alone and, furthermore, Jane and Dorothea were coming as well. Claire was not getting married without the support of her family—the female side.

He'd warned them he was travelling all night and they had less than three hours to pack. He must have been insane to think that would stop four determined females. Amazing how fast they could be ready if properly motivated. Even more staggering had been the sight of the assorted bandboxes and trunks they'd managed to fill in that short period of time.

The carriage rounded the bend and Hartfield Hall appeared, a stately home of red brick sitting majestically atop a green expanse of rolling lawn.

Jack straightened up, his eyes fixed on the brick walls he had thought he would never set foot in again. And he found that, in spite of the circumstances, he wanted more than anything to make Claire his.

Claire looked up at the knock on her door. And then stood stunned as Jane entered. Her face was dusty and she looked hot, but her smile held pure delight. 'Claire, my love! Are you all right?'

'Yes, but…Jane! What are you doing here?'

Jane dashed forward and embraced Claire, then stood back. 'We had to come. Do you think we would possibly let you marry without us?'

'Us? But who else is here? How…how did you know?'

Jane caught her hands. 'Come and sit. You look all done in. Dorothea is here of course. And Aunt. And the Duchess.'

Claire sat, completely bewildered. 'The Duchess? But I still don't know how you found out.'

'Jack told us.' She laughed. 'Rather reluctantly, I must admit. He was in such a hurry to get back to you that he was afraid we would hold him up. But we didn't. We packed quickly and left yesterday afternoon. We spent half the night travelling, with only a brief stay at an inn. So here we are! What will you wear?'

'Wear?' She must sound like a parrot. 'I hadn't really thought… Jane, you must do something! Can you not speak to Edward? He insists we must marry, but really there is no need. It is so horrible! Just like last time.'

Jane sat down beside her. 'This is exactly how it

should have been last time. Do you know how many times I've berated myself for not standing up to Edward and insisting that he let Jack speak to you again? But Edward sent him away and I let him. I was so foolish; I tried to tell myself that Marcus's strictness was rather like Edward's. If I'd had the least idea of his real character, I never would have let you marry him. I fear much of your unhappiness was due to me.'

'Oh, Jane! It was hardly your fault. I suppose by then I really didn't care.'

'But that was what was so dreadful! You didn't seem to care. And now there is a chance to make it right!'

'But, Jane…you don't understand! Edward is forcing him to marry me. Can you not speak to him?'

A stubborn look crossed Jane's normally open face. 'No. I really have no desire to speak to Edward at all, if you must know.' She rose. 'We must get you dressed.' And then the door opened and Thea, followed by the Duchess, entered the room.

An hour later, Claire entered the drawing-room, Jane and the Duchess on either side, Dorothea following behind. Her legs felt so shaky that she hoped they would support her. Light spilled across the polished wood floors of the drawing-room, making it friendly and inviting. Her mind barely registered the bouquets of flowers, which sat on tables and around the room. She only saw Jack standing near the mantelpiece with her brother and the vicar she had known most of her life.

Her stomach knotted even more at the sight of Jack, formally dressed in a midnight-blue coat and black silk breeches, the locks of his hair carefully arranged as if he'd taken great pains for the occasion.

He turned at their entrance; his eyes locked with hers.

She caught her breath, her heart thudding in her chest. His unsmiling expression was unusually stern. She dropped her eyes, feeling horribly disappointed. What had she expected? That he'd dash across the room to declare his love? No, he was only doing this because of some misguided sense of honour. Or, worse, because he only wanted her physically. The same way Marcus had.

Lady Billingsley caught her arm. 'My dear, this is quite dreadful. I knew Edward should never have let you go alone! Of course that man would follow and try and seduce you!'

'He did not seduce me,' Claire said distractedly. Every nerve in her body seemed to be aware of the man standing across the room.

'But I understood…' Lady Billingsley began.

The vicar cleared his throat. 'Perhaps we should begin.' He looked around at the silent group. 'That is, if everyone is ready?'

'We are,' Edward snapped.

'Then perhaps the parties to be joined should come before me.'

Claire, clutching the small bouquet of roses, larkspur and pinks the Duchess had thrust in her hand, moved to stand before the vicar, her legs trembling. She could scarcely look at Jack as he came to stand next to her.

'Claire.' She looked up at the vicar's round, concerned face. 'Is this what you want?'

'She should have thought of that before she compromised herself,' Edward snapped. 'Get on with it.'

'Edward! That is quite enough!' Jane rounded on him, fury in her eyes. 'If you plan to be this…this disagreeable, I would like you to leave the room! We will proceed without you!'

'Oh, my!' Lady Billingsley said in a breathless voice.

'If we start now, perhaps the wedding could be concluded before dusk,' said the Duchess, her voice dry.

A frown creased the vicar's brow. 'I have not yet heard from the intended bride.' He looked directly into her eyes. 'Is this what you want? I see no reason to proceed further unless you are willing.'

Jack stiffened beside her. 'It is what she wants.'

'Mrs Ellison can speak for herself,' the vicar said, giving him a stern look.

'Of course. Claire?'

She glanced up at him and saw the tinge of colour in his cheeks, and the uncertainty in his eyes. With a flash of insight, she realised that if she were to refuse him now she would humiliate him unforgivably. She could not do that to him.

'Yes.' She barely breathed the words. 'It is what I want.'

Relief flashed across his face.

'Very well.' The vicar frowned at the rest of the company. 'If anyone else has something to say, I suggest they wait until after the ceremony.

'We are—' he began.

'Hope I'm not too late!' Harry's cheerful voice boomed out from behind them. Everyone turned.

He looked around the room, his eyes full of mischief. 'I can see I'm not. Well, don't let me stop you.'

Jack watched Claire from across the room. She sat on a sofa, Dorothea next to her. Getting a moment alone with her since the brief ceremony had proved impossible. Not for the first time, he regretted not dragging her off to Gretna Green. A quick wedding with strangers for witnesses was hardly romantic, but at least they'd have been free of all the swirling tensions that permeated the air around them.

'So, when do you plan to leave for Blydon Castle?' Harry said, coming to his side.

'Blydon Castle?' He'd completely forgotten about it.

'It is yours now. Or will be as soon as you and Claire reside there the next six months. I doubt that will be a problem. It's exactly the sort of place she'll love. In fact, I suggest the sooner you're out of this festive atmosphere, the better it will be for both of you.'

Jack grinned sardonically, forgetting he was angry with Harry. 'So you noticed? I think Edward would have been happier to put a hole through me than see me wed Claire. He hardly knew which would disgrace the family more.'

'He's never forgiven you for your supposed escape the first time around.'

Jack cast a glance at Edward who stood stony-faced across the room. He saw Dorothea had left her place at Claire's side and was now standing with Edward. 'No. If you will excuse me, I want a word with my bride.'

Claire looked up at him, colour tingeing her pale cheeks when he came to stand in front of her. 'May I speak to you for a moment?'

'Oh, yes...of course.' She flushed. 'Pl-please sit down.'

'Alone.' He held out his hand. 'There must be some place in this blasted house we could be private for a few moments.'

She looked at his hand, then placed her own in his, allowing him to draw her to her feet. Her hand felt cold, and he wanted more than anything to pull her into his arms. Instead, he planned to tell her she was now free to do as she pleased without interference from him.

She led the way out of the drawing-room and to the library. It was less intimate than he would have liked, but it was, at least, blessedly quiet. She closed the door behind her. 'We can talk here.'

He frowned. 'You should sit down. You look on the verge of collapse.'

'Hardly. I am a bit tired, but mostly I'm tired of everyone dictating what I should do or feel.' She was beginning to look cross.

'Nonetheless, you are going to sit down.'

'I prefer to stand.'

'I prefer to have you sit.' He moved towards her, his mouth set in a determined line. She glared at him.

'You have a choice, Claire: you may walk to the sofa, or I will carry you.'

She stared into his eyes for a moment, her chin raised defiantly. 'Is this what I'm to expect from you? That you'll dictate my every move?'

'I'm not dictating your every move! I merely asked you to sit down.' His patience was wearing thin.

'You didn't ask. You demanded that I sit and then you threatened me.'

He had no idea whether he wanted to kiss her or shake her. He stepped back, before he did something rash like pull her into his arms. 'Claire, my patience is quickly running out. Will you sit or not?'

She must have seen something in his face, for her breath quickened, sudden awareness springing to her eyes. 'I…I think I will.'

She hurried to a chair and sat down, forcing him to take the chair opposite her. He stood almost as quickly, and went to lean against the mantelpiece. 'I realise you are married to me against your will. However, I will endeavour to make the situation as painless as possible.'

He nearly groaned; he sounded as pompous and stiff as the surgeon who had once removed a bullet from his arm. Perhaps he should offer her a swig of whisky as well.

He cleared his throat. 'That is, I will try to restrain from inflicting my presence on you any more than necessary. You may choose where you wish to live. I have the town house in London and there is Grenville Hall, although my stepmother prefers to reside there. There is a smaller estate in Surrey and my hunting lodge in Scotland. I've no doubt my grandmother would be delighted if you wished to stay with her. Or, if you prefer, I can purchase a property for you anywhere you desire.' He hadn't a clue what he was saying. From the confused look on her face, he suspected she hadn't either. And instead of looking relieved she was looking more and more dismayed.

'You will be living at Blydon Castle?' she asked softly.

'No. It is not mine.'

She knotted her hands. 'But I thought that…that since you married within the proper time it would come to you.'

He stiffened. 'Do you think I forced you into marriage so I could inherit Blydon Castle?' he demanded, his voice harsh.

'No. Of course I do not think that at all.' She rose, not looking at him. 'I don't understand. Why won't you inherit it? At least you should have some compensation for all the trouble I've caused you.'

He strode to her side, pulling her around to face him. Her wide, startled eyes met his. Her lips parted in surprise. 'Listen to me, Claire. This is nonsense. I wanted to marry you, for reasons that have nothing to do with the damn castle or the night we spent together. I want to hear no more about your forcing me into this marriage. Besides, in case you've forgotten I was a most willing participant that night.'

'Oh.' Her mouth looked soft and wholly kissable. Her eyes had softened and he knew without a doubt she was as affected by him as he was by her. 'I…I see.'

'Good.' His voice gentled. He should pull away, before he did something rash. Like sweep her up in his arms and carry her to the sofa. He abruptly released her and stepped back. 'It would be best if you stay with my grandmother for a while.'

'If that is what you want.' Her voice had gone flat, her expression bleak. 'Perhaps you will at least tell me where you plan to reside.' She started towards the door.

'Claire, wait!'

She halted, her hand on the knob. 'What is it?'

'I would ask you to go to Blydon Castle with me, but under the conditions of the will we would be required to live there together for six months.'

She bit her lip. 'That is very kind of you, I am sure, but I should not want to inflict my company on you for six months.'

He inwardly groaned, wondering what had happened to his famed address. 'On the contrary, I was worried about inflicting *my* presence on *you* for six months. I should not mind your company at all.' Except he had no idea how he would keep from touching her.

She glanced away for a moment, then looked back at him. 'I…I think I would rather like to stay at Blydon Castle.'

'Would you?' Relief coursed through him, and hope. 'It is only fair to warn you that it is not very modern. Some of the furniture looks like it was brought over with the Romans and several of the fireplaces smoke. Although the leaking roof was repaired recently. At least sleep is possible without rain pouring on one's head.'

A half-smile touched her lips. 'Are you trying to discourage me?'

'No. I didn't want you to think it is some sort of romantic place when in reality it's damnably uncomfortable. It needs a dozen repairs. But you'll never find a more beautiful setting—there's a view of the sea that takes your breath away. The grounds are in poor shape but once the gardens are restored...' He stopped, realising he was babbling like a fool trying to convince her to go with him.

She smiled, the first genuine smile he'd seen today on her face. It lit up her countenance and he realised, not for the first time, how beautiful she was. 'It sounds lovely.'

'It is.' He stared at her, transfixed. Then wondered what she'd do if he pulled her into his arms. How the devil he was going to keep away from her was beyond him. Or, he could court her. Away from the complications of their respective families, he could gently woo her to be his wife in all respects. He realised, with sudden clarity, he wanted more than just her lovely body or her honest soul with him. He wanted her heart as well. And he vowed, if he won it, he would be worthy of keeping it.

'Jack?' Her voice cut through his stunned thoughts. He yanked his mind back to her and saw she was looking at him, puzzled. 'Is something wrong?'

'No. Nothing.' He smiled at her. 'Everything is quite all right. When do you want to leave? I suppose you will wish some time with your family. Although they are welcome to visit,' he added politely. Some of them.

'No. Actually, I would like to leave as soon as possible. Tomorrow, perhaps.'

'Tomorrow?' He started.

'Perhaps that is too soon?'

'Not at all.' It would suit him fine. Although he had no idea why she wanted to stay with him. To escape from her family? She looked composed, but from the tight way she clasped her hands he could tell she was nervous. Perhaps she was only coming with him as some sort of compensation for his trouble. The thought made his voice more abrupt than he intended. 'We should inform your family, then.'

'Yes.' She turned away quickly, but not before he saw the swift hurt in her eyes. He followed her from the room, cursing himself under his breath.

Claire fought back the despair that threatened to overwhelm her. Whatever had possessed her to ask to go to Blydon Castle with him? It was only because the thought of having him leave her, even with the kind Duchess, had filled her with a kind of panic. And for a brief moment she had thought he might even want her with him. Then his face had closed down, shutting her out.

How was she ever to spend the next six months alone with him?

She reached the drawing-room door and stopped when she heard a familiar languid voice. 'I only hope I am not too late to stop my son from this foolishness. I have no idea what sort of trap she set, but he cannot possibly marry that woman. He is betrothed to my ward.'

'I fear you are much too late, madam.' Edward's voice was cold and crisp. 'The marriage has taken place.'

'This is quite impossible!' Lady Rotham said.

'He couldn't have!' Alicia said at the same time. Her voice rose, unnaturally shrill.

"Damn!" Jack had come up behind her.

Harry appeared at their side. His brow rose. 'I see we've added more players to the drama. I wonder what the next act holds?'

Chapter Seventeen

Dinner was an awkward affair. Claire sat next to Jack, and picked at her food, her stomach in knots. Edward and Jane addressed each other only when necessary and in overly polite tones. Lady Billingsley complained of a headache, but continued to sit at the table declaring it was a most dreadful day in between the interminable courses. Lady Rotham persisted in addressing her remarks solely to Jack. She scarcely deigned to do more than glance at Claire, unlike Alicia, who stared at Claire with ill-concealed malice in her lovely eyes. Only Harry and the Duchess persisted in attempting something resembling normal dinner conversation.

'So, when are you leaving for Blydon Castle?' Harry asked, reaching for his wine. His cheerful voice only served to make the tension in the air more pronounced.

'Tomorrow,' Jack replied tersely.

Alicia's fork dropped to the table with a clatter. At the same time Lady Rotham said, 'Impossible.'

'I don't see why, Celeste,' the Duchess replied. 'In fact it will be quite the best thing.'

'My sister will stay with her family until the place is

habitable. I will not have her health compromised,' Edward said, his voice cold.

Feeling more and more as if she was in some sort of nightmare, Claire watched Jack's face turn hard and implacable. 'She is my wife. She will come with me. Tomorrow.'

'Of course he wants her.' Alicia gave a high, tinkling laugh. Her face was flushed, her eyes over-bright. 'The terms of the will state they must live together for six months after the wedding. Or he will not inherit Blydon Castle. Everyone knows he would do anything to possess it. And of course there was the bet. So he has won everything.'

There was dead silence. 'What bet?' Edward demanded.

'Why, the bet—'

'This is not the time,' Jack told her in a low voice.

'I want to hear about the bet.' Edward's voice was starting to rise.

'Edward!' Jane said.

'Quiet!'

Jane turned pale, but said nothing more.

'What bet?' Edward turned back to Alicia.

'Why, the bet John made with Mr Devlin. The bet that he could marry the lady whose fan he pulled from the lottery. And it was Mrs Ellison's.'

'Is this true?' Edward demanded.

''Tis no use denying it, John,' Lady Rotham said. 'I fear dear Frederick told me all.'

Claire was dimly aware of Lady Billingsley's moan. Edward's sharp intake of breath. Alicia's look of triumphant malice. She stood and shoved her chair back, unable to bear any more. 'If you will pardon me.'

'Claire?' Jane also stood.

'No. Please, just leave me!'

Claire fled from the room, but not before she heard Edward's thundering, 'I should call you out for this!'

Claire sat on a bench and hugged her knees to her chest as she had done as a small child when she felt wounded. The conservatory was full of shadows and moonlight, the huge potted palms and the small orange tree making her feel as if she was in her own isolated world.

She had no idea how long she'd been there. She sighed, a tear trickling down her cheek. She was such a coward—instead of standing up to Edward and defending Jack, she had fled. The thought of staying with Edward's irrational hostility, and the stares of pity and outrage, had been too much. And most of all Jack's increasing withdrawal into stone-cold silence. She had had to get away.

She forced herself to rise from the marble bench. She supposed she must face them all some time. Including Jack. But first she must see Edward.

She slipped her feet into her satin shoes and reluctantly left the safety of the conservatory. She had barely taken a few steps when a tall figure stepped out of the shadows. She jumped, her heart thudding.

'Claire, it is only me.'

'Harry! What are you doing? Why are you lurking around here?'

'Trying to find you. I finally remembered you liked hiding out here when you were upset or mad.' His mouth quirked. 'I should ask what you are doing here. This is hardly the proper place for a newly wed bride. You should be with your husband.'

'I doubt if he wants me.' She looked at Harry, tears

filling her eyes. 'Oh, Harry. This is all such a horrid muddle. I wouldn't blame him if he wanted nothing to do with any of us ever again. And now he has been saddled with me and I…I have to go with him so he can inherit his castle and—'

'Stop this, Claire.' Harry stepped forward and caught her forearms. 'This is ridiculous. The man's in love with you—he has been for years. He wants you more than anything.'

'No…no, he doesn't.' The tears began to flow uncontrollably.

'Oh, hell!' He pulled her into his arms and awkwardly patted her back. 'Are you this much of a watering pot with Rotham?' he finally asked, a disgusted note in his voice.

'No…no.' Claire gave a watery giggle.

'I hope not.' He pried her hands from his coat. 'Now, be a good girl and go find your husband and persuade him to leave this madhouse first thing in the morning. And, if nothing else, weep all over him. He'll probably do anything you want just to stop you from ruining his coats.'

'Are…are you certain he really wants me?'

'Yes.' Harry grinned. 'I'd lay a wager on it.'

'But what should I say to him?'

'You could try telling him that you love him.' He frowned at her. 'I assume you do?'

'Yes,' Claire said slowly. 'I love him.'

'Then tell him.'

'But I couldn't possibly. He…he has never said he loves me.'

Harry let out an impatient snort. 'One of you has to start. Lord! I've never seen such a pair. You might as well be the one. Damn it, Claire. He thinks you feel obligated to go to Blydon Castle with him to make up for being forced into marriage with him. Particularly after you fled the dining-room.'

'But I told him that wasn't true.'

'Did you give him any hint about how you feel?'

'Well, no… I didn't know,' she whispered. 'I didn't really know how I felt until now.'

'What is he supposed to think? You pretended to be in love with me. You rejected his offer of marriage. You haven't exactly given him a great deal of encouragement.'

'But that night at the inn…I…practically threw myself at him…' She bit her lip. How could she possibly tell Harry she'd begged Jack to make love to her? 'He… he never said anything after that.'

'Nothing? He just walked away from you?'

'He…he did ask me to marry him. But I thought he just…'

'Good God! How many times must he ask you to marry him before you're convinced he's in love with you?' He gave her a sharp look and then comprehension dawned in his eyes. 'You want him to actually say the words?'

'Well, yes.'

He snorted. 'He probably was afraid to tell you for fear you'd throw it back in his face. I think, my dear, in this instance you need to be the one to make the first move. Otherwise, I fear the forces at work in this place will pull you apart. For once, Claire, stand up for what you want. And he is not Ellison.'

She stood dead still, stunned by the truth of his words. And then wanted to bow her head in shame. It was true; she had done everything to push Jack away from her, even after the night she'd spent in his arms when he'd

been as gentle and passionate and caring as she could
ever imagine a lover to be. The desire in his eyes was
not Marcus's possessive lust, but the desire a man had
for a woman he cared for.

'You are right.' She looked at Harry. 'I will tell him.'

'Then go now.'

'Thank you.' Claire smiled at Harry, suddenly feeling
more hopeful. She impulsively threw her arms around
him and then stepped back. If only she could speak to
Jack, then perhaps everything would come out right.

Jack turned away from the couple in the shadows,
bitterness settling in his heart. It took no imagination to
see the bond between the two, the comfort Claire received from Harry. He had no wish to see more proof
of his bride's unhappiness—an unhappiness that forced
her to seek solace in another man's arms.

He silently left the conservatory. He would leave tomorrow, and Claire would stay, whether she wanted to
or not.

Jack was nowhere to be found. No one knew where
he'd disappeared to. With a cold stare, Lady Rotham
informed Claire he had seemed quite angry and had left
the house. Discouraged, Claire finally made her way to
her bedchamber. The sinking pit in her stomach was almost worse than the nervous trepidation she'd felt on
her first wedding night.

She sat on her bed, and finally rang for the abigail.
After the girl left, she climbed into bed, her heart heavy.
She was about to blow out the candle, when Jane's voice
came from around the door.

'Claire? May I come in? I've brought you your milk.'

'Yes.' To her dismay, her voice quivered.

'Oh, my dear!' Jane came across the room in a few swift steps. She sat the cup she carried on the table next to the bed. Then she gathered Claire into her arms as she had when Claire was a young girl. 'Hush. Everything will be fine.'

'Oh, Jane, Harry said Jack loves me, but how can he? He's not here. He...he doesn't want me. Lady Rotham said he...he has gone.'

'No.' Jane stroked Claire's hair. 'No. He won't leave without you. I know he won't.'

'But...but where is he?'

'I don't know,' Jane admitted slowly. 'I thought he went to find you after you left the table. I told him you might be in the conservatory. I haven't seen him since. But his things are still here. And I cannot imagine him leaving without telling any of us. He's much too honest.'

'Oh.' Claire drew back, feeling uneasy. The conservatory? Surely he hadn't seen her with Harry? But wouldn't he have said something? And he must know she and Harry were only friends.

'Claire? What is wrong?'

'Nothing.' She shivered, unable to shake off the certainty that Jack had seen them together. She could not let the night pass without knowing. 'I think I'll wait up for him in his room.' Surely he would come there.

'I think that would be a splendid idea. Shall I escort you there?'

'If you please.' And if he was there perhaps Jane's presence would help. Jane waited while Claire found a shawl to throw over her nightdress. She followed Jane to his room, two doors away from her own. She pushed the door open. He was not there and she had no idea whether she was relieved or not. Jane squeezed Claire's hand. 'It will be fine, you'll see.'

But as Claire stepped further into his bedchamber she wondered whatever had possessed her to do this. A single lamp burned in the otherwise darkened room. As Jane had said, his presence was very much evident. A pair of riding boots sat near the bed. His dressing-gown was thrown carelessly over a chair and a linen shirt lay crumpled on the floor.

She picked up the shirt and draped it over a chair. She chose the wing chair near the fireplace, and, after arranging his dressing-gown more carefully on the chair, sat down. His dressing-gown smelled of him—sandalwood and maleness—and reminded her vividly of their night together.

She folded her legs under her, trying to quell the nervousness in her stomach. The thought of her own bedchamber was tempting, but she'd been enough of a coward tonight. She felt on edge and tired at the same time, the wine she'd consumed at dinner making her sleepy. She started when she heard footsteps, her heart leaping to her throat. But it was only one of the maids who entered. 'Your milk, my lady. You left it in your chamber.'

'Thank you.' Claire took the glass. Jane had always brought her warm milk after she'd come to live with them at the age of eleven. She settled back down into the chair and took a few sips from her glass, listening to the clock tick away the minutes. The milk had a slightly peculiar taste, and she put the glass down. In spite of her best efforts to remain awake, her eyes finally drifted shut, and she heard no more.

Jack brushed the raindrops from his greatcoat as he entered the hallway. He had no idea how long he'd tramped through the gardens surrounding the house. It wasn't until a light rain had begun to fall that he'd turned towards the house. Claire should be asleep by now, and he wouldn't have to face her until morning.

It was cowardly of him. But after tonight he felt too defeated to confront her. He wanted to wait until his mind had cleared. Then he would rationally tell her she would not be coming with him. After that he would leave for Italy, and be gone for as long as it took to banish thoughts of her from his mind.

He pushed opened the door of his bedchamber. He stepped inside, his senses alert as his eyes raked the room. Then his gaze fell on the pale figure in the chair near the fireplace. 'Who is there?'

There was no answer. He moved across the room and was shocked to see it was Claire, her head resting against his dressing-gown draped over the back of the chair, legs tucked under her. She was so still he felt a shaft of fear before he saw the gentle rise and fall of her chest. 'Claire?'

She didn't move. He touched her shoulder. 'Claire? Claire!' Panicked, he shook her shoulder. But there was no response. Perhaps she was an unusually deep sleeper. Since neither had slept much the two nights he'd had with her, he had no idea if she slept soundly or not. There was something about her stillness he didn't like. Her breathing was shallow, her skin shiny with a peculiar sheen. He bent beside her. 'Claire! Wake up!' She finally stirred. 'Claire! Come, sweetheart, wake up.'

She moaned. He frowned. 'Claire, can you hear me?'

Her eyelids fluttered open. She looked at him as if she didn't quite know who he was. She closed her eyes. Jack gave her a little shake. 'Claire, don't. Wake up!' He was beginning to worry. 'Damn it! Don't go to sleep on me.'

He could see she was fighting his attempts to wake

her. He forced her to sit upright, his arm under her shoulders. She felt limp, a dead weight on his arm. 'Claire. Come, open your eyes. You're almost awake.'

She finally half opened her eyes. 'Want to sleep.'

'No. Get up.' He rose, pulling her to her feet. She fell against him, as limp as a rag doll. Suddenly, Hobbes appeared in his nightgown and nightcap. 'A problem, my lord?'

'She won't wake up.'

'Perhaps after the…er…excitement of today it would be best to postpone the wedding night,' he suggested delicately.

'That's hardly what I had in mind! Damn it! She looks drugged. Help me get her awake.'

Hobbes moved over to look at Claire's pale face. He touched her skin and looked at Jack, a frown on his face. 'Fresh air. Perhaps some strong tea. I believe we should send for Lady Dunford.'

Hobbes went swiftly to the window and threw open the sash. Then he rang for a servant and quickly issued instructions, shutting the door before the man could catch a glimpse into the room.

Between the two of them, they managed to keep Claire from tumbling back into sleep. Clearly disoriented, she seemed to scarcely know who they were. An age seemed to pass before the servant appeared with a pot of tea. Jack, standing with Claire in his arms, felt himself praying that nothing would happen to her. He only lifted his head when he heard Jane's voice.

'What is it?' she asked.

'I fear Lady Rotham is not quite well.'

'But she seemed perfectly fine when I left her playing cards with… But you mean Claire! Oh, Jack! What has happened?' She hurried to his side, her face stricken when she saw Claire's pale form.

'She appears drugged,' Jack said grimly.

'Drugged? Oh, God! But how can that be?'

'I found her here. She was limp and lying half-across the chair.'

'She wanted to speak to you. Claire, can you hear me?' She lightly shook Claire's shoulder.

Claire's eyes fluttered open. 'Y-yes, want to sleep more.'

'Tea for you first, my lady,' Hobbes told her.

'No…no.'

They forced the tea down her as she sat on Jack's bed. And then she turned towards him, her face even more pale than before. 'I…I fear I am about to be ill.'

Hobbes scrambled for the basin, but it was too late to prevent her from heaving the contents of her stomach over the side of the bed and on Jack's coat. 'So sorry,' she gasped before another fit of sickness overcame her.

Claire woke to the sound of rain pattering on the window. Her body felt weak and shaky, her mouth dry, and her head hurt. For a moment she had no idea why she was in her bed at Hartfield, and then memories of her wedding came flooding back. And more vague memories of being violently ill all over Jack.

She must have made a sound, for suddenly Jack was at the side of her bed. She stared at him, uncomprehending why he was there, why he looked as if he'd scarcely slept all night. His loose white shirt was open at the neck, the shadow of his beard dark around his mouth.

'Claire, do you know me?' he asked hoarsely.

What was he talking about? She tried to form the words, but her mouth was too dry.

'Claire, do you know my name?' His intense eyes bore into hers.

She nodded and licked her lips. 'Water,' she managed to croak. He poured a glass from the pitcher on the stand near the bed and brought it to her. Propping her up with his arm around her shoulders, he helped her to take a sip. The water was nectar to her parched lips and mouth, but it made her stomach churn. She lay back against the pillows and gazed up into his face. Why did he look so serious and worried? And what was wrong with her?

'Am I ill?' she whispered. 'Why are you here?'

He sat down on the bed, his face still grim. 'You took too much laudanum. When I found you, you were sleeping so deeply I could scarcely rouse you. And then you were very ill from it. Why did you take so much?' he added, his voice very careful.

'Laudanum? But I never take it.' She always had avoided it as it made her feel dizzy and sick.

'But you had. It was in the milk. A half-empty bottle of laudanum was found by your bed.'

She stared at him, not certain what he was trying to say. 'I didn't put it there.'

He rose, a frown on his face. The door opened, and Jane entered followed by Thea. Jane stopped, and her face brightened. 'You're finally awake! Thank goodness! We've been so worried!' She came across the room to Jack's side and placed her hand on his arm. 'You must get some sleep.'

'May I speak with you?' he asked curtly.

The smile faded from Jane's face. 'Yes, of course. Thea, will you sit with Claire?'

Thea nodded and went to Claire's side.

Claire watched them leave, then sank back on her pillows with the feeling that something was terribly wrong.

In the passageway outside Claire's room, Jack stopped and looked down at Jane. 'She says she did not take the laudanum.'

Jane's blue eyes held worry. 'I will own I was surprised. She has always refused it, even when she had the toothache. I brought the milk to her room. She had wanted to see you before you slept.' Her brow furrowed. 'She did not bring the milk with her when she went to your room, so I asked a servant to carry it to her. And I cannot think how the bottle came to be by her bed. I am sorry, I have not yet had a chance to question the servants.'

'No matter.'

'You must rest now,' Jane said firmly. 'Don't worry about Claire; we will take good care of her.'

Sleep eluded him. Jack finally rose and insisted Hobbes shave him. He found Harry in the library.

Harry looked up from the newspaper spread before him. 'So she's awake?'

'Yes.'

'You still don't think she deliberately took it?'

'She denies it.'

'Claire would never do what you're suggesting,' Harry said quietly. 'In fact, I know she meant to speak with you.'

'So you are privy to Claire's thoughts? Amazing how she always confides in you.' Jack couldn't quite keep the bitterness from his voice.

'As a brother. There's no need for that raised brow. She's always been like a sister to me. Fact of the matter, there's no way I'd take her on. Too weepy. She has a miserable habit of bursting into tears all over my coats.'

His drawl made Jack long to hit him. 'Did you ever consider her feelings might be more than sisterly towards you? Perhaps you might play some part in her unhappiness?'

Harry snorted. 'There must be something about the atmosphere in this place that encourages melodrama. So she decides to take her own life because she's pining away for me? Why didn't she lace your brandy with laudanum? Then she could have lived happily ever after with me.' His voice was heavy with sarcasm.

Jack scowled. 'Then why the hell was she in your arms last night?'

'Are you mad? I assure you I was in my bed and quite alone the entire night.' He stared at Jack, then he gave a short laugh. 'I begin to see. You saw us in the conservatory and assumed I was comforting her for her unfortunate marriage. And she was confessing her undying love for me.'

Jack was beginning to feel like a fool. He took a pace towards the window and turned, hands clasped behind his back. 'What the devil should I think? She made it clear the marriage was forced on her. She wanted no more to marry me now than she did before. She has always considered you her friend.'

'There is a difference between a friend and a lover.' Harry made an impatient sound. He laid the paper aside and stood. 'You're as bad as Claire. She feels the only reason you married her was because Edward forced your hand. I suggest you take her away from here even if you must abduct her. And tell her the truth.'

'The truth?'

Harry raised a brow. 'The truth that you married her because you're in love with her. I suspect you'll discover your feelings are reciprocated.'

Chapter Eighteen

Jack left the library, stunned by Harry's words. Claire in love with him? It couldn't be possible. Even the fact that she had invited him to her bed he'd dismissed as some sort of aberration on her part. Perhaps it was only out of gratitude for his kindness the night before, or the fact they'd been thrown together in an unusual situation, the combustible attraction between them bursting into flame. In his experience, love and sex had very little to do with one another. He was under no illusions that any of his mistresses had felt more for him than a mutual lust, with the exception of Sylvia, who had first been a friend. And on his part he'd never been foolish enough to confuse his liaisons with love.

Until now, he'd never stopped to consider that what he felt for Claire in return was love.

Lost in thought, he nearly careened into his step-mother. 'I beg your pardon,' he said.

Her eyes swept over his face, and she raised an elegant brow. 'Despite the lack of a proper wedding night, you do not appear to have rested particularly well.'

'I rested well enough.'

'Indeed. How is your bride?'

'She is fine.' He attempted to move past her.

'A pity when one's bride resorts to laudanum to avoid her wedding night.'

Jack stopped and gave her a hard stare. 'That was hardly the case, ma'am.'

'Wasn't it?' She gave him a little smile. 'I hope not for your sake. I fear you will have a very uncomfortable time at Blydon Castle otherwise.' She moved down the passage. He stared after her with an uneasy feeling.

Who had given Claire the laudanum? And for exactly what purpose? Harry was right; he needed to get Claire out of here as soon as she could travel.

Claire sat up and found she felt much better, at least physically. The grogginess and slight nausea had faded. But her spirits had not recovered as quickly. Every time she thought of Jack's cool, unsmiling face and the way he'd abruptly left her room, she wanted to curl up inside herself. His question as to why she had taken so much laudanum—as if he thought she had done it purposely— hurt her deeply.

And he had not come to see her. The clock on her mantelpiece showed it was nearly four in the afternoon. Perhaps he was still asleep. Jane had said he'd spent the night by her bed, which had momentarily lifted her spirits until she recalled his cold manner.

She heard footsteps and then her door opened. Her head jerked up, half hoping to see Jack. To her surprise and consternation, she saw it was Alicia.

'Oh! I hoped you were awake!' Alicia walked towards the bed without asking permission and came to stand next to Claire's side. 'You look much better than you did last night.'

'I feel fine.' Claire wondered what Alicia could possibly want. She had no doubt Alicia probably hated her for marrying Jack.

'How nice.' She stared at Claire. 'I suppose I should be very angry at you. You have ruined everything, you know.'

Her eyes were almost expressionless, which somehow frightened Claire more than if she had looked furious. 'I had no intention of ruining anything,' Claire said.

'I would be married to him by now if he hadn't come running after you.'

'I never expected him to do so.' Claire had no idea why Alicia should cause her to feel so uneasy. There was something in her calm manner that was at odds with her words. Claire glanced at the bell-pull and wondered if she should summon a servant.

'Then how did he know where you were?'

'I…I don't know.'

Alicia smiled. 'I think you do. You are very clever.' She picked up the small gilt mirror from the table near Claire's bed and fingered it for a moment. Then she looked back at Claire. 'I wonder if you will be well enough to go to Blydon Castle with him?'

'I suppose I will.' Perhaps she should attempt to get out of her bed and quit her bedchamber. 'I thought perhaps I would…'

'Really? But are you certain you want to?' She set the mirror down. 'I cannot imagine why you would wish to live with a man who only married you to win a wager.'

The knock on her door startled both of them. She looked up, relieved at the interruption. Then her stomach knotted when she saw Jack. He entered her room, then stopped abruptly when he saw Alicia. His brow crashed down. 'What are you doing here?' he demanded.

Alicia turned, her face composed. 'Merely visiting poor Mrs Ellison. I fear she is still quite overset.'

'I would like to speak with Lady Rotham alone, if you please.'

'Of course.' Alicia appeared utterly unconcerned by his manner, which bordered on rude. She drifted towards the door, and turned to smile at Claire. 'I do hope you will feel better.'

He came to Claire's bed and looked down at her. 'What was she doing in here?'

'Visiting me.' She slumped back against the pillows, suddenly too tired to say more. She turned her head away, certain she could not bear another confrontation with him.

'Did she upset you?'

'No.' She clutched the quilt with her fingers. His face had that grim expression again. He had probably come to tell her he didn't want her after all.

'I fear you still are not well.' His voice had gentled. She finally stole a look at him and saw he had lost some of his anger.

'I am much better, just rather tired.'

'Do you think you'll be able to travel in a day or so?'

'Travel? Where?'

'I want to take you to Blydon as soon as possible.'

'You do?' she whispered. So he wasn't planning to leave her here. A tiny flicker of hope sprang to life. 'When?'

'The day after tomorrow.' He was still frowning. 'But I don't know that you're well enough.'

'I am much better.' She gave him a little smile, feeling unexpectedly happy, even if he was frowning at her. 'I feel a bit shaky when I sit too much. I am sure I will be fine by then,' she added.

'Are you certain?'

'Oh, yes.'

'Then I should probably let you rest.'

'Oh, no! Please, won't you stay? I have hardly seen you at all today.'

He seemed to hesitate and then sat down on the chair near the bed. 'I apologise for not coming. I did not know if you wanted my company.'

She bit her lip. 'But I did. I…I missed you.'

His expression lost some of its grimness. 'Did you, Claire?' he asked softly. He leaned towards her, his eyes darkening.

'Yes.' Perhaps she was becoming delirious, to think of inviting him to stay. Looking into his face did cause her to feel rather light-headed. But, after all, she had been about to tell him she loved him before she became so ill.

'I missed you, too,' he was saying.

'Did you?' she whispered.

'Yes.' He reached out and smoothed a tendril of hair from her face. She scarcely seemed to breathe at the feather-light touch. 'In fact, I've been thinking about how much I've wanted to touch you again. Do you mind?'

'No.' She waited, her eyes fixed on his face, as his hand caressed the soft curve of her cheek.

'You no longer feel so hot,' he said. 'Nor are you so pale.'

'I…I think I am almost well.'

'Then you really will be able to travel soon?' It was not only his hand, but his eyes and voice that caressed her as well.

She nodded, not trusting her voice as her mouth had

gone dry and every nerve of her body seemed to tingle with anticipation.

He withdrew his hand. 'Claire, if you look at me like that I'm going to be in that bed with you.' His voice was thick.

'I...I wouldn't mind.' Her eyes widened at the blatant desire in his.

He gave a choked laugh and rose. 'Then move over, for I'm coming in.'

'But you cannot. It is the middle of the day.' She yanked the covers up to her chin.

He sat down on the edge of the bed, a wicked smile crossing his face. 'Don't worry. I'm not planning on a full-scale seduction. Just enough to remind you of what it feels like in my arms.' He gently eased himself down beside her. 'Come here, Claire.'

'I...' But his arms were around her, pulling her against him. Her cheek brushed up against the fine cloth of his coat as he turned her head so her mouth was positioned beneath his. A slight smile lifted his lips. 'Do you know how damned desirable you are?'

'I...I...'

'Claire! You wanted to see me?' Harry's cheerful voice was like a bucket of water dumped over them. Jack's head jerked up, and Claire froze.

Harry charged into the room, and then stopped. 'Good God! Er, I had no idea you were occupied.' He looked amazingly embarrassed. 'I'll return later. Er, carry on.' He started to back away.

Jack rolled off the bed and rose in one graceful movement. 'I was just leaving.' The intimate warmth had gone from his voice; instead it was coolly reserved. 'Please don't let me interfere with your conversation.'

Claire stared at him, her blood suddenly flowing as cold as his voice. 'Jack, please wait...'

He glanced down at her. 'I will inform your brother we are leaving in two days.' He stalked out of the room with a curt nod at Harry.

Harry waited for a moment before crossing the room. 'Poor timing on my part. Although your message seemed rather urgent. So, what did you want to see me about?'

A tear squeezed out from Claire's lids. 'Nothing.'

His brow shot up. She slumped back against her pillows. 'I never sent for you. Could you please just go and...and leave me?'

He looked at her, a frown creasing his forehead, and then left.

Jane refused to let her come down to dinner. 'You will need all the rest you can get if you are to leave soon.'

'Jack told you that?'

'Yes. Edward was not a bit pleased. Apparently, Lady Rotham has told him the castle is practically a ruin and he's convinced you'll end up with a dreadful illness.'

'Oh, dear.'

Jane made a face. 'I fear we'll have another uncomfortable dinner as we did last night. You will be much better off up here. The Duchess has finally persuaded Lady Rotham and Alicia to come away with her tomorrow, so perhaps we'll have a bit of peace.'

'And you and Edward?' Claire hated to see them at such odds with each other.

'We are at least civil to one another.'

It didn't sound very good. But there was nothing Claire could think of to do. Perhaps if they all left Jane and Edward could make up their quarrel.

Still, it was difficult to eat by herself despite the excellent beef and the side dish of peas. She ate a few bites of the mushrooms—a dish she cared little for under the best of circumstances—and finally shoved everything aside. Even the apricot tart, her favourite, failed to please her appetite.

The maid came to take away her tray. Restless, Claire threw back her covers and climbed out of bed. Her legs still felt shaky and the slight nausea she'd experienced earlier had returned. She made her way to the chair in front of her dressing-table and sat heavily, tears of frustration springing to her eyes. Oh, why must she feel so unwell still? And where was Jack? Perhaps he'd changed his mind about taking her with him. He'd looked so grim again when Harry had interrupted them.

She was beginning to feel even sicker, and her stomach had started to cramp. She tried to stand, but the wave of nausea that hit her made her feel so faint she collapsed back on the chair. Perhaps, if she rested her head on the desk for a minute, she could make it back to bed. She closed her eyes and laid her head on her crossed arms, willing the sickness to pass.

'Claire? What the devil are you doing out of bed?'

She barely managed to lift her head as Jack entered the room. He stared at her and then was across the room in a few quick strides. His face swam before her, and she was hit by another wave of dizziness and nausea so strong, she started to fall. Strong arms caught her. 'I'm putting you to bed.'

'No.' And she was sick again at his feet.

Jack shot away from his position against the wall as Dr Burke came out of Claire's bedchamber into the passageway. 'My wife. How is she?'

The physician, a tall, thin man with a pair of intelligent eyes, frowned. 'She has been bled, and I have given her a draught to help her rest. She is calm for now. If I may speak with you privately, my lord.'

'Yes,' Jack said curtly. Icy fingers of fear clutched at his heart at the man's expression. He'd never seen a person become as ill as Claire in such a short time. He'd hovered over her, trying to help ease her pain, until Dr Burke had arrived, and then Jane had gently suggested he leave. Both Jane and the Duchess were still in the room with her.

'We can go to my study,' Edward said.

Jack started. He'd nearly forgotten Edward had stood in the hall with him. He was about to tell Edward he would speak to the physician alone, but the sight of his own fear reflected in Edward's face stopped him.

Edward led them to his study. Dr Burke put his bag on the desk, then clasped his hands behind his back as he turned to face them. He rested his stern gaze on Jack. 'Did Lady Rotham eat anything unusual tonight, my lord?'

'I've no idea. She ate in her room. Why?'

Dr Burke ignored his question. 'Lord Dunford?'

Edward frowned. 'I don't know. You would have to question the servants, or perhaps my wife.'

'Why?' Jack demanded.

Dr Burke looked at him. 'From all the violence of her symptoms, I must consider the possibility she was poisoned.'

'Impossible!' Edward exclaimed.

Jack stared at him, uncomprehending, then cold fear hit him. 'How?'

Dr Burke's expression was careful. 'I questioned Lady Dunford about whether there are certain foods which do not agree with Lady Rotham. She knew of no such foods. The possibility exists, then, that something was added to Lady Rotham's food.'

'You are saying this was deliberate,' Jack said flatly.

'I do not wish to alarm you. But I suggest all food and drink Lady Rotham eats be brought by a trusted member of the household until the source of the poison is determined.' He hesitated. 'Of course, it could be it was a mere mistake of some sort.'

Jack's voice was grim. 'I've no intention of having this mistake repeated. She's leaving with me as soon as she can travel.'

'I fear that would not be wise…' Dr Burke began.

Edward whirled towards Jack. 'She's going nowhere with you!'

Jack moved towards him. 'You are quite mistaken if you think I plan to leave my wife here in this madhouse.'

The presence of the doctor was forgotten as the two men stared at each other. He cleared his throat. 'My lords…'

They all started when the housekeeper bustled into the room.

'Oh, sir! Thank goodness you've not left! One of the footmen has just been taken violently ill. He has the most terrible pains I have ever seen. Just like Lady Rotham's!' Her plump face was filled with fear.

'I'd best have a look at him,' Dr Burke said. 'If you will pardon me, my lords.'

'Yes.' Edward gave him a curt nod.

Edward waited until Dr Burke had followed the housekeeper from the room before speaking. 'Not only will you not remove her from here, you will not go near her.'

Jack stared at him. It took all his will-power to keep

from lunging at Edward. 'She is my wife. You can't keep me from her.'

'I will.' Edward gave him a cold look. 'I am not at all certain you are not the one behind this. You were with her alone both times she became ill.'

This time Jack moved. He sprang forward and grabbed Edward by the lapels of his coat. Edward staggered back, caught off guard by the attack. 'I should kill you for that remark,' he told Edward between gritted teeth.

Edward attempted to loosen his grip. 'And I will kill you if I find out you've tried to harm her.' His usually cool eyes were hot with dislike. 'Can you deny you were to marry Alicia Snowden? That you set out to seduce my sister for revenge?'

Jack abruptly released him. 'What the hell are you talking about?'

Edward smoothed down his lace. 'Lady Rotham informed me you were about to contract a betrothal with Miss Snowden.'

Jack's laugh was short. 'I was never informed of the fact. As for your other accusation, I never set out to seduce Claire. I wanted to marry her.'

'There is your castle, and the wager.'

'The wager was called off weeks ago. I forfeited. Ask Harry. And if it will please you I'll give up the damned castle. Are there any other accusations you wish to throw at me?'

Edward ignored that. 'Nonetheless, you are to stay away from Claire.'

'You can't prevent me.'

'Oh, but I can. My servants will be instructed to keep you away from her. And if I find you near her I will have you removed from the house.'

His voice was calmer, but he had a wild look about him Jack had never seen before. 'Then Claire goes with me,' Jack said.

'You are quite mistaken.'

'Edward, what is this?' Jane's worried voice interrupted them from the doorway. She looked from one to the other, her brow creased with concern.

'There is nothing to concern yourself with,' Edward said, his voice stiff.

'How is Claire?' Jack asked sharply.

'She is still sleeping. The Duchess is with her.' Her face was tired and lined with worry. She laid a hand on Jack's sleeve. 'She will be fine; I know so. And please don't worry; we will watch out for her.'

'Thank you.' He brushed past her. He had no intention of obeying Edward's orders if he had to mow the servants down to be near her.

Jack had barely reached the stairway when he encountered Dr Burke. 'Lord Rotham, I believe I have determined the source of the poison,' the physician said without preamble.

'What is it?'

'Mushrooms. A particular type which if ingested causes severe illness. It is fortunate Lady Rotham only ate a few bites.'

'Mushrooms? We had no mushrooms tonight.'

'The cook prepared a special dish for Lady Rotham. She claims she was instructed to do so.'

'By whom?'

'Lady Dunford, I assume.'

Jane? Jack frowned at him. 'That makes no sense.'

'Nonetheless, that is the source. The dish was sent back up with very little eaten and the footman, who ap-

parently has a fondness for mushrooms, decided to par-
take of a few bites himself.'

Jack had nearly forgotten about the ill man. 'How is
he?'

'He will live, although he is quite miserable at the
moment.' The physician's face was serious. 'It is possible, of course, that this was merely an accident despite
my earlier words, which I fear were rather rash. Unfortunately, it is not entirely uncommon to gather dangerous
mushrooms.' He frowned. 'I will check on Lady Rotham
and then take my leave.'

Jack followed him to Claire's room. His stepmother
stood outside the door, apparently in argument with the
brawny servant standing near the doorway. She turned
when she saw Jack, exasperation written on her face.

'Rotham! Would you believe this man refuses to let
me see her? My own daughter-in-law!'

'I have orders to let no one in except Lord Dunford,
Lady Dunford, or the Duchess of Arundel,' the man said.

'Not even Lord Rotham?' Celeste's voice rose in disbelief. 'He is her husband!'

Jack watched Dr Burke enter Claire's room, then took
his stepmother's arm. She looked on the verge of hys-
terics. 'Celeste, we cannot discuss this here.'

'Does Dunford really think I would poison her?'

He pulled Celeste away. 'Come with me.'

He took her down the hall to her room. With relief,
he saw his grandmother behind them. The Duchess took
one look at Celeste and took her arm, then led her into
her room. 'You'd best rest yourself,' the Duchess told
Jack over her shoulder.

Even if he'd wanted to, rest was impossible. He went
to his own bedchamber and flung himself down in the
wing chair near the window. As soon as the doctor left

and he was certain Dunford was out of the way, he planned to force his way into Claire's room, servant or no servant. He had no intention of leaving Claire's protection to Dunford's devices, although, amazingly enough, he felt Dunford would do anything to protect Claire.

He stared down at the empty grate in the fireplace, lost in thought. When the hands of the clock reached midnight, he rose and left his room. The dimly lit hall was quiet—too quiet. For a moment he couldn't determine what was wrong and then he realised there was no servant in sight. He dashed down the corridor to Claire's room.

He shoved open the door. The room was dark, the only illumination provided by slivers of moonlight. It took him only a few seconds to see a white-clad figure on the other side of the bed. He started towards the bed, almost at the same time as he saw the ghostly raised hand, the glint of silver flashing in the air.

'No!' His cry was hoarse as he tackled the figure. They fell to the floor together, a small table crashing to the ground. Stunned, he found himself crushing soft feminine curves, and then was looking into Alicia's lovely, cold face. He stared at her, uncomprehending for a moment, and then her features distorted into a mask of hatred. He sensed more than saw her hand descend. He rolled out of the way. A stab of pain shot through him as the blade slashed through his thin linen shirt and caught his upper arm.

She seemed to collapse into a heap. He lay stunned for a moment, then heard voices. Harry bent over him. 'My God!' Harry said.

Jack sat up, clutching his arm. 'Never mind! Attend to Alicia! She has a knife!'

Edward had pulled Alicia ·to her feet. Her face was dazed. The knife slowly slipped from her hand. Celeste shoved past Edward and caught Alicia in her arms. 'My child! What has happened?'

Harry helped Jack to stand. He shook off Harry's arm and stumbled to the bed. Claire lay so still, his heart nearly stopped. He dropped to his knees and touched her pale cheek. 'Claire! Claire!' Then he saw the gentle rise of her chest. 'Thank God!' His voice came out barely above a whisper.

'Jack!' He felt Harry's hand on his shoulder. 'I doubt Claire would appreciate your bleeding all over her bed-covers.'

Jack started. Blood was indeed seeping on the quilt covering her. He rose to his feet, his legs unexpectedly shaky. He looked at Edward who stood behind Harry. 'I found Alicia standing over Claire with a knife. Your damned servant was nowhere in sight,' Jack said.

'He was called away. Miss Snowden claimed Lady Rotham—that is, Celeste—was ill.' Edward stared at Jack, his face shocked. 'My God! If you hadn't ar-rived…' He swung around to face Celeste who sat on the chaise longue, her arms still around Alicia, who was sobbing silently on her chest. He marched over to them. 'Why?'

'Can't you see she is upset? Leave her for now!' Celeste gathered Alicia closer.

'I want to know why she tried to kill my sister!'

'How dare you?' Celeste looked as if she wanted to attack Edward herself.

Alicia lifted her head and stared at Edward. She sniffed. 'She…she ruined everything! I…I was to marry Lord Rotham, and then I would have had Grenville Hall and…and Blydon Castle! Mama said they were to be mine someday! They…they were my…my birthright!'

'Alicia, no!' Celeste looked horrified. Then her face seemed to crumple. 'Please, just go away. You are upsetting her!'

Jack moved towards them, still holding his arm. 'Celeste, what is this?' he asked.

Celeste looked at him. 'She is my daughter—my natural daughter. She should have had all of it.' Her face was bitter. 'If Claire Dunford had not appeared again, you would have married Alicia.'

'You are wrong,' he said quietly.

'But you would have! That is why I wanted Claire gone! Then you would have had to marry me so you could inherit Blydon Castle!' Alicia's voice was almost petulant, like that of a child denied a treat.

'My God,' Edward said.

Jack turned away, sickened by her words. His head seemed to spin and the next thing he knew he had hit the ground.

'Another casualty seems to have occurred,' Harry said.

Jack stepped inside Claire's bedchamber and paused. The last rays of the day slanted across her bed. She was sitting up, propped against the pillows and gazing out of the window.

He moved towards the bed, and she turned at the sound of his footsteps. Her tawny hair hung about her shoulders. Her face was still very pale and she seemed far too fragile. 'You are finally awake,' he said.

'Yes. I have you to thank that I am awake at all.' She twisted the sheets in her fingers. 'Edward said that if you had not come to my room…'

'Don't, Claire.' The horror of what might have happened if he hadn't arrived in time had haunted him most of the night and all of today. 'Don't think about it.' Guilt twisted his gut. 'I am sorry, Claire. I had no idea Alicia was so obsessed, so mad.' He gave a short laugh. 'And none of us had the least suspicion she was really Celeste's daughter. Not even my father.'

'Poor Alicia,' Claire said softly.

'Poor Alicia? After what she did?' It was incredible to him that she could feel the least pity for a girl who had first tried to poison her and then stab her. Not to mention the laudanum—Alicia's scheme to ruin his wedding night.

'It must be horrid to feel you belong nowhere, really. And then to want something so badly…' She looked away for a moment, then turned her gaze back on him. 'What will happen to her?'

'She could be committed to a private asylum. The other alternative is to have her tried for attempted murder.'

'No, I don't want that. I don't want to live with her death on my hands.' Her gaze fell to his arm. 'You've been hurt! What has happened?'

'Nothing much.'

'But you are holding your arm so oddly.'

He grimaced. 'Alicia managed to wound me slightly when we fell together. It is a mere scratch.' He had no intention of telling her Alicia had had, at that moment, every intention of killing him as well.

'I am so sorry.'

'There's no need to be.'

She looked away again. She seemed so distant. Perhaps it would make what he had to say easier. He took a deep breath. 'I wanted to tell you I must go away for a while.'

She kept her face averted. 'I see.'

'I have some business I must attend to. I will leave tomorrow.' His stepmother had completely collapsed from the shock of Alicia's madness. He and his grandmother were left to deal with Alicia.

'Of course.' She sounded even more wooden.

He rushed ahead. 'Then I will go to Blydon for a while. I have discussed this with your brother. We both agree it would be best if you stay here for the present. You could stay with my grandmother if you wish. In your present state of health, Blydon Castle would do nothing but harm to you.'

'Would it?' She finally looked at him. He was taken aback to see the flash of anger in her eyes. 'There is nothing wrong with my health.'

'You nearly died.'

'But I didn't.' Her face was stony.

'Claire, don't…'

'Don't what?' She glared at him. 'I am quite tired of having everyone dictate to me what I must do. In fact, you are as bad as Edward! I have no intention of staying with your grandmother or at your hunting lodge or anywhere else you or my brother think I should be.'

'Claire…'

'Has anyone ever bothered to ask what I want? So, my lord, I may be married to you, but if you don't want me for your wife, then you have no power to tell me what to do!'

'Claire, listen to me, you are overwrought…'

'Overwrought? Why does everyone think I'm over-wrought when I dare to speak up for myself?' She glared at him. 'Now, I really am quite tired and if you will have the courtesy to leave me I would be most appreciative. My lord!'

She deliberately rolled over onto her side and yanked the bedcovers up over her head.

He stared at her back with a feeling of helplessness. Then he quietly left the room.

He stalked to Edward's library and pulled out the decanter of brandy on the sideboard. If ever he needed a drink it was now and damned be his head. He poured himself a glass and was about to raise it to his lips when Harry spoke from behind him.

'What is the occasion this time?'

'There is none,' Jack said shortly.

'How is Claire?'

'She is better.'

Harry eyed him curiously. 'So, why the scowl?'

'There is no reason.'

'I will try another conversational tack. When are you taking her out of here?'

'I'm not. She's staying here, or with my grandmother if she wishes.'

Harry looked at him for a moment, a gleam of anger in his eye. 'Have you told her this?'

'Just now.'

'If it wasn't that Claire would hardly thank me, I'd mow you down,' Harry informed him. 'What do you think you're doing, passing Claire off like an unwanted piece of baggage? Have you ever considered she might want to actually be your wife?'

Jack slammed the glass down. 'No. Why? Every association I've ever had with her has been a disaster. First, she was forced into a hellish marriage with Ellison because of me. Now, she's been forced into another marriage because of another damnable bet. This time, she nearly lost her life.' He gave a bitter laugh. 'Just now she accused me of dictating to her, just as her brother always has. The least I can do is grant her her freedom. She can come and go as she pleases. God knows, I have the funds to allow her that much. She'll be free from her brother's interference and anyone else's.'

'So you think walking out of her life will make her happy?' Harry stared at him as if he'd grown horns.

'Better than being forced to live with me out of some misbegotten sense of duty.' He picked up the brandy, about to take a swallow, then set it back down. It suddenly looked about as appetising as a vial of poison. 'I'm leaving tomorrow as early as possible.' He looked steadily at Harry. 'Take care of her for me.'

Harry let him pass without a word.

Chapter Nineteen

Claire's stomach knotted as her coach left the ancient town of Folkestone. Her journey of nearly three days would soon be over. She had no idea what she would find at the end.

Well, at least she was following her own wishes for once. It had not been easy breaking away. Edward had tried his best to dissuade her, but in the end he had given in and let her go.

Thank goodness Edward and Jane had reconciled. They had assured Claire she could stay as long as she wished. She had no idea what Jack had told them. She had avoided him, refusing him a last interview. Her satisfaction at his leaving without her speaking to him had lasted until his carriage had rounded the bend. Then she'd felt as if her heart had turned to stone.

Harry had cornered her a few days later. He'd ridden over from Charing Hall.

'So, it is to be a repeat of six years ago. Amazing how you've learned so little.'

Claire was sitting in the rose arbour feeling sorry for herself, as she had for the past five days. She twisted her handkerchief in her hands. 'What do you mean? I fear I have no patience for games.'

Harry rested one leg on the bench next to her and clasped his hands over it, then leaned towards her. 'I mean that this is an encore of last time. You in your castle room refusing to see him, Jack riding off, certain you don't care a fig for him, certain the only way he'll rescue you is by leaving.'

Claire scowled. 'Hartfield is not a castle. And he left in his coach.' Harry lifted a brow. 'Well, why should it matter to him whether I care for him or not? He doesn't care for me!'

'I believe I may be able to follow that.' He reached over and took her hand. 'Claire, my sweet idiot, do you remember the last conversation we had, the one on your wedding day?' She nodded. 'Well, did you ever tell him what you'd planned to?'

'No. I…I fell asleep before he came. And then everything went wrong after that.'

'It is not too late.'

Claire stared down at her hands. 'Of course it is. He has probably left for Italy by now.'

'He's at Blydon. He's been there trying to force himself to put the place up for sale.'

The image almost made her cry. 'Oh, how sad!'

Harry shook his head. 'Isn't it? If only you were there, then he wouldn't have to do it.'

'But he doesn't want me.'

'Claire.' He sounded as if he was speaking to a simpleton. 'He wants you. He's afraid he'll ruin your life again. Actually, he is ruining it, with your help. In fact, you're both going to be miserable. So why don't you finish up what you were going to do before fate in the form of Alicia interfered?'

She sat in the arbour a long while after Harry left. She could do that. Go to Blydon Castle. The worst he could do was tell her to leave, which would break her heart. Of course, it already felt shattered in a thousand pieces so what difference would one more make? At least she would force him to listen to her first.

So now she was in a coach travelling over dusty, rutted roads. And if Harry was wrong… She had spent the entire night before she left tossing and turning, trying to imagine what he would say. But there was no going back.

The coach rattled around a bend and the twin towers of a castle appeared, the ancient grey stone bathed in the last glorious rays of the day. And then the coach stopped under the arches of the courtyard in front of the stone façade.

Sally, the little maid who'd come with her, stirred. Her colour had returned. She'd spent most of the trip moaning in the corner, sick from the motion of the coach. The footman flung open the doors and Claire alighted, followed by Sally.

Claire stared up at the rows of tall narrow windows, her legs starting to shake. The castle had a silent and rather forlorn air about it. What if he had already left? She'd sent no word she was coming. She forced herself up the steps and waited as the footman lifted the heavy knocker on the massive oak door.

After what seemed like an eternity, the door slowly creaked open. A middle-aged woman peered out, her face puzzled. Claire stepped forward. 'I am Lady Rotham.'

The woman stared at her for a moment, then her plump face creased in a smile. 'My lady! His lordship said nothing… You must come in.' She pulled the door open. Claire followed her into a vast hallway. The woman bustled around Claire, showing her to a dark-panelled drawing-room, calling for a pot of tea, then hustled off, leaving Claire staring after her in bewilderment.

She looked around. The heavy, carved furniture was old, as Jack had said, but the warm light of the setting sun spilling across the worn wood floor filled her with an unexpected sense of welcome.

She jumped at the sound of footsteps. But it was only the housekeeper, returning with a pot of tea. She poured it for Claire, who managed to find out her name was Mrs Gunning. And then she was left alone.

She seated herself on a heavy wooden chair and sipped her tea. Then she heard footsteps again. And this time the footsteps were very familiar. She rose, her heart racing.

Jack stepped in. He stared at her, his face expressionless. He wore buckskin breeches and a dark brown cloth coat, and from the flecks of mud on his boots she thought he must have come directly in from outside. 'Claire. What are you doing here?' he asked quietly.

She swallowed. 'I…I decided this is where I want to live. You did say I could live anywhere I wanted.'

'I did.' He stepped closer to her. She saw he looked tired, shadows under his eyes as if he hadn't been sleeping well. 'So what made you decide to come here?'

'I've always wanted to live in a castle.' She met his gaze squarely.

'I remember.'

'This is the only one I…I know of. I hope you don't mind,' she said a little breathlessly.

'No.' He looked at her for a moment. 'You do know

that if you want this castle I must reside with you for the next six months.'

'I know. I hope it doesn't interfere too much with your plans. That is, you were planning to go to Italy.'

'Italy will most likely still be there in six months.'

'Yes.' The way he watched her made her feel vulnerable, and afraid and excited all at once. Perhaps it was true—he did want her. Even if it was only physically. In time, he might want her in every way. She forced herself to step closer to him. 'I will need a room.'

His mouth lifted. 'You will. There is one near mine that is habitable.'

'That will be fine.' His words were not at all suggestive, but she felt heat rise in her face nonetheless.

'I'll have Mrs Gunning show you to it.' His eyes were still focused on her face. 'I'm afraid I am not prepared for company. We dine early, but the fare is simple.'

'I don't mind.' It was on the tip of her tongue to tell him she was not company, but perhaps she was being presumptuous. At least he had not told her she must leave.

'Very well. I'll call Mrs Gunning. I promise I'll even change for dinner.' He turned and walked towards the door. He paused and looked back at her. 'I'm glad you're here,' he said softly, then left.

Claire hesitated in the doorway of the dining-room. He was standing near the mantelpiece with a glass of wine in his hand. He was now dressed in satin breeches and a corbeau coat, the candlelight reflecting off his dark hair. Claire stepped forward, her heart thudding. She had dressed with unusual care in a rose gown she'd rarely worn, its rounded neckline revealing more of her creamy breasts than she liked.

But tonight she wanted to play every card she had. He set his wine on the dining table as he came towards her. His eyes swept over her, and she saw the flame that sparked in them. He took her hand and brought it to his lips, then released it.

'You look lovely, Claire.'

She formed her lips into a smile, despite the trembling in her limbs. 'Thank you.'

'Come and sit.' He led her to a chair next to the head of the long, carved table. 'I thought we could converse more easily if we sat together instead of shouting at one another down the length of the table.'

'Yes.' She gave him a quick smile as she sat down. She wasn't sure she could make any sort of rational conversation.

'I hope you found your bedchamber adequate?'

'It is quite lovely.' Were they going to hold nothing but this polite conversation? It was making her more edgy than ever. But what was the proper time to blurt out that she loved him? After the soup? Over a piece of fruit? Perhaps dinner was not the most appropriate time after all.

He raised a brow. 'Lovely? I wouldn't go that far. If I recall, the room is in dire need of new hangings and the chest looks as if a pack of rats had gnawed it.'

She gave a shaky laugh. ''Tis not that bad. At least I didn't actually see any creatures in the room.'

The footman entered. They waited until the servant finished laying the course. Jack picked up his wine and stared into it for a few seconds, then set it back down. 'So, how did you escape from Edward?'

'I told him I was leaving. He was not happy at first, but Jane persuaded him to let me go.'

'He should not have let you come by yourself.'

'I insisted.'

'I will not have you travelling unaccompanied again. I am responsible for you.'

His arrogant tone set her back up. 'Are you, my lord?'

A slight smile touched his lips. 'I most certainly am your lord. I will expect you to notify me of your plans in the future.'

'I did not think you much cared what I did.' The words sprang to her lips before she could stop them.

'You are quite wrong,' he said softly. 'I very much care what you do.'

'Do…do you?' To her complete mortification, her voice quavered. She quickly looked away.

His hand caught hers. 'Claire, my sweet, don't cry. There is no need.'

She wiped her eyes and tried to smile. 'Harry says I've ruined more of his coats weeping on him.'

Jack's hand tightened. 'There is one thing I must make clear if you plan to stay here. You are to ruin no more of Harry's coats. If you feel an impulse to shed tears on someone it had better be me.' His voice was light, but the look in his eyes told her he was very serious. 'Do you understand?'

She nodded. 'I promise.'

'Good.' He released her hand. 'Now, I suggest we eat before the food is even more cold than it usually is.'

She scarcely noticed what she ate, although she must have been hungry for she was surprised to find she had eaten most of her dinner. The footman finally removed the last course. She took a glass of wine, hoping it would calm her shaky nerves.

The candles flickered, casting shadows in the room. She stared down at her glass, the air tense with unspoken emotions.

Jack shoved back his chair and rose. He took several paces towards the mantelpiece, then turned. 'Claire, come here.' His voice was husky.

She obediently rose and went to him, coming to stand in front of him. What she saw in his eyes made her breathing erratic. He took a step towards her. 'So you are here because you want my castle?'

'Yes.'

'I am part of the bargain, you know.'

'I…I know.'

He stepped closer. 'And you don't mind?'

'No.' Her mouth had gone dry, her mind completely blank.

'I'll want everything,' he said softly. 'Everything a husband wants from his wife.'

'I know that, too.'

His laugh was shaky.

'Then come upstairs with me.' He held out his hand.

She put her hand in his. His fingers closed over hers, warm and strong. A flame of desire shot through her, so strong she was light-headed.

He led her from the dining-room, through the silent stone great hall, and up the winding, candlelit staircase. He paused only to push open the door to a room, and then led her inside, closing the door behind them.

They were in a large bedchamber, dominated by an old-fashioned bed. A light burned on the table next to the bed.

He pulled her around to face him, then touched her cheek. 'Are you really here? Or is it a dream? I dreamed of you only last night. You were in my bed and in my arms. Tell me I am not dreaming now.'

'No, you are not dreaming.'

'I want to kiss you. Just to see that you are real.'

'Jack, there…there is something I must tell you.'

'Let it wait.' He bent his head towards her, and then, with a groan, crushed her to him. He kissed her as if he were drowning, and she was his only hope. She clung to him, caught in a whirlpool of sensations as his mouth and hands possessed her. He kissed her face, her cheeks, then trailed his mouth down her neck to where her breasts plunged into her bodice. He lifted his head and, with a sound of impatience, pushed the silk of her dress aside. She gasped as his lips found her nipple, her whole body contracting at the sensation.

He raised his head, his eyes dark and heavy. 'God, you are real. Did I hurt you?'

'No.' His concern, despite the wild desire she saw in his eyes, almost made her want to weep. 'No. It…it was very nice.'

'Nice!' He half laughed, half groaned. 'I must do better. Much better. I promise I'll try to be gentle.' He took her hand. 'Are you still willing to come to my bed?'

'Yes.'

'But first your gown. It is lovely; I've wanted nothing more than to get my hands on it all night, but it must come off.'

'Oh, yes.' She waited, her impatience growing as he fumbled with the buttons at the back of her gown. His hands slid it from her shoulders and it fell to the ground in a pool of rose-red silk. Then she heard his sharp intake of breath. He pulled her around to face him.

He tilted her chin towards him. 'What is this, Claire? No stays? No petticoat?'

Her whole body trembled at the hot fire in his eyes. 'No.'

'How very wanton of you.' A slow smile curved his mouth. 'So, you planned to seduce me for my castle?'

'I...I thought it might help.'

'Most certainly it will.'

He tugged at her shift; she lifted her arms, allowing him to slip it over her head.

She felt more than a little vulnerable as he gently removed her hands from her breasts and he stepped back, his gaze moving slowly from her face to her breasts and then down to the curve of her hips and thighs. There was desire and passion and, most of all, wonder in his eyes, as if he beheld a rare and beautiful treasure.

He stepped forward and knelt in front of her, first removing her shoes, then slowly rolling her stockings down one leg and then the other. She looked down at his dark head and her hands tangled in his thick silky locks. She bit her lip, hoping she wouldn't groan in frustration before he finished with her stockings.

He rose and took her hand, and led her to the side of the bed, then gently picked her up and laid her on the coverlet. He bent over her and cupped her cheek, then his hand followed the path of his eyes, first caressing each breast, then travelling to the curve of her hip. Her body was on exquisite fire and when his hand did nothing more than tangle in the soft curls at the juncture of her thighs, before skimming lightly down her leg, she whimpered in frustration.

'In a moment, sweetheart,' he whispered. He rose to his knees and struggled out of his coat. She watched without shame as he removed his waistcoat and shirt, the tension in her belly and between her thighs growing. The muscles of his chest under the dark mat of hair rippled as he fumbled with the fastening of his breeches. It was only when he started to slide them down his narrow hips that Claire averted her eyes.

He laughed softly. 'There's no need to be so shy of

me.' He moved closer, now completely naked. 'Touch me.' He took her hand and guided it down to his hard shaft. Her fingers lightly touched him in wonder, then more boldly closed around him. He seemed to spring alive under her hand. She slid her hand down its length, marvelling at the feel of it. He moaned, and she glanced swiftly up at his face, her hand dropping away.

'Did I...I hurt you?'

'No. Never. It is only I am about to lose control. Claire, I need you now,' he said in a choked voice. She turned onto her back, and he slipped into the bed next to her. He rose above her. Then, with his knee, he gently parted her thighs. He slid into her with a swift thrust, his hardness filling her. She arched, her body aching to enclose him fully in her, but he suddenly bent his face towards her, cupping her face in his hands. 'Open your eyes. I want to see your face when I am in you.'

She obeyed. His eyes were filled with passion and want and an unexpected tenderness. She moistened her lips. 'Jack, I...I must tell you something,' she whispered.

'Later.' He began to move in long, measured strokes, plunging her into a world of exquisite sensation. Her body followed his relentless rhythm, her own thrusts increasing in intensity until she exploded in a climax of surrender and passion. She cried out.

His own climax followed and then she was in his arms, her head resting on his chest, his arm holding her to him. They lay in silence. He turned to look down at her. His hand stroked her hair. 'What is it you wanted to tell me?'

Claire's fingers touched the rough shadow of beard near his mouth. She swallowed, feeling shy. 'I...I didn't quite tell you the truth about why I came.'

'What do you mean?' His hand stopped its gentle motion.

'I…I really don't want your castle. That is…' She could feel his body tense as if waiting for a blow. 'I…I came because I…I love you.'

She shut her eyes against the silence. Then he said, 'What did you say?'

'I love you.' There; he could not possibly mistake her meaning. She waited for his words of disgust or pity.

She turned to look at him. His eyes were intent on her face. 'Claire, do you mean that?'

'Yes. I…I know you don't love me, and I promise I will not ask for too much…but…'

'Stop.' His mouth closed over hers and then he raised his head and gave a strangled laugh. 'My love, do you know how I've longed to hear those words from your lips? For years.' His eyes were warm and tender with laughter. And a happiness she'd never before seen there. 'For I love you, Claire. I think I have from the moment I first saw you six years ago. I was such a fool; I should never have let you go then.'

'I was the one who refused to see you.'

'I should have abducted you. I am sorry.'

Her laugh was shaky. 'I forgive you.' She twisted her fingers in the dark mat of hair on his chest. But she had something else she must ask. 'Were you planning to let me go this time?'

'Yes,' he said quietly. 'I could not force you to live with me and hate me for it. I consoled myself with the thought that as long as you were wed to me there would be no more marriages arranged by your brother. And I could see that you were safe.'

Tears filled her eyes. 'Safe, perhaps, but dreadfully unhappy. Oh, Jack, I had no idea you cared for me…I thought you were only being kind and that I was a dreadful burden.'

'You are. I'll expect you to compensate for it on a daily basis.'

'Will you? How?' And then she flushed as she saw the wicked smile on his face.

'I'll be glad to demonstrate,' he said.

And she opened her arms to him.

Epilogue

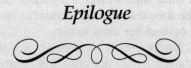

Claire slowly rose as Harry was shown into the drawing-room. Her increasing figure made it difficult to move much faster. His gaze swept over her, coming to rest on her rounded belly. A huge grin broke across his face. 'I see everything must be going quite well.'

'Oh, it is.' She flushed and laughed. 'We wanted to surprise you. We've only told Jane and Edward and Thea and, of course, the Duchess.'

He moved across the room to take her hands. 'I can't say I'm really surprised,' he drawled. 'I saw how Jack looked at you.'

'Harry!' She felt her face turn pink.

'So when is the happy occasion?'

'In another three months. I'm afraid by then I will hardly be able to move. Jack has forbidden me to do anything but needlework or an occasional walk, and I'm getting very plump.'

He smiled. 'You look beautiful. Marriage quite agrees with you—at least, to the right husband.'

'Yes.' She gave him a shy smile. 'I have never thanked you for sending me here. Oh, Harry, I never knew he cared for me. He was going to be noble and let me go so I wouldn't hate him!'

Harry stepped back, his face rather apprehensive. 'You're not planning to cry again, are you?'

'No. I promised Jack I would only weep on him.'

'Good. I only hope he has a wardrobe full of coats. Or maybe he should carry a cloth about as one does with an infant.'

'Harry! I hardly ever cry any more,' Claire said with dignity, although it was not quite true. Since her pregnancy, she'd been prone to tears at the most unexpected times, although most of the occasions had had nothing to do with unhappiness. Her husband had been quite satisfactory in stopping them using a number of interesting methods.

'Where is he? I've brought your wedding gift.'

'Isn't it a bit late?' Jack asked, coming into the room. Claire's heart still leapt at the sight of her husband. He had been out in the fields and was dressed in well-fitting buckskin breeches and a bottle-green coat. His face had lost much of its harshness in the months since she'd arrived.

'Perhaps, but I think you'll find it worthwhile. I decided to let you have time alone before interrupting. I see you've managed to use it wisely. My congratulations.'

Jack threw Claire a wicked glance. 'We have. Thank you.'

'Come out with me, then. It's waiting outside.'

They followed him out of the drawing-room and down the steps into the cool morning. Harry's coach still stood in front. A groom was walking a coal-black horse up and down.

Jack stopped dead still, Claire beside him. The groom

led the horse towards them. The animal's head came up; his nostrils flared at the sight of them.

'Satan?' Jack's voice held disbelief. The horse's ears pricked forward. Jack whistled and the horse tugged on his lead and broke free, coming to Jack and nuzzling his hand.

'I don't have anything for you,' he said. He patted the horse who thrust his nose at Claire with no better success at locating a morsel. Jack looked at Harry. 'What are you doing?'

'This is your wedding gift,' Harry said. 'Thought you might like him back. Poor fellow, he's been moping around the stables and gives hell to anyone who tries to ride him.' Harry grinned at Jack's stunned expression. 'Besides, I owe you some compensation for my, er, less than sporting efforts to win our wager. Although I must admit you won in the end.'

Claire frowned at him. 'What efforts?'

'There was the mouse, of course, and the charming Sophy at Vauxhall. Not to mention Lord Hawke's study. I never expected Jack to go through the window.'

'Harry! I thought you were a friend!' Claire said reproachfully. 'He scratched his hand and his face!'

Jack moved to her side, his arm going around her thickening waist. He looked down at her, a smile quirking his lips. 'Don't be too hard on him, my love, for I suspect he was the one responsible for our marriage.'

She looked up at him, puzzled. His smile was tender and full of laughter. 'The night of the fan lottery, you very vehemently assured me you never threw your fan in, did you not?'

'Yes.' She turned to stare at Harry. 'You took my fan?'

His grin was sheepish. 'I will confess. A pure gamble

on my part. I was certain if he chose your fan he'd never persuade you to marry him. I am pleased I was wrong.'

'So, you see, we have Harry to thank after all.' Jack's arm tightened around Claire as he gazed down at her.

She smiled up at him. 'Yes, we do.' She turned again to Harry, feeling rather teary. 'Thank you.'

He looked alarmed. 'Perhaps I'd best show Satan to his new home. Your bride appears to need, er, soothing, Jack.' He motioned to the groom who came forward and took Satan's lead, and they headed for the stables.

Jack laughed and pulled her into his arms. He looked down at her, his eyes full of love. 'This usually works quite well,' he said. His lips met hers, and soon Claire had completely forgotten why there was the least need for tears.

* * * * *

MILLS & BOON®

*M*akes
any time
special

Enjoy a romantic novel from
Mills & Boon®

Presents...™   *Enchanted*™   TEMPTATION®

Historical Romance™   ✚ MEDICAL ROMANCE™

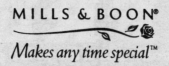

COMING SOON

A limited collection of 12 books. Where affairs of
the heart are entwined with the everyday dealings
of this warm and friendly children's hospital.

Book I
A Winter Bride by Meredith Webber
Published 5th May

SECH/RTL/2

2 FREE

books and a surprise gift!

We would like to take this opportunity to thank you for reading this Mills & Boon® book by offering you the chance to take TWO more specially selected titles from the Historical Romance™ series absolutely FREE! We're also making this offer to introduce you to the benefits of the Reader Service™—

- ★ FREE home delivery
- ★ FREE gifts and competitions
- ★ FREE monthly Newsletter
- ★ Exclusive Reader Service discounts
- ★ Books available before they're in the shops

Accepting these FREE books and gift places you under no obligation to buy, you may cancel at any time, even after receiving your free shipment. Simply complete your details below and return the entire page to the address below. *You don't even need a stamp!*

YES! Please send me 2 free Historical Romance books and a surprise gift. I understand that unless you hear from me, I will receive 4 superb new titles every month for just £2.99 each, postage and packing free. I am under no obligation to purchase any books and may cancel my subscription at any time. The free books and gift will be mine to keep in any case.

H0EA

Ms/Mrs/Miss/Mr ....Initials.....................................
                                                            BLOCK CAPITALS PLEASE

Surname ....

Address ....

....

....Postcode..................................

Send this whole page to:
UK: FREEPOST CN81, Croydon, CR9 3WZ
EIRE: PO Box 4546, Kilcock, County Kildare (stamp required)